ANIMOSITY

Also by David Lindsey
in Large Print:

The Color of Night
Requiem for a Glass Heart

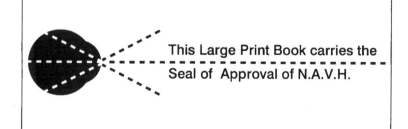

This Large Print Book carries the
Seal of Approval of N.A.V.H.

ANIMOSITY

David Lindsey

Thorndike Press • Waterville, Maine

LARGE TYPE

LINDSEY D

3 1257 01378 9416

Copyright © 2001 by David L. Lindsey

Published in 2001 by arrangement with Warner Books, Inc.

Thorndike Press Large Print Americana Series.

The tree indicium is a trademark of Thorndike Press.

The text of this Large Print edition is unabridged. Other aspects of the book may vary from the original edition.

Set in 16 pt. Plantin by Myrna S. Raven.

Printed in the United States on permanent paper.

Library of Congress Cataloging-in-Publication Data

Lindsey, David L.
    Animosity / David Lindsey.
      p. cm.
    ISBN 0-7862-3324-9 (lg. print : hc : alk. paper)
    1. Man-woman relationships — Fiction. 2. Artists' models — Fiction. 3. Sculptors — Fiction. 4. Texas — Fiction. 5. Large type books. I. Title

PS3562.I51193 A84 2001b
 813'.54—dc21
                             2001027336

For Joyce,
my second self,
ex dono Dei.

Chapter 1

He watched the rain on the night street from his second-floor window. It was only a mizzle, gathering on the broad leaves of the linden trees along the narrow street until the leaves sagged under its weight and shed the huge, spattering drops. It had been a cold winter in Paris, but spring came early and wet.

Ross Marteau turned and went to a work-bench in his studio. He picked up the last slice of apple from the plate where he had cut it up with a paring knife and put it into his mouth as he looked around. The bronze sculpture of a nude woman, posed walking away and turning in a backward glance, was gone. But there were small clay maquettes of it everywhere. He had overseen the installation of the *Turning Woman* commission two weeks earlier. The client was thrilled. There was a party in the elegant conservatory of his home in St.-Germain-des-Prés where the sculpture was the center of attention. Champagne. Friends and sycophants cooed in admiration. The woman, the client's young wife, was flattered. Everything her husband was proud of, her taut flesh

7

and firm musculature (his), her high-riding breasts (his), her entire, finely distributed anatomy (his), was there to stay. In thirty years if people forgot, or if they never knew her, they could look into the lush light of the conservatory and see what a fine thing she had once been.

So the studio was dormant. Job done. The dust had settled for good. The tools and paraphernalia of clay modeling were scattered about, waiting to be organized and put away. He would do that, later. The place needed sweeping. It had been weeks since he'd bothered with it. This morning's coffee sat in a cold pot on a hot plate near the back of the studio, where there was an open shower, a toilet behind a muslin curtain, a rust-stained porcelain sink.

Chewing the slice of apple, he walked back to the window, leaned against the frame, and looked out again. And there she was, under her umbrella, gliding along beneath the dripping lindens, her raincoat glistening, her stride strong and quick. She turned without looking and crossed the wet street to the sidewalk below him, then disappeared into the foyer below.

He looked toward the door and waited. He heard her coming up the turning stairs, quick, impatient steps. No hesitation on the landing as she reached the last stair, and then the studio door flung open. There she stood, holding her dripping umbrella, her creamy face and a sheaf of auburn hair pulled to one side and falling over the front of one shoulder, making her seem as though she were the only thing in color, a pastel woman in a black-and-white world.

"Goddamn you," she said. "You *son* of a bitch."

She looked around the studio, her hazel-eyed glare slicing around the space until she found his things piled in a corner.

"God," she said, looking at his clothes hanging on a makeshift wooden rod underneath the long slanting skylight.

"You knew I was going to," he said. "You knew."

"We'd talked about it."

"That's right. Exactly."

"You didn't say when. You didn't say today." She was furious.

"I didn't really have to, did I?"

"We didn't agree it was final."

"Agree? Christ, Marian, we haven't agreed on anything for a year now, longer. As for final, it's been final for six months. We've just never had the guts to admit it to each other."

She was trembling.

9

She dropped the umbrella and fought off her raincoat, threw it over one of the maquettes. She was poured into black tights, from ankles to waist. She wore a white blouse with a pleated front, its long tail gathered under her rib cage and tied in a knot. Her sandals were wet. Her hands were wet, and she wiped them on her blouse to dry them. Strands of auburn hair hovered in agitation around her face. She was breathing heavily, having quick-walked from their flat near Métro Raspail.

She put a long hand on one hip, wrist up, and looked around, searching for the next thing to say, and then snapped her eyes on him.

"This is . . . vicious," she said.

Vicious. She liked that word. Ironically.

"It's over." He paused. "It's over for me."

She glared at him. He imagined her hair, hot with her anger, heating like the coils on his hot plate in the corner. He imagined the auburn strands beginning to glow.

Abruptly she turned her back on him, hand on hip, the other cupping her forehead, a gesture of wild distress. He looked at her tight buttocks as she stood with one leg cocked at the knee. The woman had a beautiful body, that was all you could say about it. He was ashamed to admit that it was

10

harder to leave a body like that than one that was less stunning. How long had he stayed with her just because of the body?

She spun around.

"What . . . are we going to do?"

"I'm through here," he said. "I'm going home."

She looked as if he'd slapped her. With these seemingly innocuous words he had locked her out of his house, and out of his life.

"No," she said.

"Marian, I can't do this anymore. This past year's been excruciating. There's nothing left . . . between us." Pause. "Not for me."

"You think I'm going to just let you walk away from three years together?"

"Nearly."

"What?"

"Nearly three years."

"Goddamn you! It's three years of *my* life, too."

"Look, we gave it our best shot —"

"Shot! That's what you call three years together . . . a 'shot'?"

"Okay, wrong choice of words. You're right. But I can't do this anymore. I'm weary of insults, weary of grievances, weary of accusations of wrongs, imagined or real."

"Weary of me."

He didn't say anything, an insulting silence.

"What's your record with a woman, Ross? This it? Three years? I think it is, isn't it? Was it always their fault, too, Ross? Did you lecture them, too . . . tell them how you couldn't take it anymore? Tell them how weary you were . . . of them? You arrogant son of a bitch!"

He was exhausted. They had just been through two days of this, a marathon siege of verbal hostilities that had bloodied their souls and murdered the last simulacrum of caring that might have remained between them. It had all been said in those forty-eight hours, words long held in check, words oft repeated, words that should never have passed their lips or even left the mean corners of their hearts.

"I can't be with you anymore," he said, "and I don't want to be."

She looked at him, stricken. The expression on her face was wrenching, and it shocked him. What constitutes a mortal wound to the heart? What does it look like, looking back at you? It really was the end for them. And now — at this moment — she knew it, too.

There was a partition of free-standing

wooden shelves near the doorway where he kept a mélange of junk that he had gathered in the flea markets during the past year. He was an incurable collector of stuff, and wherever he traveled and stayed for any length of time he accumulated the priceless and the worthless together, its commercial value having no bearing on his desire to have it.

Marian leaped at the shelf and snatched a vase from it. It was a pottery vase with a crazed turquoise glaze that Marian herself had made in the first year of their relationship. He loved the piece and carried it with him whenever he had to relocate for any length of time. He put it on a shelf or a mantel or a ledge, and all the other things that he collected while he was there were gradually drawn to the vase as if it were the magnetic hub of their cumulation.

In one quick sweep of her body she wheeled around and flung the vase with all her might against the largest of the *Turning Woman* maquettes. The vase exploded, blowing green shards into the air in a radiant burst of turquoise fireworks. He heard the pieces falling all around him like hail and saw them skittering across the rough wooden floor.

Marian was in a rage, hyperventilating.

He saw what happened next before it happened, as if he were watching a play he had seen before. He knew the script, saw it in an instant, whole, complete, though he was incapable of doing anything about it.

Eyes swollen in wrath, Marian lunged at the table where he had been eating the apple and grabbed the paring knife. He remembered her posture in that instant as if he had sculpted her: long body stretched out, right arm reaching for the paring knife, one black-tighted leg extended behind, the other bent for support, buttocks compacted with tension, a flame of auburn hair falling across her right eye. It was a narrative posture of aggression.

He didn't remember how she gained her balance to throw the knife, but he remembered her hand outstretched toward him, almost as if reaching for him. But she wasn't reaching. She had released the knife. It tumbled sloppily through the air toward him because she didn't know what she was doing, didn't know how to do it properly, just slung it somehow in his direction. There are scientific odds to tumbling. When the knife reached him, what would those odds be that it would hit him handle first? Or blade first? Or flat? Or any one of the 360 degrees of angles in between?

He put up his hands and turned to the side.

The blade went into his right deltoid muscle as straight and smooth as a bullet. And buried to the hilt.

Chapter 2

He took a taxi to Val de Grâce, a hospital not too far off Boulevard Saint Michel. He left the paring knife in his shoulder, figuring that if they took it out themselves, it would give them a better knowledge of the internal damage. He knew it wasn't serious, but by the time he got to the hospital it was hurting like hell, and he was feeling a little queasy. He'd thrown a sports jacket over his shoulder to hide the damn thing.

When Marian recovered from the shock of what she'd done and realized she hadn't killed him, her anger resurged, and she grabbed her raincoat and umbrella and stormed out of the studio, screaming that she wished it had gone into his throat.

He was surprised at how long he had to wait at the hospital with a knife in his shoulder. Eventually they took him into an emergency room, removed the knife, cleaned the wound, applied four stitches, and gave him some pain reliever. They said that because the wound was deep the pain was going to be significant, and the danger of infection was a concern. They wanted to see him again the next evening.

One of the nurses recognized him from the *Paris Match* article of two months before. It was embarrassing because the article had been one of those "Personality" shorts recounting the continued rumors of his rather noisy breakup with Marian. The gossipy copy was accompanied by two photographs of him and Marian outside Brasserie Femme one night as they stopped all pedestrian traffic by giving each other a thorough tongue-lashing, their posture aggressive, their faces contorted, no shame in thrall to their self-centered hostilities.

The nurse was far too interested, and Ross guessed that she'd make a telephone call after he was gone. Another little something for the media.

When he got back to the studio around midnight, he swallowed one of the pills the doctor had given him, turned out the lights, and lay down on the bed. The city glow came in from the skylight, and he could see the drifting mist.

He had forgotten to ask the doctor if the painkiller would make him sleepy, but he lay there and stared at the ceiling, waiting to feel it. He wasn't sleepy otherwise, too much adrenaline.

Ross Marteau had made a comfortable

living as a sculptor for nearly twenty years now. He'd traveled all over the world, knew extraordinary people, acquired a respectable renown. As a sculptor, critical acclaim had eluded him and probably would continue to, but success certainly had not. He worked hard and depended on discipline to accomplish what his talents allowed.

But he wasn't driven to soul-rending struggles of angst in pursuit of art in the way that he understood great men were often driven. He ardently loved sculpture and considered himself a craftsman, even a master craftsman, but he had fallen in love with success from the very first moment he'd encountered it as a young sculptor. As a result, he had abandoned his early ideals and built a lucrative career on the smarmy nudes and busts of rich women and of rich men's wives and mistresses. A Marteau nude provided a flawless classical technique, a keen eye for anatomy, and a wise sense of balance between near genius and flattery. It was the gift of subtlety in flattery that had kept his commissions schedule full. It was his *near* genius — his recreant decision always to sell out for the big money rather than to plunge fervently into the deep well of his latent gifts — that made him bury his self-loathing behind a crust of cynicism and restless discontent.

Nor had he had any more integrity in committing his loyalty to a single woman than he had in accepting the responsibilities of his neglected talent, as Marian had so quickly pointed out. In the past several months, as it had become increasingly clear to him that his relationship with Marian had deteriorated beyond repair, he had begun to think about the fact that he had never married or had a lasting relationship. He didn't so much worry about it as wonder about it.

He had always been a serial monogamist. He didn't like being alone. Or rather, he preferred being alone with someone. His work required a certain amount of solitude, with necessary bursts of gregariousness, but in the long haul he wanted the company of a woman. Not, usually, just any woman. He had never been like that. Well, when he was younger there had been a time when he couldn't get enough of the models who paraded through his studios, but those days were long ago and in another world. And models, he had soon learned, were another world all their own.

He woke up during the night with his shoulder throbbing so intensely that he could feel the reverberations all the way down the right side of his body. He pulled himself up and sat on the edge of the bed and realized he was still dressed. Wearily he took off his clothes. Without even looking at his watch to see if it was permissible to take another pill, he opened the amber plastic bottle, took out another one, and swallowed it. Then he lay down again and passed out.

He didn't fly home immediately. It was spring in Paris, the sweetest of all seasons in the sweetest of all cities, and he hated to leave. He spent a week feverishly cleaning out the studio that he had leased for the year. His shoulder proved to be a greater disability than he had anticipated. Eventually he had to hire a couple of men to come in and help him. When he had packed all of his tools and crated the maquettes, he shipped everything home. He settled with his landlord and moved out. Marian hadn't contacted him since the stabbing, but he knew she would. He didn't want to have anything else to do with her.

He moved across the Seine to St.-Germain-des-Prés. He got a suite in the small, secluded Relais Geneviève near the Seine and convinced the hotel management to let him stay under an assumed name. He slept for the greater part of two days.

The weeks that followed were the first

genuine vacation that he had had in years. Though he had never really thought about it until now, he realized that he had worked on back-to-back commissions for nearly eight years. He decided that as long as he was making major changes in his life, now was the time to interrupt that hectic pace.

He called Gerald Beach, his client in San Francisco who had commissioned him to do yet another nude. Back-to-back young wives for older men. God, there was no end to pride and desire. He told Beach that there would be a delay of a couple of months before he could begin but promised him that he would still have plenty of time to bring the project in on schedule.

Then he deliberately devoted himself to idleness.

He browsed the Left Bank bookstores and bought whatever caught his curiosity, books on ancient history and psychology and religion, a how-to book on building stone walls, a biography of a lesbian abbess in Renaissance Florence, the complete poetical works of e. e. cummings, a basic history of illuminated manuscripts.

Without intending to, he fell into a routine, spending his mornings at a table that he informally appropriated in the hotel's garden. The kitchen brought him light lunches. In the afternoons he roamed St.-Germain-des-Prés, rummaging through its antique shops, stopping into cafés and wine bars whenever he felt like it. Discipline was studiously avoided.

A month passed in this way. His shoulder recovered well enough, but he took note of the slowness with which he regained his complete use of it. His body wasn't bouncing back from the wound with quite the same nonchalance that his mind had accepted it. His muscles protested and refused to let him ignore what they had been subjected to. He was strong in his upper body. A thick chest and hefty shoulders were genetic bequests that he had always taken for granted. This little acquaintance with disability, however slight it might be, was something new for him.

Another month of idleness drifted by before he began thinking of going home. As healing as the two months of loafing had been, he was not made for a life dedicated to it. The Beach commission began worming its way into his daydreams, gradually occupying more and more of his thinking until he finally had to admit that he was itching to get on with it. He needed to be back in his own studio, surrounded by the clutter of all the things that made him comfortable.

He called Beach in San Francisco and arranged to have his wife photographed by a woman who for years had provided him with the kind of images of his subjects that he needed. It was the first step in beginning the new commission. By the time he got home the photographs would be waiting for him. After spending a few weeks studying these, he would have Beach and his wife fly to San Rafael for several weeks of live sketching.

Two and a half months to the day after his last encounter with Marian, he flew home.

Chapter 3

Texas

He landed at Austin's Bergstrom International Airport, took a taxi to the charter hangars, hired a small plane, and headed west. Instead of going directly to San Rafael, he asked the pilot to swing south for half an hour and then bank northward again and snake his way up through the beautifully rugged Balcones Escarpment. It was this terrain — marked by high, rolling hills wooded with oak and juniper, which the locals call cedar, and mountain laurel and mesquite, and veined by several small chalky jade rivers — that Texans knew affectionately as the Hill Country.

As they flew low through the valleys, he could clearly see the limestone outcroppings of the old Mesozoic reefs that ran a ragged course from southwest to northeast, their beamy gray ledges presenting a monolithic ridge along the shoulders of the hills. When the early Spaniards first came into central Texas while establishing their network of trails known as the Camino Real, they thought the old limestone escarpment resembled the balconies of Spanish archi- tecture and began referring to the region as *los balcónes.*

From the air, the explosion of flowers that attracted caravans of tourists to the Hill Country every spring looked like pastel powder strewn down the hills and across the meadows and out onto the roadsides, a bright scatter-fall of coral and canary and heliotrope, shades of orange, white and cream, amethyst, and scarlet. It was a hell of a thing to see from the vantage point of the low-flying plane, an unexpectedly colorful welcome home.

Eventually he nodded to the pilot, and they turned back over another ridge of hills and another series of valleys, humming on beneath dazzling white cirrus clouds. As they drifted upward to clear a ridge, San Rafael suddenly appeared below them, dark patches of shadows from the clouds mot- tling the town that straddled the green in- testine passage of the Rio Encinal and crawled up out of the long narrowing valley onto the surrounding wooded hillsides.

San Rafael was a jewel of a town estab- lished by Spanish friars as a mission in the eighteenth century. It grew slowly as a com- munity gathered around the mission, then burgeoned and flourished during the latter half of the nineteenth century when the hillside streets of the town began to fill with block after block of Victorian homes.

With the advent of World War I, the town's fortunes turned and San Rafael languished for decades, almost becoming a ghost town, isolated from the clock and the calendar.

Then in the early 1970s visitors from Austin suddenly recognized the old historic town for being the sleeping architectural prize that it was and began to take the town's future into consideration.

Soon serious preservationists founded the San Rafael Historical Association, and the architecture of the community was documented. Developmental restrictions were put into place and stringently enforced. The hippie tribes that had drifted into town during the sixties were gradually supplanted by artists, writers, and artisans who were drawn to San Rafael by its history and beauty and isolation and, initially, its inexpensive real estate.

The town didn't grow so much as it rejuvenated itself. New construction was obsessively limited and regulated. Every old building, however humble or derelict, became a target for preservation. The old became — without appearing to be — new, and everything new was strictly required to adhere to the architectural milieu that was already there. Access to San Rafael was deliberately restricted. The highway leading to it remained the same small, two-lane paved road that had wound through the valleys of the Hill Country in the 1930s.

By the time Ross bought his place there, the new San Rafael was still discovering the place it would become. During the course of the following twenty years, however, it not only found itself, but was reincarnated: It thrived; it prospered; it became a retreat colony for the artistic cognoscente. Then, magically, it became chic. Art galleries and antique shops moved into old historic buildings, the famous and wealthy bought summer homes there, a spa nestled into one of its hillsides, and an amphitheater sprang up in a neighboring valley. Stylish, intimate restaurants served much-fussed-over southwestern cuisine in rustic but well-appointed settings. The price of real estate was now out of sight, and if you weren't already a resident, you had to stand in line to become one.

But San Rafael was still a small town, too, and all the simple pleasures of a small town were still there in the quiet streets, the mom-and-pop cafés, the occasional neighborhood icehouse, and the dim, quiet bars. Real life still existed there, it was just in the background.

While the plane taxied to the small terminal office of the airstrip south of town, Ross surveyed the private planes of the summer society nosed into the new hangars along the asphalt runway. There were more than ever, it seemed. Every year there were more than ever.

The cab pulled through the wrought-iron gates into his property and crept along the gravel drive that led to the house. He rolled down his window and took a deep breath of the warm spring air. The resinous fragrance of cedars hung like musk in the building heat of the afternoon, and the ratcheting burr of cicadas throbbed sonorously, resembling the deep-throated drone of Tibetan monks.

For years an old German couple had served as caretakers of the house and grounds while he was away on trips, and as the cab pulled up to the low-slung Spanish-style house with its thick stone walls and mottled tile roof, he saw that they had already unlocked the place and left the windows open.

The cabbie helped him unload his bags,

then drove away, leaving him standing on the *galería* that ran the length of the house. In front of him the lawn, the only "kept" part of the property, sprawled out from the house like an irregular green pool, shaded by the broad reach of old oaks that covered much of the entire three-acre compound. Beyond the lawn, he had let native brush grow dense and natural over the whole property, all of which was enclosed by a stone wall dating from the late eighteenth century.

He turned and propped open the screen door with a river rock that sat on the edge of the porch, then carried his bags into the house. The low ceilings and thick, plastered stone walls retained a surprising amount of coolness even late into the day, as well as a faint, lingering sweetness of the mesquite wood he burned in the fireplaces during the mild southwestern winters. He wandered slowly through the silent rooms, re-acquainting himself with the shape and color of things, with the way the light came into the house through the deep casements of the windows and played on the dun-colored walls. He stopped here and there, noticing little things forgotten and confirming the presence of things he had missed.

He went into the kitchen, which was redolent with the sweetness of fresh, ripe peaches from Mrs. Scherz's orchard that she had left heaped high in a crockery bowl in the middle of the kitchen table as a welcome home gift. He took one of the fat peaches and went out through the back screened door to the patio. The mockingbird was the first thing he heard, still and always at her perch on the very top of a resplendent bougainvillea, its cerise bracts tumbling over the arbor bordering the courtyard. He bit into the peach and crossed the patio to a path that cut through the brush to his studio a short distance away.

When he bought the property and its three derelict stone buildings in the oldest, historic part of town, research revealed that the land had once been part of Mission San Rafael, which still occupied a five-acre enclosure on the adjacent property and still shared a common rear wall with his compound. He wasn't able to identify the original use of the ruins he purchased, but the largest of the three buildings became his studio.

An old, rough-barked mesquite threw a lacy shade over the studio's courtyard and heavy wooden door, to the left of which was a niche in the stone wall where a marigold grew from a clay pot. He retrieved a key from behind the pot and unlocked the door.

The place was quiet, beshadowed, and slightly musty; its cavernous height and thick walls made the slightest sounds echo, and the strike of his own footsteps hung in the air of the high space. Coarse, natural muslin drapes covered the tall windows on both sides of the room, and Ross went to the first window on his left and threw back the drapes. A steep shaft of light plummeted to the limestone floor in sudden, brilliant silence, and dust from the long-closed curtains floated and swirled in the brightness. He made his way around the room, throwing open the drapes on each of the eight towering windows.

When the room was lighted, he walked slowly from one end of the studio to the other, eating his peach, surveying the clutter he had left behind a year ago, and savoring the peculiar pleasures of returning home after a long absence. It wasn't until he made his way back to the front door that he noticed the crates he had sent from Paris. There was a lot to do before he could even begin thinking about the new commission.

The very next day after arriving he got an

e-mail from Marian demanding that he pack up everything she had left there and send it to her immediately. He was relieved that she hadn't insisted on coming over to get the stuff herself.

So he spent the better part of the first week searching for the remains of Marian's presence. It was like cleaning up shattered glass. Everything had been shared for so long that it was easy to overlook the things that were exclusively hers. He went through the rooms again and again, finding pieces of Marian's life that stubbornly persisted in hiding from him in plain sight.

When that was done and the crates were shipped off, he began on the studio. Mrs. Scherz had kept the house in good shape, but the studio had remained closed, waiting for him. So he pitched in to put things in order, unpacking the Paris crates in the process. Another three days were consumed by these chores. With all of this tended to, he allowed himself a couple of days to simply wander around the compound and assess the condition of things.

He was surprised to find that despite his relief at having freed himself from Marian, the house and the studio felt different to him from when he'd left them. There was a sense, almost a smell, of absence that hadn't been there before. He tried to put it out of his mind.

One afternoon he picked up the telephone and called Amado to tell him he was home.

Chapter 4

Franz Graber, whose family was among the several large waves of German immigrants to settle in the Texas Hill Country in the mid–nineteenth century, had given his tavern on the river the sentimental name of *Mein Paradies*. But no one had ever called it that. It was known to all merely as Graber's. It occupied a rock building on a quiet street sheltered by towering pecan trees that cast a deep, unbroken shade through the long Texas summers.

It was early evening as Ross approached the tavern along the broken sidewalk. A small green neon sign depicting the disregarded name flanked by a cactus and a palm tree hung above the front door, casting a desultory lime wash upon the stone facade. Twenty steps away a broad concrete staircase turned and descended to the narrow Rio Encinal, which coiled sluggishly through the center of San Rafael, its banks overcast by old cypresses that rose darkly from the embankment. A little farther along the river a scatter of restaurants and bars threw colored lights onto the water. They belonged to the modern town. Graber's still belonged to the 1940s. It had changed so little over the decades that it continued to be rediscovered by different generations of patrons who developed an affectionate loyalty to it.

He waited at the bar in the crowded front room while Nata, Graber's Mexican waitress of most seniority, went out to the courtyard to see if any tables would be available soon. He got a Pacifico, his favorite Mexican beer, from the bar maid and had just turned around to survey the crowd when he saw Nata across the room, raising her chin at him from the doorway that led out to the sprawling patio.

Every chair and table in the garden was full, and the tin lanterns draped between the palms and pecans and oaks dappled the setting with pools of amber glow. During the day the patio was alive with parakeets and parrots that roamed among the trees and vines, shrieking and whistling and strutting their plumage. But now they were silent in the darkness.

He sat down at the marble-topped table and took a deep breath of the evening air. It felt vaguely of the river and carried a sweet waft of the honeysuckle that banked up against the stone wall twenty yards away.

Scanning the courtyard, he nodded at a few familiar faces and sipped his beer. When his eyes reached the back door of the tavern again, Amado was standing there, looking into the patio twilight. Ross raised his hand, and Amado saw him, grinned, and started over.

Amado Mateos was an elegant man who possessed a tranquil manner that one seldom saw anymore. In an age in which no one had enough time, Amado appeared to have an abundance of it. He dressed with a cavalier carelessness in expensive clothes, and in the torrid summers in San Rafael he wore mostly tropical linens in shades of cream and ivory, all of which set off nicely his longish dark hair that was now graying heavily at the temples.

"Ross!" Amado approached the table and shook Ross's hand and slapped him good-naturedly on the back. "Welcome home," he said, pulling out a chair and sitting down. He nodded at the beer. "The first Pacifico since you've been back in the New World, huh?"

"Hardly."

Amado laughed.

The two men had been close friends since they met as students in Paris. A native Mexican, Amado had spent his entire life in Europe, where his father represented a Mexican corporation. Now he divided his time among his principal home in London, where his novels were published, his family home in Mexico City, and San Rafael.

For the next half hour they brought each other up-to-date on what had happened in their lives in the past six months since they last met in London. When Amado asked about Marian, Ross said, "Long story." Amado nodded and let it go at that. He could be patient.

Nata came to take their orders, and they both chose one of Graber's serious Mexican dinners. Though always savory, these dishes were notoriously unpredictable. Graber's cooks were all Mexican nationals, and their interpretations of the advertised dishes could be idiosyncratic, sometimes bearing little resemblance to the descriptions on the menu. If you didn't like surprises, you didn't order food at Graber's.

They ate slowly and kept talking while the tables around them emptied and filled again. Eventually they finished, their plates were taken away, and they ordered another beer. Amado unwrapped his cigar and lighted it with a match. As he drew the tobacco to life, smoke billowed and its pungent aroma replaced the light fragrance of honeysuckle, and the mood of the evening changed.

Finally Ross told him about Marian.

"Jesus Christ," Amado said softly, his eyes fixed on Ross from across the table. "Well . . . damn . . ."

Amado knew Marian about as well as anyone besides Ross, and he was well aware that her outrageous tantrums were always just a flash of the eyes away.

"You know," Amado said after some thought, "if a man and a woman hope to have any magic at all between them, they have to be willing to be a little blind about each other." He paused, drew on the cigar. "Regrettably, that practically invites grief into the equation, doesn't it? Well. It's a lovely paradox."

He shook his head and smoked, regarding Ross with a languid gaze. "She was handsome, Marian was, but God, she was fierce, a passionate woman." He paused. "You have a predilection for fierce women."

"Sure as hell seems that way."

"I'm serious."

"Maybe."

"It's ironic."

"I don't know."

"It is, because you're particularly ill suited to deal with a woman of that kind."

"*Particularly* ill suited."

"You're too self-absorbed," Amado said flatly.

He looked at Amado.

"This isn't news to you, Ross," Amado persisted. "You're brutally honest with yourself, aren't you? About most things, anyway. It's your trademark. But, in this one thing you deceive yourself. You don't want to deal with it."

"Maybe you shouldn't deal with it, either," he said pointedly.

Amado ignored him. "How many times have we had these conversations, over the corpse of one of your relationships? Doesn't it make you wonder about yourself, that you've been to so many women's funerals — metaphorically speaking?"

"No," he lied.

Amado adored women, all women, every kind of woman. He was the only man Ross had ever known who had never spoken a disrespectful word about any woman and who could talk about them with a nearly clinical eye and do so without a hint of salaciousness. He was an unabashed romantic about them, and if he was disappointed or treated meanly by a woman — a rarity — he attributed it to the frailty of human nature, not to the foibles of their sex.

"Ah, and speaking of a woman," Amado said, nodding toward the door to the tavern.

Two women were just then entering the patio, following the stumpy, earnest Nata, who was taking them to their table. Ross recognized Anita Beaton, a seasonal resident from Los Angeles, a thin, angular woman who kept her railish fingers on the pulse of San Rafael's arts establishment in which she mixed at the upper echelons. She was precisely the kind of woman Ross found it easy to be rude to. Her sole interest in life was the cultivation and commerce of gossip. She trolled the taverns, chic restaurants, and dinner parties of San Rafael's summer circuit and created and traded scandals and rumors of scandals. She was every bit the vulture that she resembled.

But it was the woman who accompanied her who was the object of Amado's reference, a woman so striking that she actually sucked all the attention away from Anita, who became, in her presence, a mere tagalong.

She was just shy of being able to be described as tall and had an olive complexion that appeared even darker in the diffused lights of the lanterns. Her hair was dark and thick, and she wore it in an unfussy style at shoulder length. She avoided everyone's eyes as she walked beside Anita, who was doing her best to catch as many eyes as possible. When Anita stopped to chat with an actress whose recent box office success had resuscitated a stumbling career that had almost rendered her invisible, the dark woman moved on, following Nata to their table even though Anita had clearly wanted to introduce her.

"Céleste Lacan," Amado explained. "Arrived about a month ago with Anita's name. You know, one of those tenuous connections one carries to another country. Anita knows a good thing when she sees it, and took Céleste under her bony wing."

"Where's she from?"

"Your city — Paris."

"Really? What's she doing here?"

Amado was still watching her, smiling appreciatively. "Looking for a summer home."

He gave Amado a skeptical look.

"According to Anita," Amado went on, "she's originally from Mexico City. Father was a Scot who went there to work with Petroleos Mexicanos back in the forties. Her mother was a Mexican, an aspiring actress who actually made several films. Céleste was an only child, packed away to London to be educated when she was a young girl. At nineteen she was abruptly called home when her father was kidnapped by guerrillas. He was killed when the oil company dickered too long about the ransom. Mama was left financially comfortable. She and Céleste moved to Europe . . . lived in various great cities. I gather Mama was a bit of a free spirit. A crazy little thing. I think Céleste was the levelheaded one and had her hands full with Mama.

"Mama died three years ago. Céleste married a Mr. Lacan shortly after that . . . marriage fell apart shortly after that . . . estranged . . . separate homes."

Ross glanced at her as she ordered a drink from Nata.

"You've met her?"

"Once at a cocktail party at Anita's. Once at a gallery opening. Visited with her fifteen minutes or so each time."

"What's she like?"

Amado thoughtfully savored a mouthful of maduro smoke.

"Imagine you're looking at the new moon," he said. "There's the sharp, bright crescent . . . and there, next to it, tantalizingly unavailable to you but faintly visible, is the greater moon, veiled in shadow. That's Céleste Lacan. You know when you're talking to her and looking at her that the greatest part of her, the most intriguing part, is . . . just there . . . hazily visible, veiled in shadow."

"That's dramatic."

"And apt."

Ross looked at her again through the pools of lantern light. Anita had rejoined her and was telling her something. Céleste was listening, her back straight as she leaned forward slightly, one elbow on the table as her fingers idly combed through her hair, the other arm in her lap, her breasts resting on the marble top of the table.

She was listening politely, but without genuine interest. She didn't have a film star's polished attractiveness, but if you scanned past her in the course of surveying the garden, your eyes would snap back for a closer look. Beautiful wouldn't be the first word to come to mind.

"She's attracted some attention here," Amado said. "Anita's found it convenient to be her friend and introduce her around. I'm guessing Ms. Lacan will soon find it best to make her way around town unescorted."

Amado smiled.

"Anyway, she's the big excitement so far this season," he said, "but I think it'll be a long summer. The swallows seem to have arrived in greater numbers this year."

Chapter 5

Ross quickly settled into his usual routine when he was in San Rafael. Years ago he had decided to allow the Angelus bells that regulated the mission's daily life to regulate his own daily routine as well. He deliberately arranged his workdays around their tolling.

They woke him at six o'clock. He got up, made coffee, and walked to the front gates to get the newspaper. When he came back, he made a light breakfast and took it out to the patio. Sitting on the deep bench of the arbor, he read the paper while he ate breakfast under the bougainvillea. At eight-thirty he took everything back into the kitchen, put away the dishes, filled a thermos with coffee, and walked through the woods to the studio.

For the next several hours he studied the photographs of Mrs. Beach that had been waiting for him when he arrived from Paris. When the bells tolled at noon, he walked to the house, ate a cold lunch while he listened to a new CD by the tango group Tosca, and then returned to the studio.

In the afternoon he began sketching from

the photographs. He didn't listen to music while he worked. He preferred the sounds that came in through the doors and windows, which he always kept open: the rasp of cicadas, which could be nearly deafening in the hottest part of the summer, interspersed with the somnolent cooing of mourning doves and the gabby vocal flights of a solitary mockingbird.

When the bells tolled again at six o'clock, he closed the studio and climbed into his Jeep and drove down Las Lomitas, the narrow lane that ran by the front walls of his property and descended in a series of turns into town. He drove through Denegre Park, a greenbelt with jogging trails shaded by oaks and sycamores that flanked Rio Encinal, and followed the river upstream for nearly a mile before turning onto a smaller street that led to Graber's.

Inside the tavern he stopped at the bar to pick up his first bottle of Pacifico before heading back to the patio.

He wasn't gregarious, but he liked watching people and listening to them talk. And he liked the parrots that Graber let roam around his jungly patio. Sometimes he and Amado agreed to meet there, but it was a hit-or-miss kind of arrangement. For Ross, this time in late afternoon was simply an opportunity to get away from his own mind for a few hours by turning his attention to other people.

About half the tables in the sprawling patio were occupied as he made his way to a table near the rock wall just above the river. He sat down, looked for the parrots, and found a couple of them sitting on their perches under a small palm. One of them was staring stupidly at nothing, as still as a painted stone, while the other negotiated his perch like a hapless land animal, falling upside down and trying to right himself using his strong beak, squawking and screeching and flopping his broad scarlet wings like flailing flags.

"They're quite beautiful, aren't they?"

He looked around and was surprised to see the woman he had seen here several nights before with Anita Beaton.

"They can have nasty tempers," he said to her profile. She was looking at the birds.

"I've heard they can live to be very old."

"Sometimes," he said, studying her. Then she turned to him. "Fifty, sixty years," he said.

"I'm Céleste Lacan." She reached across the table, and they shook hands.

"Ross Marteau," he said. Her hand was cool and wet from the bottle of beer she was holding. She stood there, not quite smiling, but looking as though she might.

"Are you meeting someone?" he asked.

"No, I just came in . . ." Her voice trailed off as she looked around.

"Would you like to sit down?"

She glanced at the table.

He opened his hands. "I'm by myself."

He thought she was going to offer an excuse, but then she tilted her head to one side in acquiescence.

"Thank you," she said, and before he could stand, she pulled out a chair and sat down. She was as tall as he had judged her to be the night he had seen her, with high hips and almost broad shoulders. Not a fragile woman. He thought of her Scots father. He could see her mother's blood in her coloring and the structure of her face.

"I saw you here with Amado Mateos one night, didn't I?" she asked.

"Probably."

"He's a very civilized man. I like him."

He nodded, took a drink from his bottle. He was staring at her, but most good-looking women were used to it, and he doubted she would be an exception. She had a firm jawline and high cheekbones. Her eyebrows were prominent and dark, and the left one had a small mole at the outside corner. She wore no makeup, perhaps a little mascara.

"This is a quiet corner," she said, looking around the patio. "Appropriate for a quiet man, I suppose."

In profile her forehead sloped back slightly — another Indian feature — to a low hairline.

"A quiet man?" he asked.

She turned back to him. "A hunch."

"Mostly it's just a good place to watch people without having to be involved. It's a good observing spot."

"So you sit here . . . just observing."

"Well, I've never considered it a 'just' sort of activity."

She smiled at that, and he saw a trellis of lines at the outside corners of her brown eyes. She was a woman in transition, passing into her early forties and doing it very well indeed.

"I've gotten the feeling that watching other people is a major preoccupation in this town."

"Well, San Rafael's a small place, so new-comers and the summer celebrities attract a lot of attention. We're easily amused."

She sat quite straight, as she had done that first night, her forearms resting on the table as she held her bottle in both

48

hands, looking at him.

"But aren't you something of a celebrity yourself?" she asked.

"This is San Rafael, Texas." He smiled. "Being a sculptor isn't high on the wow scale around here."

"Well, it is with other people who come here for the summer. Anita says you're a famous recluse . . . and famously reclusive."

"Anita's going to work herself to exhaustion tending to other people's business."

"I've been reading about you," she said. He thought she was watching for his reaction. Her voice was smooth, in the lower registers. There was an accent, but its vowels and inflections gave confused hints of British English and French and Spanish. It was pleasant to listen to, but unidentifiable.

"Reading about me?"

"*ARTJournal, American Artist, Art International* . . ."

"Oh, the critics," he said, tilting his head at her and wondering why she wanted to explore those particular sores. "Well, I won't disagree with them."

She gave him a puzzled frown.

"That surprise you?"

"You're referring to the not-always positive critiques?" she asked.

"Not-always positive. Those, yes."

"What do you mean, you won't disagree with them?"

He took a big swallow of beer to stanch the sour taste this subject always left in his mouth. He decided to just meet the issue head-on with her.

"I used to believe," he said, "that the only time an art journal bothered to cover my work was when they wanted to illustrate an aesthetic morality tale for their readers. You know, a reminder of what it looks like to sell out. They're pretty consistent: They usually refer to the 'enormous potential of his early years,' and then they examine the mediocrity of my work, and then they offer a few disdainful words about the high fees I 'demand.' Often they conclude with a philosophical lament on squandered talent."

Another mouthful of beer.

"After years of this," he went on, "I decided I needed to be honest with myself, take a long hard look at my career. I began to think, Well, now, there's a grain of truth in some of this, isn't there? Maybe more than a grain. I have made compromises, haven't I? Yeah, sure. I have taken commissions purely for the money, haven't I, even knowing from the beginning that the client's going to want something really smarmy? Yeah, sure I have."

He didn't know why he was answering her like this instead of simply shrugging it off with a flippant remark as he had done habitually over the years.

"Then I had to admit to myself that, really, I had sold out more often than I'd stood my ground. In fact, I'd done it for so long that I finally had to admit to myself that the damn magazines don't really have it in for me after all. They're just telling it like it is."

She stared at him curiously. He could see it in her face. She seemed to be trying to figure something out. Was she surprised by something? By his stone-cold self-appraisal? By his lack of pride? By his cowardice at not having tried to turn his career around? What?

"Look," he said, "I don't make any excuses for my work. And I don't pretend that I'm being misunderstood, either," he added. "I've made my choices with both eyes open. I do what I do. They write what they write."

One of the parrots shrieked and Céleste flinched, and a bedlam of screeching and whistling and chirruping rolled through the upper stories of the trees as the parakeets and macaws contributed their opinions of the parrot's comment. When it all died down, there was an awkward silence between the two of them, and the murmur of conversations from the surrounding tables rushed back into the vacuum that he had created by his remarks. He heard someone laugh and smelled the pungent waft of a cigarette.

She was staring at him, her mouth slightly puckered to one side as she nibbled thoughtfully at the inside of her lower lip. Who knew what she was thinking or what her reasons were in bringing up the unflattering articles? But he didn't see how she could have done it innocently. Still, she seemed oddly affected by his response. To hell with it. He wanted to move on.

"Are you in the business, then?" he asked.

"You mean . . . the art business?"

"Yes. Is that why you were reading about me?"

She shook her head. "Oh, no. Not at all. I used to be a researcher for Christie's in London. That's my background, my university training, art history."

"But you don't do that anymore?"

"Not since I've been married, the last few years. Still, I keep up, casually, with what's going on. Since I knew I was going to be here for the summer — I'd read about you in the Paris papers during the past year and knew this was your home — I looked up a lot of articles about you."

"People do that, I suppose," he said.

She sipped from her long-neck bottle, the first taste from it that she had had since she'd sat down. He guessed she didn't really like beer but drank it as an accommodation to the favorite local beverage.

"You know," she said, "I really didn't know . . . how you felt about those articles. I just assumed that sort of thing was something you . . . an artist, shrugged off."

For some reason he wanted to believe her. Just like he wanted to believe everything else she said. Why? If she was really as savvy about the art world as she claimed, then she should've . . . Oh, to hell with it.

"Forget about it," he said. "I will."

She was looking at him as if she didn't believe him. At least he thought that's what she was thinking.

"How did you stumble onto Graber's?" he asked.

"Anita."

"Was that your first time here the other night?"

"Oh, no. I'd been here a couple of times before."

Then, as they looked at each other, there was a quirky and unexpected moment of clarity when he felt as if he saw right into her mind and understood the substance, if not

53

the actual essence, of what she was thinking: She was having second thoughts. About him. What he didn't have any sense of was what her opinion of him had been in the first place. Though he had no doubt that she was amending a preconception, he had no idea if that was good or bad.

"I wonder," she said, still looking at him, "would you mind letting me see your studio sometime?"

That wasn't what he had expected to hear.

"Of course not," he said. "Anytime."

"I'd love to see it."

"Sure. Call me first, though. You'll need directions . . . and to make sure I'm there."

He took a fountain pen from his pocket and lifted his bottle from the round blotter-board coaster on which it had been sitting and wrote his telephone number along the curving edge, away from the wet circle left by his bottle. He gave it to her.

"Thank you," she said, and then she hesitated as if she were about to say something else, something her face implied, entirely different from what they had been talking about. But the moment passed, and her expression softened. "You know . . . it was good of you to ask me to sit down," she said. She looked at the telephone number on the coaster, and then she looked up at him again. "I'll leave you to your observations."

"Take care," he said.

She stood and walked away, past the honeysuckle and the parrots, past the random tables of others, through the sun-dappled shade of the garden. He watched her until she disappeared into the tavern.

At dusk he ordered half a roasted chicken, black beans, grilled green onions, and fresh corn tortillas. It was dark by the time he finished, and the parrots had fallen silent, and the mumble of human voices took over the evening.

When he stopped by the bar inside to settle his tab, Nata had some information for him.

"I see she finally found you," she said, taking his money and ringing up the change.

"What?"

"That woman — she's got some Mexican in her, huh?"

Nata herself was a small wiry Indian from Sonora who had never been seen by either lover or confessor without her silver earrings, little hands from whose fingertips dangled oval medallions engraved with scorpions.

"What do you mean she finally found me?"

Nata counted out his change into his hand with a smirk. She crossed her arms on the bar and leaned toward him.

"She's coming in here four or five times a week for a month now. Same time. Your time. She has only one beer the whole time. I don't know why she gets it. She don't seem to like it. She don't talk to nobody. You're the first one she says *anything* to." Nata grinned. "I think that woman has been waiting for you."

Chapter 6

He spent the next couple of days concentrating on Mrs. Gerald Beach's body. Her name was Lily, an old-fashioned diminutive for a thoroughly modern woman with a thoroughly modern body.

The images his photographer had sent him were clinical in detail. She knew exactly what he wanted, and what he wanted was no surprises. When his client showed up for her live sketching sessions, he wanted to know the architecture of her body as if he'd built it himself. If there was an odd wrinkle in her groin, he wanted the photographer to show it to him. If there was a thickness at her waist, he wanted to see it and he wanted to know how it behaved when she squatted. If her buttocks were uneven, he wanted to know to what degree and how they behaved when she took a step or turned at the waist. If her breasts didn't match, he wanted to know so he could decide which poses presented them to their best advantage.

The more he knew about his subject's anatomy before she showed up for her live sketching sessions, the less time the sessions would require. And the more accomplished he would look at the end of each day when she would inevitably want to see what he had done. He could fudge, but he had to be clever about it. These women knew very well what they looked like, and his flattery had to be subtle enough to avoid outright embarrassment at the fact that what he was drawing was not exactly what he or they were seeing.

Lily Beach, however, was genetically lucky and too young to have to worry about discordant tissue. After several days of sketching isolated parts of her body from the photographs in which she had posed standing, sitting, kneeling, bending, re-clining, leaning, crouching, stretching, reaching, and sprawling, lighted six different ways and from a dozen different angles, he was finally getting to know the essential peculiarities of her anatomy, such as they were.

More than a few times during these days his mind wandered to Céleste Lacan. She was poles apart from Lily Beach in appearance and, he guessed, in personality, too. She kept breaking into his thoughts entirely unbidden: the empathy in her face when she realized that she had touched upon the tender subject of his critics, the way she straightened her back, the flash of hesitation in her eyes, and her decision not to say whatever it was she had started to say before she stood to leave. He thought of her, and wondered about her, sometimes forgetting altogether the very fine musculature of Gerald Beach's wife.

One afternoon, relieved by the noon Angelus bells, he drove his Jeep down the hill into town to a shoe shop on Morelos Street, where he dropped off a favorite pair of old work shoes that he wanted to have resoled. On the way back he stopped by a barrio taco stand in Rincon and grabbed a couple of tacos that he ate right there, sitting in the Jeep under the shade of a mesquite tree.

By one-thirty he was back in the studio, settled into his old leather armchair, his feet resting on a worn-out ottoman, and his sketchbook propped on the incline of his thighs. Lily Beach's photographs were scattered all about him as he worried with one of his drawings in an effort to get the correct angle of her neck. He had been at this a little more than an hour when he heard footsteps on the stones in the courtyard. He looked up just as Céleste Lacan stepped through the opened door.

"Hello," she said simply. The light that fell in through the door illuminated the right one-third of her body, leaving the rest of her in the shadow.

"I guess you didn't need any directions after all," he said, taking his feet off the ottoman and standing. She'd caught him by surprise again. Could she even see him there in the relative darkness? He closed the sketchbook and tossed it into his chair behind him.

"I know, I told you I'd call," she said, coming toward him, passing through one of the shafts of light. "I'm sorry. I just came by on an impulse." She stopped halfway to him. "If this is a bad time, I certainly understand —"

"No, no," he interrupted her. "It's not a bad time at all. I could use a break."

"It's not what I said I'd do, so —"

"No, really. Believe me, I'd tell you if it was a problem for me."

"Okay, good, then." She smiled, accepting his assurances. She came on toward him, surveying the studio as she approached. She wore a dark long skirt with a tan short-sleeved blouse tucked into the waist. Her hair was hastily gathered at the nape of her neck in a careless chignon. She held an oak twig with a cluster of leaves still attached that she must've picked off a tree along the path from the house.

She stopped in front of him but looked up at the high ceiling and drew in a slow, deep breath. "I love the smell of the stones." Her eyes roamed the studio. "It's an old place, isn't it?"

He told her briefly about the compound, what it had been, how he'd got it, and what he'd done to it. When he stopped she began to wander in no particular direction, stopping to look at old maquettes of various sizes that lay scattered about from former commissions, a dusty monkey skeleton dangling from a wire on a wooden stand, the model of an arm or foot. She paused and smiled at a vitrine that contained a collection of outspread birds' wings, and she lingered over a framed display of obsidian insect carvings.

"You're a gatherer," she said, her back to him as she examined a tray of feather-light cicada husks arranged in diagonal rows. Not a collector, a gatherer. That was a nice distinction. And she seemed to be pleased at the idea.

"I like stuff," he said. "Sometimes you can just pick it up for nothing, wonderful stuff, and sometimes you have to pay for it. But it's all interesting . . . and it's all . . . stuff."

He saw her smile to herself as she turned and moved on, and he moved along with her, watching her. She said nothing else to him, and he was content to observe her in silence as she continued prowling among his workbenches and cluttered tables. He knew what she was doing because he had done it himself in the studios of other artists. She was indulging in a kind of intellectual scopophilia, spying on the minutiae of non-essentials with which he liked to surround himself on a daily basis, curious to know if these secret singularities could somehow reveal to her his personality in a way that nothing else could. That was fine with him. He had the feeling — based on nothing more than gut instinct — that this woman was going to glean a lot more from what she saw than most people. He felt oddly stirred, as if he were allowing her to glimpse him naked through the narrow opening of a door slightly ajar.

It struck him how peculiar it was that they were meandering around the studio together in silence. But he rather liked the idea of them doing it, and he liked it that she didn't feel obligated to fill the silence. She seemed comfortable among the things that made him comfortable, too, and he was secretly gratified when she stopped to examine with obvious appreciation some small thing that he had acquired for no other reason than that it gave him a simple or indefinable pleasure. As he accompanied her and watched as she paused at some artifact or trifle — and often he was surprised at the minutiae that caught her attention — he felt a growing responsiveness to her. It was easy enough to explain: Like most people, he found her tastes and curiosity most attractive when they confirmed and coincided with his own.

Occasionally he caught a waft of faint fragrance. It wasn't perfume.

At one point she stopped and looked in silence at the wooden modeling platform that stood in the center of the studio. It was two feet high and twelve feet square, large enough for several models at once. Only an uncovered daybed and a straight-backed chair occupied the bare boards. The empty stage contrasted sharply with the rest of the cluttered studio, but she gave the stark platform more time than anything else. She stood still, looking at it, lost in thought. Then she moved on without comment.

When she found herself back at the chair where he had been sitting, she bent and picked up a couple of Lily Beach's photographs. She held one in each hand and looked at them, her eyes taking in the whole of the long, pale, privileged body of his client. She dwelled on the pictures longer than he would have expected — and this time he really wished he knew exactly what she was thinking — and then she bent and dropped them on the floor where she had found them. She scanned the other pictures from where she stood, and as she turned away he saw her take note of the sketchbook in his chair.

"Lovely," she said to him, but he didn't know whether she was referring to the studio or to Lily Beach. She cast her gaze about the studio once again, then stopped her eyes on him.

"Do . . . do you have a little while to talk?" she asked.

She sat on one of the high wooden stools, the heels of her sandals hooked on the bottom rung, her back nearly touching the bench, and he sat on the top of a wooden cabinet of flat files, facing her. She almost seemed as if she wanted to confide in him.

The sunlight reflected off the deep stone window casement beside her and washed into the room between them. They looked at each other across a span of brightness in which an occasional gnat drifted about in disoriented vacillation, like an animated mote.

"I need to be honest with you about something," she said, reaching up and tucking a strand of hair behind her ear. "I would have come here sooner, but I knew I had to do this and . . . well . . . I wasn't looking forward to it."

She was uncomfortable, maybe even embarrassed, but not upset. He waited.

"I'm not here out of simple curiosity," she began, "there's another reason."

"Which is . . ."

"I want to commission you to do a sculpture."

He waited a beat for that to soak in.

"You mean that's why you came to San Rafael, to see me about this?"

"Yes."

"Not looking for a summer home."

"No."

This was pretty unorthodox, but it explained a lot.

"Why didn't you just tell me this at Graber's the other day?"

"It would be a sculpture of my sister," she said, ignoring his question.

Her sister?

"What kind of sculpture?"

She flicked her eyes toward the photographs of Lily Beach. "A full-length nude."

The sister was younger, then? How much younger?

As if she knew what he was thinking, she

reached into the pocket of her skirt and pulled out a photograph, looked at it, and then handed it to him.

"This is Leda," she said.

It was a color snapshot of a young woman sitting at a table on a terrace. A section of the terrace balustrade was visible in the background, and beyond that the sea, unmistakably the Mediterranean. If Céleste possessed an appeal that some people might have found difficult to appreciate, her sister's beauty was indisputable. It really was the sort, as the cliché had it, that made careers and wrecked lives. He had seen a lot of beautiful women, and this one was, by just about anybody's standards, drop-dead gorgeous. The only thing anyone might find difficult about her appearance would be turning away from it.

Her dark hair fell over her shoulders, and her complexion was the same rich olive of Céleste's. But it was the structure of her face that immediately caught his experienced appraisal: It was startlingly symmetrical, so balanced that a mirror image of either half would exactly match its original. A rare attribute. There were no flaws in her features, and Ross thought it would be difficult for anyone to suggest an improvement.

"She's beautiful," he said.

"Yes," she agreed, "but Leda's . . . not like any other beautiful woman you've ever seen."

He felt a pang of disappointment at this remark. He'd heard something like it, variations of it, so many times over the years that it rang empty and silly in his head. Beautiful people, and the people who loved them, always thought they were special. Even if they had the good sense to hide this conceit, it was still there, embedded within them, feeding their self-regard, informing their own belief in the blind magic of a genetic accident. But it hadn't been his experience that they were indeed special. Gorgeous young women, most specifically those who wanted to have their bodies sculpted, were all too dreadfully similar.

"That must've sounded trite to you," she said. There was no hint of apology.

"What makes you say that?"

She held him with a look. "Surely you don't think you're the only one capable of reading other people?"

"Was I that transparent?"

"I'm that observant," she said.

The retort caught him by surprise, and he felt an unaccustomed twinge of uncertainty.

"I realize you've seen a lot of beautiful women in your career," she went on, "and I guess you've formed some pretty strong opinions about what's 'typical' about them. They must bore you now." She paused. "I doubt if you see anything special in them anymore."

"Special," he said, recovering his thoughts. "That's an idea that tends to lose its meaning in certain circumstances, doesn't it?"

"Does it?"

He wanted to make his point without sounding sardonic.

"Imagine," he said, "that there's a room where a thousand women have been gathered because their beauty has distinguished them, made them special. In the context of that group, 'special' begins to lose its meaning. Because they're all special, each of them ceases to *be* special. To be 'special' in that room, you'd have to possess a quality defined by a completely different set of criteria."

She thought about this a moment. She looked at the twig as she twirled it in her fingers. When she lifted her head again, they looked at each other from shadow to shadow through the shaft of light.

"In that room," she said, "Leda not only would still warrant your new definition of special, she would easily qualify as exceptional. A rarity, in fact."

Chapter 7

It was a remarkable thing to say, and she must have seen the skepticism in his face.

"You find that hard to believe?" she asked.

"It sure as hell raises expectations," he said.

There was a small change in the shape of her eyes, a smile in her mind.

"What if I told you," she said, "that you could still learn something new about beauty."

"Something you could teach me?"

"No, I think you could learn from Leda."

"Then I'd say I can't wait to meet her."

The twig stopped twirling, and she looked away toward the window. Nearby, in one of the oaks, a mockingbird gabbled to herself in a low, ruminative voice. He studied Céleste's profile. Though she sat in shadow, the next window beyond her provided a backdrop of oblique, hazy brightness. She seemed, suddenly, enormously intelligent, as if she possessed a powerful secret and were trying to decide how to convey it gently to an uninitiated intellect.

"You're cynical about it," she said, still

looking out the window. "About beauty, I mean." Her tone was neither challenging nor accusatory. It was thoughtful — almost, even, understanding.

"I'm not cynical about it," he said. "You can't be cynical about an amoral thing like that. It just exists, all by itself. The fact that we find it in this thing or that person, and not in that thing or another person, is amoral, too. It just happens. Like thunderstorms. The reasons for it, the deeper reasons for it — beyond atmospheric conditions, beyond DNA — remain a mystery. I have a lot of respect for mystery. I'm not cynical about that."

Outside, the sun was burning in a cloudless sky, and the broad depth of the windowsill was at its most brilliant point because of the angle of the sun. In contrast with the sharp light, they sat in the darkest shadow. A warm breath of the afternoon moved in through the opened windows, occasionally displacing the cool from the stone walls.

She turned to him. "But there's something derisory in your attitude about —"

"Human nature, not beauty."

She waited. Suddenly he saw her in extraordinarily sharp focus, even through the shadow. He could see the moisture in her eyes, not tears, but the viscous liquid environment of her sight.

"And you include yourself in that harsh assessment?" she asked pointedly.

"Especially myself."

This seemed to be a new thought to her. Though she had been insightful about him, even eerily intuitive, she hadn't expected he would include himself in his own cynical philosophy.

"You'll talk to Leda, then," she said, shifting abruptly back to her sister and the subject of the commission.

"Sure. Is she here, in San Rafael, too?"

"She will be in a few days. She'll be staying the summer with me."

She hesitated, and this time he could see her carefully considering what she would say next.

"Leda and I have different fathers," she said. "When Eva — my mother — and I moved to Europe after my father's death, I was old enough by then to be on my own, and I returned to London where I'd been in school. Eva finally settled in Rome." She paused. "Eva was an exotic woman. Dramatic. She was like nectar to certain kinds of men. Always the wrong kinds."

Her hastily wrapped chignon began slipping from its moorings, and she absently reached up with one hand and prodded it back in place with fingers that instinctively knew the maneuvers. It was a thoughtless reflex, a universally feminine motion.

"One day I went to Rome for the holidays and discovered that Eva had had a baby. It was only a few months old. Leda. Eva had hired a nurse and was going on with her life. I don't think she even knew who the father was."

Céleste looked down at her hands in her lap, thinking. He wondered how she was deciding what she would tell him and what she wouldn't. Why would she select one word rather than another, why this phrase rather than that one?

"I didn't feel any attachment to this child," she said, looking up, straight at him. "Or any affection. And I didn't want any part of the kind of life that she represented. I fled back to London and that was that. For the next dozen years I saw them only rarely. That was fine with Eva, who didn't really want a younger woman — and potential rival — hanging around complicating her affairs.

"When Leda was fifteen Eva sent her away to school, as she had me. Switzerland. When Leda finished school she stayed on in Geneva for university. Eva didn't make her feel any more welcome in Rome than she had me, and was glad to pay her to stay away. She was in her last year in university — about three years ago — when Eva decided to drive to Switzerland to see her for the Christmas holidays. She and the man she had taken with her were both killed in a car crash in northern Italy."

Again the chignon began to come apart. Irritated, she started taking it down while she went on talking, removing hairpins and combing her fingers through her falling hair.

"When Eva's will was settled I was astonished to discover that she'd made me Leda's legal guardian. I would have that responsibility for another four years. It wasn't a situation that either of us liked."

Céleste paused and toyed with one of her hairpins.

He didn't know where any of this was going, but he was discovering that he would rather watch and listen to Céleste than just about anything else he could think of. Her accent was delightfully interesting and pleasant.

"Have you ever been a model?" she asked suddenly.

He shook his head. "Well, maybe a few times, for friends. Years ago in school."

"For busts. Portraits."

"Yeah, sure. We all did that for each other when we couldn't afford models."

"But you've never taken off your clothes."

"No, never done that."

"Well, that's another matter altogether, isn't it?"

"I guess so. You say that as though you've done a good bit of it."

"Yes, I have."

"You didn't like it much."

"Oh, but I did. I more than liked it."

"What does that mean?"

"It was satisfying." She hesitated a beat. "It's not an insignificant thing to do."

She spoke as if there were something mystical about it. He'd known a lot of models over the years, but he sure as hell hadn't known any mystics among them. For the most part, they were pretty earthy women.

"The point is," Céleste went on, "Leda wants to do this more than anything else in the world, but I have serious reservations about it."

"Why?"

There was a little pucker at one corner of her mouth as she thought, but the expression in her eyes was impenetrable.

"Tell me," she asked, "have you ever done anything of which you are profoundly ashamed?"

Jesus. She could go off in some strange directions. He didn't know anyone who was such an engaging mixture of plain speaking and surprise.

"Oh, I think everyone has done something at some time in their lives tha—"

"No, no," she interrupted, "nothing glib. That's not what I'm talking about. I said 'profoundly' ashamed."

It was a hell of a question.

"I can't say that I have."

"You 'can't' say —"

"A figure of speech," he said. "No, I don't think I've ever done anything of which I was profoundly ashamed."

She gave him a disturbing smile that wasn't a smile but took the shape of one, as if she had caught him in a lie. Then she shrugged as if to dismiss it all and changed directions again.

"Mr. Marteau —"

"Let's drop that, okay?"

She paused, then continued, but without using his name at all. "Leda doesn't fully understand what she's doing here, and I think she could be making a serious mistake."

"I thought you were trying to get this done for her?"

"She's going to do it with my 'help' or

without it. I'll sign the check. That's my job. But I don't see any reason to ignore the risks, either."

"What are you worried about?"

"Not about posing nude, no." Her eyes were dark, the pupil lost in the iris. "My fear is that Leda will never be nude. She'll always be naked — in your eyes, and in her eyes. And certainly in the eyes of everyone who will look at the sculpture."

He was beginning to feel that Céleste viewed everything through a lens that provided her with a perspective that was not only uniquely her own, but also completely off the charts of behavioral norms. He would be making a mistake if he ever presumed to believe he could anticipate how she would feel about anything.

"I'm not trying to be obscure or evasive," she said. "Actually, my problem is that I want to say more than I should."

This last remark was colored by sadness or regret or longing, he really couldn't tell, but the edge of discontent was unmistakable. The relationship between the two sisters was not a simple one.

"I imagine this is rather more about us than you would've liked to know."

"But these are things you wanted me to know, aren't they?"

76

He wanted somehow to put the conversation on a different footing. He was beginning to feel that he was being manipulated, though he couldn't really say how or to what end. But he wasn't too comfortable with it.

"It must seem that way," she said.

"It does."

"Well, I wouldn't make too much of that," she said. "Sometimes I simply talk too much."

"I doubt that. I don't think you say much that you don't intend to say."

The light between them was softening. Her face was somber now, which he felt odd about. It was as if she were making arrangements for a funeral.

She reached out, her arm penetrating the light, and laid the twig of oak leaves on the deep windowsill.

"Then I'll just call you," she said, "when Leda's ready to talk."

It was late in the afternoon when they finally reached this point, and he asked her if she would like to stay for a drink. But she made an excuse that sounded like an excuse, and she didn't bother to make it sound like anything else. He walked out to her car with her, and she left.

That night after he ate dinner and cleaned up the kitchen, he went into the sunroom and put on a Miles Davis CD. He turned off the lights, lay down on the sofa, and kicked off his shoes. As he looked out from the dark to the small lights around the patio, his mind wandered to Céleste. He had never been so entertainingly finessed. Yet in the end, somehow, he didn't feel manipulated at all. Or maybe he did, but he just didn't mind.

When he woke the room was silent. It was after two o'clock. The timer had turned off the patio lights, and everything was blue black, with highlights of indigo. He got up, turned off the CD player, and walked down the corridor to his bedroom. He undressed and got into bed. He tried not to think of her anymore.

Chapter 8

For the next three days he worked steadily on the Beach project, filling several sketchbooks with studies of poses, working his way toward a decision about how best to present Mrs. Beach's wonderful proportions.

Amado had gone to New York for a week with a friend who had "a lovely back," so Ross hadn't seen him since Céleste showed up at Graber's and then at his studio.

In the afternoons after he'd finished in the studio he worked on the grounds, trimming dead wood out of the trees and bundling the trimmings in neat piles to be hauled away. In the evenings he dawdled through his art books. He had missed his books during the year he'd been in Paris, and he was enjoying revisiting his old favorites.

And every night he resisted the temptation to call Céleste.

On the morning of the fourth day he was fine-tuning a sketch on the drawing board when the telephone rang. It was Céleste.

After they exchanged a few pleasantries, she said, "Leda came in early yesterday morning. She's caught up on her jet lag now, and she's eager to meet you. When is a good time for us to come over?"

"Make it easy on yourself," he said.

"This afternoon?"

"Sure."

"Three o'clock?"

"Fine."

The afternoon was bright and warm and still. The cicadas were raising a din in the woods surrounding the studio. He had ordered a small load of limestone blocks from a quarry north of Austin, with the intention of trying his hand on some small sculptures just to stay in practice with stone. His last four major commissions had been in clay. The blocks had arrived that morning — but only a partial load, the rest would be delivered in a couple of days — and were stacked under an oak tree between the studio and the kiln shed.

He had gone out to inspect them and had just stepped back into the studio when he heard footsteps on the stones of the courtyard. He turned toward the open door as the silhouettes of the two women filled the panel of light.

"Ross?"

"Yes, come in," he said, wiping off the chalky limestone dust from his hands with a rag from one of the workbenches. He squinted at the bright backlighting behind the silhouettes of the two approaching women.

"This is Leda," Céleste said as the girl extended her hand to him. He was concentrating on her face, anticipating the symmetrical features he had seen in the photograph. And there they were, emerging as his eyes adjusted to the contrasting light. Reality surpassed the image in the photograph. She was exquisite.

As he took Leda's hand she said, "I'm happy to meet you," in the same softly accented English as Céleste's, and he felt something oddly out of balance in her handshake. Leda was smiling at him, but he was instantly aware that it was a complicated smile. There was more to it than a simple, affable expression. Her eyes were penetrating and anticipatory, and he realized that she was watching for his reaction. And then he sensed it before he understood it: The beautiful young woman before him was not entirely beautiful.

He felt Céleste looking at him, too, but he didn't take his eyes off Leda. While he still held her hand, she turned her shoulder slightly, allowing him to see the swollen convexity in the curvature of her spine, the buffalo hump of a hunchback.

Jesus.

"It was my idea," Leda said quickly, "keeping this from you. I was afraid you wouldn't talk to me at all if you knew."

Stunned, he continued to hold her hand. Suddenly he was furious that they had done this, that he had been made the butt of their deception.

"We have a lot to talk about," Leda said with the flat practicality of someone used to dealing with the radical reaction her appearance caused in others.

When she tried to withdraw her hand, he held on to it. She tried to pull away again, but he continued to hold her. Her brow creased with uncertainty, then alarm.

The expression on her face jolted him again, wrenching his reaction in the opposite direction as he instantly realized that his shock, his very speechlessness, was an insult to her, a confirmation of her freakishness. His anger collapsed into embarrassment. And fascination.

He released her hand suddenly, too suddenly.

"Sorry," he said. He hesitated. "Okay, then . . . you want to talk. Let's sit over here."

He gestured toward his old leather armchair and an uncomfortable Victorian settee with threadbare upholstery. He couldn't imagine what she was going to say, but he remembered Céleste's concern. Jesus, he understood now. Her fears about how Leda's sculpture would be viewed were unquestionably justified. A nude sculpture of this young woman would most likely create a curiosity in the viewer that was not unlike the curiosity that drew people into a carnival sideshow.

"I know this is a surprise," Leda said, turning toward the settee.

As she stepped by him he saw that the dorsal hump was canted to one side and was surprisingly acute, rising sharply from the horizontal midline of her shoulders. He also noticed that there was something askew with her pelvis as well, though she had no trouble at all walking or moving about. But there was a crablike motion to some of her maneuvering, a result he guessed of the effort she had to make at all times to maintain her balance.

"Céleste warned me that this would be a mistake," she said, sitting down on the settee. She had to sit forward, midway to the edge of the seat, and quickly and expertly slanted her legs and crossed her ankles in a certain way to achieve a kind of grace, the result of years of necessity and practice.

"I'm sorry if I was . . . awkward," he said,

waiting for Céleste to take her seat beside Leda before he sat in the old leather club chair.

Seeing the two sisters side by side was remarkable. Céleste lounged back into her corner of the settee and crossed her long legs at the knee, making them seem even longer, her whole appearance and manner a stark contrast to her sister's lumpish perch.

The disharmony of Leda's stunning face and her tortured physique was, he had to admit to himself, a second incongruous image in this disturbing dyad and was morbidly intriguing. Her face alone would demand a double take anywhere. And then the realization that this extraordinary face was connected to a severely distorted body, which in itself would have attracted stares, too, demanded yet another double take.

Almost simultaneously it struck him what a disturbing effect this aesthetic confusion must have had on this young woman's life. The psychological turmoil must have been indescribable, if, indeed, it still wasn't.

"There's really nothing very much to elaborate on," Leda began. Her voice had the clear quality of youth. "Simply put: I want a nude, full-body sculpture. I want it to be a literal representation. No subtle glossing, just reproduce what you see in front of you."

He cut his eyes at Céleste. She was placid, her expression open, waiting. He looked back at Leda.

"I'm not going to insult you by asking if you've thought this through," he said, "but could you go over some of that with me?"

"Some of what?"

"Why you want to do this."

"Why?" she asked. "Does that matter?"

"If I'm going to do this, it matters a lot."

"To you."

"Yes."

"What if I don't tell you?"

"It's not a challenge. It's only a question."

"What if I lie to you?"

"Well, I wouldn't know that, would I?"

She stared at him a moment as if to consider whether she thought him worthy of a further explanation. Clearly Leda didn't have a frail ego. He didn't have to work very hard to surmise that living with the freakish physical combination of her unique body had been the major influence shaping her personality. That and living with — or rather being rejected by — the radically selfish Eva. Whether she was mature beyond her years, or merely bitter beyond her years, remained to be seen.

85

"I'm all too well aware," she began slowly, "of my strangeness, of the effect this body has on people."

She paused, but not from uncertainty. Rather, she seemed quite relaxed about it, but not without some near-the-surface passion.

"Every day of my life," she said, "is lived in the reflection of other people's reaction to me. I have to deal with that in every face I see. No exceptions. Ever. How do people react to you? You're not even aware of a re-action, are you? Well, I can never enjoy that kind of oblivion. I see them stealing looks at me, then turning away when our eyes meet. When someone is *forced* to confront me — in the case of a sales clerk, for instance — they're so intent on *not* looking at my hump that their eyes virtually lock on to mine in a kind of stupid, unblinking startle."

She considered something a moment, her eyes going distant in thought.

"You know," she continued, "I've read ar-ticles, feminist rants, about the debasing act of 'the male gaze.' " She glanced at Céleste. "She and I both studied art history. Useless degrees for the most part, but it's good for the intellect, and you learn about culturally vital things like 'the male gaze.' Anyway, being something of an authority on the idea

86

of 'the gaze,' I can say this much. . . ." Her beautiful mouth turned down in a caustic sneer. "I'll take the male gaze. Oh, yes, please, I'll suffer *that,* and they can have the look *I'm* familiar with, the gaze of repulsed curiosity — the involuntary stare reserved for the queerly disfigured." She stopped. "There are indignities," she said, "and then there are cruelties."

He cut his eyes at Céleste and found her staring back at him with a blank expression that conveyed nothing at all. When he looked again at Leda, she was waiting for him.

"So . . . you see," she went on, like a teacher addressing a pupil for whom she had been waiting to return from a momentary daydream, "the thing is, I know that people wonder what I look like underneath my clothes. 'What does she look like *there?* Is she "normal" . . . *here?*' Well, I want you to show them. I want you to be their eyes for me."

What in the hell could he say at this point? What did one say to such an idea?

"And there's another reason," she added. "I also want to do this because *I* want to see myself in three dimensions instead of the one dimension of me I see in mirrors. I want to be able to touch myself in places I can't touch now. I want to see what others see."

She paused and held out her hands, palms facing him, and when she spoke she spoke slowly and her voice was richly soft and lovely and seductive.

"I want to walk around myself and put my own hands on this goddamned thing . . . and feel it, feel the whole . . . ugly . . . mass . . . of it."

She concluded in a husky whisper as if she had recited a tender declamation of affection, and her eyes rested in the mid-distance as if in a reverie.

Silence.

Then suddenly she moved her shoulders with a subtle shiver, like an actress snapping out of a trance induced by immersing herself in her character's long soliloquy.

"How's that for an answer?" she asked brightly with a soft, innocent smile on her beautiful mouth.

Had that really been her answer, or was it merely a smart-aleck performance? He didn't have any idea what she might be thinking or feeling, but he was dealing with a dozen different thoughts at once. What an incredible proposition she was offering him. It was crazy. Nearly everyone would find the completed sculpture controversial. Some would see beauty, some the poignant riddle of Leda's unique reality, some would see only the grotesque. There was no doubt that it would be disturbing. And it could prove to be emotionally unsettling for him, too, as well as for Leda. What would he uncover, literally and psychologically, even spiritually? He looked at her, her youthful, extraordinary face waiting for his response with a wan, angelic smile of anticipation. Was she emotionally unstable? If she was, would that matter?

Seeing that he wasn't going to respond, she elaborated.

"This idea has preoccupied me for a long time, Ross," she said, apparently unafraid of the familiarity that her sister had carefully avoided. "I *will* do it." She paused for emphasis. "I need you for this. Specifically you."

"Specifically me?"

Leda raised one hand near her face to hold his attention. It was a beautiful hand, he now noticed, and he recalled the feel of its narrow shape in his own.

"Please," she said. "Céleste has been holding me back, convincing me to wait until we found the right sculptor. Not just anyone, she said, should do this. She's talked to others, in Paris, in London. To be honest, you're the first sculptor she's agreed to let me speak to."

Céleste seemed to be more involved in this process than she had led him to believe. He wanted to say something about that, but it seemed nitpicky. It was a bizarre commission, and he could understand the two sisters being nervous about it. He was even a little flattered that he had been "selected," whatever the hell the criteria were, and especially that it had been Céleste who had made the decision. He could see her in his peripheral vision, as quiet as a basilisk, apparently feeling no obligation to smooth over the differences in their stories.

In an instant he knew he was going to do it.

Chapter 9

"This isn't going to be an easy thing to do," he said. "For either of us. It's going to require long hours. It can be physically numbing."

"I know that."

"And it'll be intimate," he said. "I'll have to take measurements of you, detailed measurements with calipers."

"I told you, I'm used to being looked at."

Céleste dropped her eyes as if she knew what was coming. Leda went on.

"Up to now," she said, "only children have had the innocence to give me a good long stare. You'll be the first adult ever — aside from doctors — to get a proper eyeful of me, to look at all of me, all that you want. God, it'll be a relief to have you take your time with me."

These last words were spoken with a kind of passion that made him uncomfortable. It wasn't said with bitterness, but with an enthusiasm that seemed inappropriate. Would he have preferred bitterness from her? Would he have preferred her to be as emotionally distorted as she was physically? What did he expect from her?

"What do you want from this?" he asked. "I mean ultimately, once the sculpture is completed, and people are able to do as you wish, to touch, to feel, to see from every conceivable angle, what do you expect to happen?"

"You mean, do I expect it to be an exorcism?" She lowered her chin and furrowed her brow in theatrical gravitas. "A release from the . . . 'spiritual agony of this body'?"

Her self-mockery was biting, but at the same time he thought he sensed that an exorcism was exactly what she was hoping to experience in the process. But she gave him a flip response.

"Look, I just want to do it. I don't want to analyze it."

"Your body has a mind attached to it," he said. "I don't have any interest in sculpting just the bones and muscles. Ideally, at least, there's more to it than that."

"Ohhhhh," she purred, "that's awfully highbrow. Were you able to capture the mind of the woman you just finished sculpting in Paris?"

If Ross had been ten years younger, he would have flushed at this impudence. But he had developed calluses. The flick of the scorpion's tail had to hit him harder than that.

"Have you seen that sculpture?" he asked.

"Actually, I have. I went to look at it."

"Her husband didn't want to see any more than what he got," he said.

"Then he wasn't disappointed, was he?"

"No."

"I don't want to see any more than that, either."

"But I do," he said.

She shrugged indifferently.

"In your case," he said, returning Leda's penchant for bluntness, "we have a mixed bag. Beauty isn't the only thing we're dealing with here. There's something else, isn't there? Inevitably this will be controversial. Believe me, I can live without the disputation this is likely to create. If I'm going to have to put up with that, I want to make it worth my while. For me it's got to be more than just another commission."

He stopped to let this sink in a moment, and then he added, "If I can't do it the way I want to do it, then I won't do it."

He could see her simmering. It was a puzzling standoff. After all, he had asked her only a relatively innocent question, an effort to get a little deeper into an understanding of how she felt about her body. Her response could have been finessed in a dozen different ways, yet she chose to make a confrontation out of it.

Céleste hadn't moved. He couldn't have guessed what she was thinking in a thousand years. He continued to look at Leda.

"Okay," she relented, though she was clearly resentful, "I'll get into that, but can we save it until later? I'll give you plenty of insight, if that's what you want."

"Fine."

"Then you'll do it?"

"Yes, if we can work out the other arrangements."

"Can we start immediately?"

"No, that's not possible."

"What's the matter?" she snapped before he could explain. "Was all that pompous talk just the peacock shimmering his tail?"

If he had had any doubts left, this last taunt wiped them away. Leda was a deeply bitter woman, and working with her would require a patience he didn't usually allow his often pampered clients. The distortions in Leda's life went far deeper than flesh and bone.

He ignored her wisecrack and told her about the Beach commission, the deadline, the obligation to honor a commitment.

"Okay, what about a compromise," Leda offered. "I understand that you can't just drop what you're doing, but I'm going to be here for a few months, and then I have to go back to Paris. It seems a shame to waste the time. I know you usually begin with photographs, but if I'm going to be right here in San Rafael anyway, why don't you just start sketching me as a diversion from your other commission? You can't work on the other thing *all* the time, can you?"

As he looked at the two women sitting across from him, it struck him how dramatically different they were from his usual clients. Most people came to him because they wanted something beautiful, something quickly recognizable as beautiful without any need for laborious interpretation by the viewer. Not so here. Nor was vanity a factor here. Neither of them was looking for approval or acceptance from a particular crowd. Rather than simply wanting a trophy that they hoped would also have an aura of sophistication attached to it, Leda was passionately tied to the commission, even though she hated to admit it.

Leda wanted something honest — or so she had said before she decided to deny it — and in pursuing this, she had provided him with a gift of occasion, a chance to reach for something deeper, something greater, than a mere facile copy of a beautiful body.

"Okay," he said, "you're right. I think we can do that."

Her face was instantly transformed by a glowing smile, a beautiful thing to see, and she literally squirmed on the settee.

"I promise," she exuded with gratitude, "that you'll regret this."

She was so excited, she didn't even notice the unfortunate misstatement, and then she was pressing him about when they could begin. He finally agreed to start the next morning. She would need to be at the studio at ten o'clock.

"Okay, that's settled, then," Céleste said, uncrossing her legs and sitting up. "Now Ross and I have to talk about the terms of the agreement, about the finances. You can stay or not."

It seemed an unnecessarily abrupt change in the direction of the conversation, but Leda didn't even appear to notice.

"No, I don't want to stay for that," she said, suddenly disinterested.

"You can take the car back," Céleste suggested. "Ross can drive me home when we're through."

Leda looked at him.

"That's no problem," he said. "I'll be glad to."

Leda held out her hands for the keys, and Céleste gave them to her. They took a few moments to go over the directions back to

Céleste's house in Palm Heights. When she had it straight, Leda stood, avoiding his eyes as she got to her feet with a kind of rolling, heaving effort. Her hulking back was so dominant, he wondered how he had missed seeing it the very first instant she arrived. He stood also, and she said good-bye and walked away toward the door.

Though her mobility was strong and sure, her hips were noticeably canted, her center of balance difficult for him to locate. The hump on her back made her seem shorter, thicker, even, strangely, powerful. She walked out of the studio without looking back or saying another word.

After she had crossed the courtyard, he looked at Céleste, who was now sitting up straight on the settee, her legs together, forearms resting on her knees, looking at him.

"There you have it," she said.

"I should've known not to push her," he said, sitting down again. "She'd already said more than she would've liked."

"You won't have any trouble learning more about her," Céleste assured him.

"Is she concerned about taking off her clothes?"

"She hasn't said anything to me about it."

"Do you think she is?"

"Frankly, I doubt it." She sighed. "Let's do settle the final business with the agreement. If you're going to begin tomorrow, then let's tie together the loose ends."

"There aren't any loose ends," he said. "We'll settle everything later. We'll just consider the early sessions as exploratory efforts. We'll see how it goes."

She nodded, looking at him. "You wanted to do it the minute you recovered from the shock of seeing her, didn't you?" she observed.

"How about a glass of wine?" he said.

He got a bottle of Barbera d'Asti from a cool bin in the stone wall at the rear of the studio and brought it back with a couple of glasses. She was standing by one of his several worktables, looking at a maquette, a reclining nude. He put the glasses on the table and began opening the wine.

"What's the story behind this one? She looks Middle Eastern."

"Egyptian. It never got past the maquette."

"Why?"

"Well, it was odd," he said, pouring the wine and handing her a glass. "Her husband commissioned it. He was a businessman in Alexandria. The woman died in a swimming accident just after I finished this. He was devastated. He didn't want the bronze casting completed. After he paid me, I offered to send him the maquette, but he didn't want it. He made me promise to destroy it. I promised."

She was surprised. "You like it that much?"

He looked at the maquette, every millimeter of which he had memorized and could easily re-create again by closing his eyes.

"I liked her that much," he said.

She regarded him over the top of her glass as she took her first sip of wine. "You didn't feel bad about lying to him?"

"He was grieving," he said matter-of-factly. "He didn't know what he was saying. It would have been a mistake."

"That's a decision you can make?"

"I did."

She turned back to the maquette. It was a large one, one-half life size, which took up the entire end of the table. She cupped the curve of the woman's hip in the palm of her hand, feeling the shape of it with her fingers, sliding her hand down the slope of her hips to the figure's waist.

"That wasn't the lie that mattered to him anyway, was it?" she said.

"No," he said, looking into his glass, "it wasn't."

Chapter 10

She had an uncanny ability to go right to the heart of things, and more than that, she seemed to understand what she was dealing with. What was there about this particular maquette that had attracted her? There were other nude maquettes and sculptures around the studio, and Saleh had been dead nearly six years. He had long since learned the art of hiding his feelings, of concealing the gall of remorse. And the painful chapter with Marian had intervened, too, obscuring the personal connection even more. But Céleste had known, by whatever sense within her, she had known.

Yet when he acknowledged that her intuition had been correct, she let the subject drop. She had simply wanted a confirmation. He wondered what she would have done if he'd denied any connection to this model other than the relationship of client and sculptor.

She turned away from the maquette and moved to the other end of the workbench, leaving her glass with a last sip of wine in it sitting against one of Saleh's thighs. She leaned the back of her hips against the heavy table and rested her hands on the table's edge. Looking toward the doorway, where the afternoon light had moved the shadow of the studio across the courtyard, she stared out at the coppery light of late afternoon.

"The other day when I came over," she said, "your house was open. I knocked and went in."

"And you looked around."

"I did," she said without embarrassment, "but I didn't see any evidence of a woman there, aside from paintings and sculptures of them. I didn't see anything of the woman you left in Paris."

"How do you know I 'left' her in Paris?"

"Because I didn't see any sign of her."

He told her briefly about Marian, about their struggle to keep what they had had alive, about their failure to do so. He even told her the way it ended. She listened, her eyes lost in a gaze toward the dying light.

"You've not been married, then?"

"No." He thought he would leave it at that, and then he changed his mind. "When I was younger, ambition got in the way. Then it was selfishness. And, later, bad luck — or maybe stupidity. The only woman who could have made all those excuses evaporate was already married."

He finished the wine in his glass and put it down beside Céleste's. He stepped over and stood beside her and leaned back against the table, too. He crossed his arms, and both of them looked toward the opened studio door and the changing light.

"Do you ever wonder about growing old this way?"

"Yes."

She looked at him. "And what do you think about it?"

"Sometimes I don't much like the idea."

"And other times?"

"At other times it seems to be all for the best."

"Why?"

"Well, it might be lonely, but there's probably less grief in it, too."

"And less joy."

"Maybe."

"I'm not sure I can separate the two so easily," she said, "grief and loneliness."

"What about your marriage?" he asked, deciding not to avoid it any longer. "What went wrong?"

She made no immediate response, but he sensed a cold change in her. He watched her as she forced herself to back off, to try to be at least as revealing about herself as he had been. It didn't appear to be easy for her.

102

The luminance outside was fading quickly, and colors, often subtle in the studio anyway because of the cavernous interior, were leaking away with the light.

"I don't know why I married him," she said. "I find it extraordinary that I did. I didn't have the excuse of youth. I wasn't even 'blinded' by love. I swear to you, I can't explain it to this day."

"Maybe you were that afraid."

"Loneliness," she said. "That's pitiful, but it may be true."

"Why haven't you gotten out of it?"

"Well," she said flatly, "that's even more complicated."

She made no effort to explain, and he had enough sense not to press her on it. He simply waited, and in a moment she went on.

"When it comes right down to it," she said, "in my weakest moments, I sometimes wonder if there's not more of Eva in me than I've wanted to believe. I'd always claimed my father's sentiments and temperament. I watched Eva hurl disastrously through life, and I told myself that my father and I were wiser than that. I told myself that he and I understood dimensions of life that she didn't even know existed. When we reached a precipice in life, we calculated the risks and stepped back. But not Eva. She plunged over, just for the thrill of falling. She and Leda."

Pause.

"I used the belief that I was like my father as a talisman to ward off those weak moments when I was afraid of being like her. It got me through some hard times, but I sometimes wonder if I was only deceiving myself."

"Can't you just admit the marriage was a mistake and walk away from it?"

"Oh, I admit the mistake."

She left the second part of his question hanging there between them. This time he didn't want to let it go.

"And what about walking away?"

The light beyond the doorway was ripening into sunset.

"It's . . . just complicated," she repeated, unwilling or, perhaps, unable to go on.

Suddenly he saw resolution struggling with genuine anguish. He could see her determination to avoid the appearance of being a martyr. He didn't know what was going on, but he guessed she was in a lousy situation or, worse, maybe even a horrible situation, and she would rather leave him with a wrong impression than let him glimpse her closely guarded yearning for simple companionship. He was sorry for his carelessness with her feelings, that it had been so easy for him to be insensitive.

"I understand complicated," he said.

"Do you?"

"I understand . . . that complicated doesn't always make sense. I understand that it can be hypnotic . . . that you can endure more than you could ever have imagined, for reasons you could never have imagined."

He unfolded his arms and turned to her.

"I understand," he said, "the loneliness of complicated." He reached out and put his hand on her bare arm and gently moved his finger over the smoothness of it. She let him touch her, and then she turned her eyes from the doorway and looked at his hand on her arm. At first she watched him stroke her as if she were observing it happening to someone else. He had the sense that she had forsworn her own feelings for so long that she was accustomed to standing at a distance from her own emotions.

But then she turned to him and tentatively placed a hand flat on his chest. Slowly, as if she were unsure of the effect, she gently laid her face beside her hand. It was a natural thing for him to put his arms around her. He could feel her breasts, could feel the rise and fall of them as she breathed, could feel their warmth through the thin summer cotton. He imagined the shape of them, the shape of their nipples, and their color.

He held her for a quiet moment before he slowly dropped his hands down to her sides and, moving only his fingers, gradually began gathering the skirt of her dress. She didn't stop him. Bending down, he touched his lips to the side of her neck, which she tilted away to accept his kiss. He felt her stomach tighten. They kissed hesitantly, softly.

When her skirt was gathered around her waist, he lifted her onto the worktable and slipped her panties from her hips and down her long legs. With her eyes open now, watching him, she lay back on the table as the last of the amber light sliced through a narrow angle of the deep window casement and cut across her stomach. He kissed her there, below her navel, his lips moving down and into the gilded crease of her groin.

It was a willful and reckless thing they were doing, troubled by entanglements on both sides that were unresolved and unforgettable. Even as it was happening, he knew that what they were starting was as fragile as the fading light around them.

His bedroom jutted out from the original

stone-and-stucco house in a long pentagonal footprint sheltered by the heavy canopies of old oaks. The bed sat in the outermost extension of the room, surrounded by floor-to-ceiling screened panels that allowed the southeasterly cross breeze to drift over the bed.

They talked aimlessly about art and themselves, of people they had known, and of places they had been, and of certain disparate memories that came randomly to mind, recalled by some word or thought expressed by the other. They were naked and perspiring slightly, and every cool waft of breeze prickled their skin.

"I remember this kind of heat from Mexico," she said, lying next to him. "For a while I lived in the Yucatán, and the nights were like this."

"Memorable."

"Oh, Christ, I'll never forget them. I was so young . . . and the nights were so . . . old. It was perfect, and I knew it was perfect, and I knew it wouldn't last."

They were sharing a single tall glass of gin and tonic with ice. A saucer of sliced limes rested on his stomach, and they were eating them as they talked.

"What happened?"

"Oh . . . nothing dramatic. Life. It was the

first time that I realized — that I *knew* — that really special things in life wouldn't be allowed to last forever. It was such a grown-up realization for a little girl."

In the silence between their thoughts and their words, cicadas and crickets throbbed and whirred in overlapping rhythms, and on the other side of the screens fireflies floated up and down like sparks in the dark heat.

She reached over and got several of the lime slices in one hand and held her hand above her and squeezed, letting the juice drizzle over her breasts and stomach. He heard her take in a quick breath, and then he smelled the clean, citrus fragrance.

They finished the gin and dozed off and awoke sometime in the long darkness, and he tenderly began to lick the lime from her breasts and stomach until they were once more caught up in a single hectic emotion. Later, exhausted again, they slept.

The next time he woke she wasn't in bed. He heard water running in the bathroom, splashing softly in the sink. He waited, but when she returned in the darkness she didn't come back to bed. She went to the screened wall and looked out. He watched her dusky silhouette for a moment, and then he thought he heard her crying. He sat up.

"Céleste?"

His voice startled her; she was still.

"Are you all right?"

She cleared her throat. "I'm fine."

"What's the matter?"

"Bad dream."

He started to get out of bed, and she heard him.

"Please," she said, "I'll be there in a minute."

He waited, looking at her form against the slaty blue darkness. After a while she came back and crawled onto the bed. She came over next to him and put her arm around him and pulled herself close. She kissed the side of his neck softly and was quiet.

He stared into what was left of the still hour before dawn.

Chapter 11

The morning light hit him obliquely across one eye, and he felt the warmth of it on the side of his face. His first reaction was surprise that he had fallen asleep. He looked over at Céleste, who was on her stomach, turned away from him so that he could see only the outline of her cheek and chin. Her hair was pulled to the side, leaving her shoulders and back bare, a glance of sun picking up the striations of silver in the spirals of chestnut. The deep fluting of mourning doves nearby carried through the screen walls on a soft breeze.

He carefully got out of bed and slipped on a pair of pants and went into the kitchen. When he returned to the bedroom with two cups of fresh coffee, the bed was empty. The bathroom door was open, and he could hear the faint splash of water.

Carrying the coffee, he went into the bathroom, a big, square white room flooded with light, and saw the door to the outside open. Just outside the bathroom door he had built an outdoor shower, a generous tiled alcove where he bathed most of the year. Céleste was under the spray, her back to him. He stood looking through the screen door at her, a saucy cerise bougainvillea hanging down over the tiled wall above her. It was a beautiful thing to see and to keep.

Then he saw the bruises on her back, two distinct smears just above her kidneys, another one on her right buttock, another below it on the outside of her upper thigh.

She turned off the water and turned around in one smooth motion and saw him standing there.

Their eyes met and stopped, and he saw the calm resignation in her look and the water beading her face, her hands paused flat against her temples in the process of clearing her hair from her face.

"Coffee," he said, breaking the spell.

"Great," she said, and completed the motion of her arms and reached for the towel hanging on the tiled wall. She dried her face, patted her hair, and wrapped the towel around her. He handed her one of the cups of coffee.

"Let's sit under the arbor," he said.

They walked around the corner of the shower and onto the patio and sat on the wooden bench that followed the arc of the arbor. For ten or fifteen minutes they made small talk, but what he had seen in that moment in the shower — and what she knew he had seen — had now stolen between them like a solemn cloud passing in front of the moon.

"You're going to find makeup on your sheets," she said finally. "I cover them with that."

He didn't rush her.

"My husband lost interest in me," she said simply. "Then he reinvented himself, re-invented me, too, discovered me all over again. These, the bruises, they're the color of the new relationship."

"Jesus Christ. I thought you were es-tranged."

"I would call this estrangement, wouldn't you?"

"How long has this been going on?"

"It started, I don't know, a year ago. But I don't see him often. We do live apart."

"Some of those are recent."

She didn't say anything. There was some-thing about her bare shoulders that made him think of a girl, not a woman. He didn't know why, but she just seemed young, sit-ting there, wearing the towel that way. The mockingbird began gabbling in the bou-gainvillea above them, her strong, clear voice a painful apposition of storybook morning cheer and depressing reality.

"I told you it was complicated," she said, still not looking at him. She put down the coffee on the bench and tilted her head to one side and wrung water from her hair.

"Do you like it?" The words were out before he even knew he wanted to ask them, and he regretted them even before his voice died.

She stopped, her face turned away, her head tilted, her dripping hair in her hands.

"God . . ." She sighed with a tone of weary disappointment.

"I'm sorry," he said instantly, "that was . . . that was dumb." He felt like an idiot.

She straightened up without looking at him.

"You know, I've got to go," she said. "It's getting late."

"Wait —" He reached out and touched her bare shoulder. "Céleste, look at me." She turned to him. "I *am* sorry for that. I'm sorry that it even entered my mind, and that I was so stupid."

The look of disconsolation in her eyes was heartbreaking, and he felt as if his brutal remark had inflicted its own bruises, the kind that would not heal as easily as the ones on her body.

"No, it's all right," she said softly, "I understand."

After she dressed, he gave her the keys to his car and walked with her through the house and breezeway to the garage. He had to move the Jeep out of the way, and when he walked back to the car she kissed him, a gentle but heavy-laden good-bye, after which she avoided his eyes. Then she got in the car and drove away along the gravel drive.

But there was something sad between them now, a disturbing dissonance that he had introduced along with his insensitive question. The single word *regret* hardly expressed all that he felt by what he had done.

Chapter 12

When Leda arrived at the studio alone less than half an hour later, she was wearing a lemon yellow two-piece dress, a fashionable style that had required special tailoring for her. Her abundant hair was worn full and wavy, a dark loop of which fell vampishly over one eye, a conceit that was adolescent in its notion of sexiness and at the same time oddly attractive.

He deliberately hadn't prepared anything for the session, thinking it might set a more relaxed mood if they talked while he went about the mundane preparations of getting together his materials.

"I hope you had a good night's sleep," he said, bringing his sketching stool over from a corner of the room.

"Apparently I got more sleep than Céleste did," she said pointedly.

He ignored the remark as he got a fresh sketchpad from the cabinets and selected a variety of pencils from the drawers.

"We won't be at it too long today," he said, bringing everything over to a modeling platform.

"Is that where you want me?" she asked, regarding the platform and the daybed, which he had covered with a vermilion damask spread.

"Eventually."

The space around the platform was open so that he could move his small bench entirely around it, choosing an infinite variety of angles for sketching. He straddled the short bench, put the pencils in the wooden tray, and attached his sketchpad to an easel mounted on the end of the bench.

"You can choose any position you like to begin with," he said, starting to sharpen his pencils, "I can move this thing around you for different views. That way you don't have to change positions so much. Less tiring."

"I don't need any special accommodations," she said.

"This is the way I work with all my models. Same process."

She walked slowly around the platform. He continued with the pencils, deliberately tending to the business of sharpening, not looking at her. He thought she glanced at him frequently as she casually circumnavigated the stage, looking at the bed and the chair in the center of it, eventually returning to where she had begun.

She dropped her shoulder bag on the edge of the platform and sat beside it, both feet on the floor. A row of quarter-size white shell buttons marched up the center of her lemon dress from hem to waist.

"Did you talk about me after I left yesterday?" she asked.

"No," he lied.

She smiled an "I know damn well you did" smile but let it go.

"Have you been curious about what you're going to see when I take off my clothes?"

"Of course." He was whittling a point on the last pencil, his lap scattered with shavings. "Why?"

"I just wanted to see if you'd lie about that, too."

"I choose my lies carefully," he said, tossing the last pencil into the tray in front of him. He crossed his arms and looked at her. "Let's talk about how to get started."

"I take off my clothes."

"There's a screen back there," he said, nodding toward the rear of the studio. "Hangers for your clothes, a bathroom, a new robe."

She turned to look at the bed in the center of the platform.

"Why don't I just undress there," she said,

turning back to him. "I want you to watch me undress."

"It's not necessary."

"I think it is. I want you to see me move. How I move. Why I move the way I do. I want you to understand the mechanics of it, where my center of balance is."

It was a remarkably perceptive suggestion. Eventually he would have asked for all of this anyway, for just the exact reasons she stated. Eventually she would have to do these things over and over. She obviously knew this. She didn't want to be humored. He had the feeling that she had been waiting for this moment for years, and she wanted to get right to it.

"Fine," he said. "I don't have to have anything particular. Not yet, anyway."

"Good. Then let's get started."

Taking her shoulder bag, she stood and walked to the corner of the platform where there was a step. She went carefully up the step and walked to the bed. She put her handbag on the chair and got a rubber band from inside it and pulled back her thick hair and fastened it in place.

"I want you to see my neck," she explained.

Nine women out of ten, when undressing, begin with their blouses. Not Leda. She sat

118

on the bed facing him, kicked off her sandals, and bent over and picked up the hem of her skirt and began with the bottom button. This particular maneuver emphasized the hump on her back, and he had the feeling she did it deliberately for that reason, so that he would see it at its most grotesque angle.

When she got to her crotch she threw open the sides of her skirt, revealing her bare legs and her butter yellow panties. He was surprised by their color and by their delicate cut and lace panels. Her skin was a lighter shade of olive than Céleste's. She sucked in her stomach to get the waist buttons, and then she stood and removed the skirt. As she turned to the side to lay it over the chair, he could see the odd angle of her hips.

Now he expected her to begin removing her blouse, but instead she put her fingers inside her panties and pushed them down, reaching out with one hand to steady herself on the bed as she stepped out of them.

"I can wear regular panties," she said, squaring around to face him. Her pubic hair was closely clipped, her vulva clearly visible.

Next she began with the bottom button of her blouse and went up rapidly. To take off the blouse she had to remove one arm from its sleeve and then use the loose material made available by this gesture to flip the blouse over her hump and then off the other arm. Again she turned to put the blouse over the chair, and as she bent slightly in profile he got his first clear view of her naked hump. It seemed enormous, far larger than it appeared to be clothed. The pitch at which it protruded from the body was much more acute than he had imagined, and the flesh covering it appeared to be stretched to the point of splitting open. It was immediately apparent also that she had to compensate for it with every move she made in order to maintain any grace of motion at all.

She wore no bra, which would have to have been custom-made to accommodate the hump and would surely have been a medieval-looking contraption. But she hardly needed one. Her breasts were the classic shape of the Esquiline Venus, high, strictly conical with no globular roundness toward the undersides, nipples centered and facing straight forward.

"Just for the record," she said, doing a slow runway turn for him as if she were a model, "technically I'm afflicted with Scheuermann's disease, or *kyphosis dorsalis juvenilis,* or, simply, kyphosis: 'humpback' in

Greek. A severe example of it. And here" — she put her pretty hands on either side of her hips, the right one of which was canted maybe twenty degrees higher than the left — "I have something for which there is no official name. At least, no medical syndrome name. My sacrum is mushed on the left side. Not enough to affect my gait, if I pay attention to it. And if I stand just right when I'm dressed you can't tell. About the hump, of course" — she turned in profile again and looked at him, an upright buffalo woman — "nothing can be done at all."

In profile like this, her appearance was shocking. He was surprised by his own reaction, and though he knew he could hide his feelings, he was nonetheless disturbed by them.

She squared around to him again. "Everything works just fine, thank you. Except childbearing is problematic. That is, it would be if conception itself weren't problematic. There's the sexual-aesthetic issue. Not a lot of young men clamoring to get naked with a hunchback."

It was a cruel remark.

She stood still in front of him. Her hips and pelvis were quite beautiful, as were her legs. Her buttocks did not suffer from the misalignment in the pelvis, though one or

121

the other of them was always more taut depending on her stance. He guessed that this "normal" look would change relatively quickly. Much of her anatomy was attractive by virtue of her youth — her breasts, for instance — but would suffer rapidly from the stress that her disability would naturally cause as muscle groups were constantly called upon to compensate.

He was surprised that she wasn't bent forward in a more pronounced way. The curvature of her spine was high, however, so that she carried the hump higher behind her shoulders rather than in the center of her back, thereby avoiding the crone's stoop. She stood more or less upright. But that would change with time, too.

"In your mind's eye," he said, standing up from his bench and starting to walk around her, "how do you imagine yourself posed for this sculpture?"

"Naked," she said. "Beyond that I don't give a damn. I want to smoke."

"Go ahead."

He watched her as she went to her purse and bent over to fish out her cigarettes. She lighted one with her back to him, but he saw her hand trembling. Her posterior view was not distorted, the hump being within the width of her shoulders, and the small tilt of her hips easily disguised by the ageless stance so natural to humans of putting one's weight primarily on one leg, causing the opposite hip to dip and creating an arc line of the higher hip to sweep up toward the breast. The leg, relieved of its weight, is slightly cocked, creating a graceful swing of the hip. *Déhanchement,* the French called it. Leda was obviously well aware of this artifice. He suspected that she had spent a great deal of time in front of mirrors.

She turned around and put one hand on her hip and stood there letting him look at her, smoking.

She said, "Altogether, my back and neck aren't that bad. I look in the mirrors and I think: If I could just slice off the damn hump, just follow the line of the normal back, it would be done. I could deal with the sacrum."

He didn't say anything to this but continued moving around her. As he moved out of her peripheral vision, he saw her tense ever so slightly. He had expected that. It was easier for her if she could see him looking at her. If she was looking at him, she could be defiant: Go ahead, I give you permission, look at me all you want, I don't give a damn. It was her own brazen decision to let him stare.

But when he moved out of her eyesight, she lost all control. What was he looking at now? The sag of a buttock? The taut cartilage of the hump? The odd juncture of the armpit and the declension of the down side of the hump?

He stayed behind her for a moment to see how she would react. She smoked, her hand still on her hip. She tilted her head back slightly and looked upward, the wrist of her other hand cocked, holding the cigarette between her first two fingers. But she was tough. She didn't give way — beyond the slight trembling of her hand — to any nervous ticks or lose control and snap something about why he didn't hurry up or was he getting enough of a look at her to satisfy his curiosity. She let him look.

He stepped around in front of her again and straddled the bench.

"Okay, let's get started," he said.

Chapter 13

He didn't try to pose her at all. He just told her to relax and try to hold her positions for a couple of minutes while he did a series of quick sketches. It would be a good beginning.

He took his sketchpad off the easel on his bench and circled the model's platform while Leda began holding various postures. She was quite good at it, and after a while she began to settle down. It made a difference in her choice of poses, and much sooner than he had expected she seemed quite at ease without her clothes. Toward the end of the session he thought she seemed not only at ease, but even to be enjoying it.

For his part, the quick sketches were not as easy as he'd expected. Just when he thought he was beginning to understand the relationship between the volume of the hump on her shoulders and the skewed angles of her pelvis in regard to her center of gravity, he'd move to another angle and realize that he'd misjudged. At times Leda's deformities appeared more severe than he had first thought, even, at some angles, terribly grotesque. At other times they seemed hardly to matter at all.

Her legs were shapely, very attractive, long beneath a high waist. Her stomach was flat and not malformed, so that in some positions the compression of her left iliac fossa was not even discernible. Despite the acute angle of the hump, her chest and breasts were unaffected, so that when viewed from the front at an angle that hid the protrusion, she was stunning.

But that required careful positioning. Most of the time there was no way to look at her without having the hump influence the way you saw her. From some angles, in fact, when the pelvis and hump were at their worst vantage and her face was turned away, she had a numbingly freakish appearance. At those moments he realized what courage it took for her to endure this. She knew that sooner or later he would see her in this way, repellent by most standards. And if this project went on to its intended conclusion, it was inevitable that the completed sculpture would make that angle available to every viewer as well. Regardless of what she had said her reasons were for wanting to do this, he knew that she must have glossed over its true importance to her. The whys of what she wanted to do were surely entangled, if not inscrutable, even to her.

"That's it," he said after nearly an hour, tossing his sketchpad on the platform. "A good start for the first day."

Leda was reclining on the bed on her side, propped on one elbow, her left leg drawn up so that her foot rested against the inside of her knee of the outstretched leg. She reached out to the chair, but instead of getting her clothes she took another cigarette out of her purse and lighted it. He realized this position was comfortable for her, the hump serving as a kind of built-in pillow against which she could lean.

Noticing this made him feel odd. Somehow it dehumanized her. There was something of the creature about this accommodation to her deformity. He thought of the massive gray body of the Brahman cow, reclining on its side, its hummock riding above its shoulders, its heavy body comfortable with the oddness of its bizarre shape because that was the only kind of body that it had ever known.

"How was it?" she asked, propped on one elbow, smiling at the sexual double entendre.

"I think I got some good stuff," he said, coming around in front of her. When they stopped he had been at her feet, looking up the length of her body, studying the effect of foreshortening.

"I mean, how was it looking at me? What did you think?"

"I found it hard to locate your center of balance. . . ."

"No, emotionally . . . what was your reaction?"

He looked at her. He could tell there was no way of getting around this. She wanted to know sooner or later if he could find her attractive. This was either going to work or not, and she was probably right about getting all this kind of thing out of the way right up front, at the beginning. He came around and sat on the edge of the platform. She was an arm's reach from him.

"Do I find you physically attractive?" he asked. "Of course I do." As he said this, trying to sound honest and nonchalant, he realized that he wasn't, in fact, lying. She was physically attractive. And she wasn't. And this, he knew, was the truth that drove her crazy: the paradoxical effect on others of the sum of her odd parts.

"You do," she said, "and you don't."

She moved her legs around and dropped them off the side of the bed and, struggling a little, sat upright facing him, her feet on the floor. She smoked, and gradually, pretending an indifference she could not possibly have felt, she let her legs loll open. He had seen professional models sit in this way all of his life, the frankness of seasoned women who had repeatedly shown him everything they had and no longer cared. He was invisible to them, a cipher, modesty was no longer necessary.

But Leda was doing it for other reasons, operating from a psychology that he couldn't even begin to understand.

"How many naked people have you seen?" he asked.

She shrugged and dragged on her cigarette.

"I've seen hundreds," he said. "I've studied them in minute detail, from every conceivable angle. Close. Heads, breasts, thighs, buttocks, armpits, stomachs, elbows, necks, knees. I try to figure them out . . . the mathematics of them. Everyone has her own physical equation. I've done it for thirty years. Let me assure you, everyone — even the 'pretty people' — are unattractive somewhere. That's the real truth about the human body: imperfection first, before anything else."

"Really?" Sarcasm. She knew a thing or two about imperfection.

"There's something unusual about your

face," he said, and for just a flicker of a second he saw fear in her eyes. Her face was something about herself that she valued without reservation, a part of her anatomy about which she felt justified in being proud, even vain. She didn't want to hear anything negative about it.

"You know it's beautiful," he went on. "You said so. But there's something else you may not have noticed . . . it's symmetrical."

She swallowed, but she didn't answer.

He explained to her the unusual phenomenon of a perfectly balanced face. She showed no reaction, looking at him blankly.

"Well, that's marvelous," she said flatly. "I feel . . . excited."

They regarded each other in silence.

"Look," he said after a moment, "I won't insult you with pop psychology, if you'll spare me the 'bitter victim' routine. I don't understand what your life is like, but I don't think sarcasm is going to enlighten me, either." He stood. "Close your legs and get dressed."

She leaned over and put out the cigarette in a glass ashtray on the floor beside the bed. Still leaning over, her beautiful face looking up at him, she said, "You're right. That's not going to get us anywhere, is it?" She straightened up, her hands on her thighs.

"I'm still, uh, a little nervous."

She was shamefaced, and he was suddenly remorseful. He could have, and should have, done that differently.

"Forget it," he said, picking up his sketchpad, fiddling with his pencils. "Look, it's lunchtime. I usually put together a plate of sliced fruit, some cold meats and cheeses, white wine. Why don't you have a bite with me before you go."

"No," she said, standing shakily and reaching for her clothes, "I can't stay. I did this. That's all I needed to do, to know that I could."

He stood and turned away as she began putting on her clothes. Dressing was more pedestrian than undressing. The moments of high tension and anticipation had passed. It was different, and he didn't want her to feel the difference between the two after the exchange they had just had. He flipped through his sketchpad. He knew she would be cutting glances at him. That was something he noticed about her. She was watching him as much as he was watching her.

After she finished dressing, she came down from the platform and went over to the drawing board, where he was going through the sketches. She stood to one side

131

behind him, and he went back to the first page and began turning slowly through the drawings as she watched over his shoulder. Some pages were covered with several studies, some with only a large single drawing. He'd always been good at quick studies, and he'd covered a lot of territory.

After they had looked at the last drawing, he started to close the book, but she reached around him and stopped him. She turned back a few pages and stared at one of the sketches.

"So this is me."

It wasn't a question.

"When I was younger," she went on, "I used to spend a lot of time in front of the mirror, naked. I couldn't believe it. I wasn't born like this, you know, I got this way gradually, from twelve to fifteen. It was a nightmare. I was obsessed with what was happening to my body. I just couldn't get enough of looking at what was happening to me. I'd use two mirrors, three."

She paused.

"I've contemplated my body from angles, from perspectives, that most women die without ever even wondering about, much less seeing."

She paused.

"But I've never, ever seen myself like this."

He couldn't tell if she was angry or shocked or humiliated . . . or any of these.

She reached out tentatively and touched one of the pencil sketches and smeared it a little.

"What do you see you've never seen before?" he asked.

"I see what you see. Always, before, I saw what I saw."

He wanted to ask her what she was thinking, but something stopped him. He wanted to turn around and look at her, but something stopped him from doing that, too.

There was a long silence.

"Well," she said at last, stepping away and around the drawing table, "tomorrow again? Same time?"

"If that suits you."

"It suits me," she said. She was already walking away.

He watched her cross the studio and approach the doorway that led outside. As she turned slightly to step into the courtyard, the yellow dress went black in silhouette against the brightness, and the hump on her back, caught in three-quarter profile, filled the doorway. It was a startling image. For an instant she was not a woman, but a creature.

He sat at the kitchen table, his empty plates pushed to the side, the sketchbook propped up against the heavy crockery bowl of peaches. He had been back and forth through the pages, studying the drawings, marveling at the extraordinary idea that had been brought to him. He was excited, more excited than he would let either of the sisters know, and not a little worried about the prospects of dealing with so strange a figure.

His concern was technical, yes, but that wasn't his most troubling challenge. Far more disturbing was the problem of how he was going to present Leda to the viewer. How in God's name did he pose her? He shared all the concerns that Céleste had expressed and many more. If he was careful, if he was meticulous, if he was sufficiently obsessed, the finished sculpture could be an explosive event in his career. It wasn't too early to begin worrying about the plethora of variables that would have to be considered, weighed, and controlled. He had no doubt whatsoever that the finished piece would justify everything he could put into it.

Chapter 14

"Thanks for loaning me your car," she said.

She stood in the doorway of the studio, her dress translucent from the bright light behind her. His eyes followed the narrowing vertical space between her legs all the way from her ankles to her crotch. The sheer fabric floated a millimeter away from her hips.

"Glad to," he said, turning away from the drawing board, where he was noodling half-heartedly with his sketches from the Beach photographs. It was hard to whip up any enthusiasm for these now. After his sketching session that morning with Leda, Lily Beach's body seemed bland and predictable in its proportions, a committee-designed frame without variety or surprise.

"What are you working on?" she asked, approaching his desk. She was wearing a shirtwaist dress of summer cotton, short sleeve with a collar. It was a style she seemed to favor, probably because it flattered her.

He studied her face, looking for some residue of resentment from his insult that morning. He saw nothing. She was going to pretend it hadn't happened.

She stood by the desk while he flipped through his sketching sheets, showing her what he was doing, what problems he was having, how he was hoping to solve them. She seemed genuinely interested and asked questions that were perceptive. She knew what she was talking about. He caught wafts of fragrance from her. Not perfume, but something softer, like the lingering scent of underclothes stored in sachet.

When they had finished talking about the sketches — she hadn't said a word about Lily Beach's flawless body — she moved away idly and wandered over to the modeling platform. She stood there, her back to him, looking at the bed where Leda had posed for the first time that morning.

"How did it go?" she asked, turning around.

"Great, as far as I was concerned."

"Do you mind if I see the sketches?"

He picked up the sketchpad and took it over to her. She sat on the platform and opened the cover. She stared at the first sketch. It was a slight image. She began going through the book, taking her time, page by page.

As he watched her, one long leg crossed over the other, the sketchbook lying on her thigh as she focused on the drawings, it occurred to him that she may never have seen Leda naked, and he reminded himself of the strange and complicated relationship the sisters shared. Nothing about them was easy to understand, but he was drawn to them, to each of them, for very different reasons.

There was an inexplicable familiarity about Céleste that made him like being with her. It was as if she were a piece of himself that he hadn't realized was missing until he met her. Realizing this made him feel all the more remorseful for the hurt he had inflicted on her that morning.

When she closed the sketchbook, she put it on the platform beside her and stood. She crossed her bare arms and took a few steps in his direction.

"What did she think of those?" she asked.

He told her of Leda's reaction, and she listened intently as if she were mining each sentence, every phrase, for an ore of meaning that lay deeper than the obvious.

"What did you think about while you were sketching her?"

It was a peculiar and unexpected question, but after jumping to his disastrous conclusion that morning, he decided to answer it straight on, without reading any implications into it.

"Mostly I was thinking about how to get her on paper, how to locate her center of gravity, which wasn't easy."

She didn't seem to be satisfied with his answer, and she studied him as if she were looking for something hidden in what he had just said.

"Did you notice anything — not to do with her deformity — anything that . . . anything about her that you've seen before?"

"That I'd seen before?" What was she getting at?

She looked away for a moment, collecting herself, then she turned back to him with an air of resignation.

"There's something here, Ross, something that's going to startle you, but you've got to know. Leda and I are Sylvie Verret's sisters."

For an instant the name didn't register with him. Then, suddenly, Sylvie's face rushed up from the long sloping darkness of the past. Good God. What the hell was going on here? Suspicion bloomed like a drop of dye falling into clear water.

As he stared at her he could indeed see the resemblance through the years, the mouth set firmer, the jawline grown heavier, the eyes — still warm, still seductive — grown sadder. Yes, he saw Sylvie, and in his numb surprise Sylvie's face was slowly superimposed over Céleste's until she became neither of them and both of them, a new woman. This was an incredible turn of events.

"Jesus . . . Christ," he said softly.

He had lived with Sylvie when he was a young sculptor in Paris in his late twenties. She was his model first and then, eventually, his lover. It was a combination that he learned to avoid as he grew older and more sensible, but Sylvie was his first great lesson in the dangers of confusing the two roles.

Sylvie was a quiet young woman with a beautiful body of olive complexion. She was unabashedly sensual in a brooding way. She felt passionately about many things, about most things, actually, but she never displayed her emotions in front of others. Always quiet, she was demonstratively passionate only in her sexuality. In all other things her emotions were entirely internal, rigidly constrained.

But Sylvie's reserve, which at first was magnetic in its ability to draw you to her, proved to be the weight that kept a smoldering anger in check. She never lost her reserve in the presence of others, but when she was alone she exploded. When their affair began to disintegrate, he would come home to the studio to find his models and maquettes shattered, his drawings shredded, their apartment destroyed.

When he confronted her she fell into an intractable silence. She never, not once, admitted what she had done, never acknowledged her secret eruptions of destructive wrath. When confronted with the damage, she simply stared at it, mute.

Then, at night, she would come to him with sexual offerings freighted with implicit apologies and remorse. It was a tornadic relationship with wrenching, and ultimately calamitous, emotional storms.

It ended badly for them, the first really disturbing breakup of his life.

"What's going on here?" he asked. He couldn't fathom it.

"I know this looks suspect," she said, "but when you look at it from our point of view it's not really so mysterious. In the years after your breakup, as you became famous, Sylvie would talk about you a lot. You know, what might have been . . . if things had been different between you. Leda and I heard a lot about you."

"Where is she?"

"Sylvie's dead. Too much cocaine, finally. Three years ago."

It startled him that she no longer existed.

"To tell you the truth, I guess I'm surprised she lasted that long."

"So was I."

He felt sad for Sylvie. The poor, beautiful thing was born for tragedy.

"Three years ago," he said. "Wasn't that about the time your mother was killed?"

"Actually, a couple of months before. It would have been a traumatic few months if any of us had cared for each other. As it was, it was just all bitterness and inconvenience."

He thought a moment. "You say she talked about me a lot?"

"Yes."

"When?"

She looked at him blankly. "What?"

"I thought the four of you were alienated from each other, your mother leading her own life in Rome, Leda isolated in Switzerland, you in London. But just then you said that over the years Sylvie talked about me a lot to you and Leda."

"Yes . . ." She hesitated.

Was the look on her face reluctance? Or confusion? He frowned at her.

"Sylvie . . . she was . . . she kept in touch with all of us," she stammered. "She was, I guess you could say she was nomadic. Always just having come from somewhere or about to leave for somewhere. She saw all of

141

us from time to time. She was pretty much the only thing that tied us together over those years."

This didn't sound like the Sylvie he remembered. The Sylvie he knew was very much a loner and wouldn't have been the kind of woman who nurtured fractured relationships and served as the family's binding center. She simply wasn't capable of that kind of stability.

Before he could follow up on that, Céleste quickly went on.

"Anyway, we'd always been aware of your career, noticed where your life was going. There was always Sylvie's few years with you, a shared history that caused us to pay special attention when we came across the newspaper items, or the magazine articles."

"Jesus, why didn't you tell me all this up front?"

"I suppose for much the same reason Leda didn't want me to tell you about her deformity. We were afraid you'd never even talk to us."

He looked at her. "Well, I'm . . . I don't know . . . it's incredible." He paused. "I see the similarities now, of course. But I didn't put it all together."

"I thought you'd surely see the resemblance in Leda once you began working with her. She's much more like Sylvie than I am."

"It was so long ago."

Silence.

"After last night I thought —" She stopped as if she had decided not to pretend it hadn't happened. "About that, last night, you know, I couldn't have imagined that would happen. Ever. I never intended that to happen."

Before he could say anything she went on. "Anyway, after last night, I thought you needed to know this."

He nodded. There was nothing more to add to the surprise he still felt. It sure as hell made a difference, though what kind of difference he didn't know.

Céleste moved a few steps away to Saleh's maquette. She put her hand on the maquette's stomach, ran her fingers over its smoothness. There was something else.

"I feel bad about last night," she said.

"That was my fault," he said, and then he hesitated and added, "but, to be honest, I don't wish it hadn't happened." He paused. "I hope you don't regret it. If you do, then I'm sorry for that."

"No, I don't, not the way you mean."

"But you do wish it hadn't happened."

"Only because . . ." She closed her eyes

143

and drew in a slow, deep breath. "Only because I think we'll both regret it later."

"Why?"

"I don't . . . I don't know," she said impatiently, "the point is, I'm not the business here. Leda is."

The way she said it, the fact that she felt she had to say it, was a disappointment.

"I didn't consider last night 'business,' " he said. "It didn't have anything to do with anyone else."

She dropped her eyes to the maquette and took her hand away.

"I think that's all I should say about it."

"What does that mean, exactly?"

"It means . . . ," she said, suddenly irritated, "it means . . . that . . ." She was flustered. "I . . ."

They seemed to be getting it all wrong. Last night they understood each other's deepest feelings with hardly a word spoken. Now they were talking too much and saying too little.

"Céleste, listen . . ." He wanted to touch her, but he stopped, fearing that he might make matters worse. "Why don't we just not make anything complicated out of this."

God, what an understatement. It could hardly be more complicated. Still, he went on with it.

"Last night was an honest thing," he said. "At least on my part."

She was silent, but she was looking at him intently, with an anguished expression that told him she had conflicts about what they had done that went far deeper than anything they had talked about or that she was willing to talk about.

"I wasn't confused about that," she said, and she swallowed and moved her tongue for moisture and was about to speak again, but then she didn't. They looked at each other, and he was bewildered to see that she was deeply unnerved, as if something eerie had happened in the last few moments and he simply hadn't seen it.

"Céleste . . ."

"If" — she started moving, walking past him — "you could just take me home."

He drove her back in the Mercedes. She hardly spoke a word apart from giving him terse directions, spending most of her time with her head turned away, staring out the window. She was living on the palm-lined Santa Elena Avenue in the exclusive Palm Heights district, a pristine quarter of Victorian homes in the foothills on the western side of town. She was leasing a two-story house that sat up off the avenue on an incline so that the driveway and sidewalk leading from the street ascended the height of a couple of terraces. The front of the house was sheltered by a giant magnolia.

He pulled up into the driveway and stopped at the sidewalk.

She put her hand on the door handle, but before she opened it she looked at him, her emotions now under control.

"We don't know what we're doing here," she said. "We're taking risks and we don't even have enough sense to be afraid."

The dark words caught him by surprise. What was she talking about? Risks? Afraid? Why was she attaching words like that to one night's passion? Before he could organize his thoughts around a response, she opened the door and got out. She didn't even glance back at him as she hurried to the sidewalk that led to the house and disappeared under the deep shadow of the magnolia.

Chapter 15

"What?" Amado frowned across the table at him. "This is bloody incredible."

It was late evening at Graber's. The sun was well down behind the cypresses, but there was still a frail peach light in the sky, fading quickly. The lanterns had just come on, and here and there people were beginning to order dinner.

Amado's serene comportment was not often disturbed, but the revelation that Céleste had a sister of such unusual description and that these two women were Sylvie Verret's sisters, and that Leda wanted a sculpture of herself, all of this seemed too incredible to him.

His surprise brought him up out of his natural lounging posture. He sat up straight in his chair and rested his forearms on either side of his bottle of Pacifico, his cigar in his right hand. He was wearing a loose-fitting white linen shirt, looking very elegant, very tropical.

"You're not seriously thinking of doing this?"

"We had our first session this morning."

Amado was aghast. "But what about your commission?"

"I'll get it done."

Amado gaped at him. "Why?"

"Why are you so surprised by this?"

"Ohhh" — Amado gave him a taken-aback look of incredulity — "come on, Ross. Why are you acting as though this is the most normal thing in the world? It's bizarre! You're going to do a nude sculpture of a deformed woman who's the sister of a woman who almost ruined you?"

"That was twenty-five years ago, Amado."

"Not nearly long enough, I should think. Besides that, this will be enormously controversial, and you know it."

"Christ, the girl's situation is genuinely poignant. Can you imagine what it's like to be in her body? Can you imagine the . . . damn, just the drama of sitting in a restaurant, catching the eye of some man who's obviously salivating over your incredibly beautiful face — and you *know* what's coming next. There's always going to be that inevitable 'other' reaction. She has to dread situations like that. I mean, every single encounter she has with a man has got to be heartbreaking."

"What about Sylvie? Do you see Sylvie in this girl?"

148

"I see the similarities, the complexion, the mouth. Her eyes. Her body is like Sylvie's, aside from the deformity. But Leda's more beautiful than Sylvie, more beautiful than Céleste. The girl's extraordinary."

"You didn't think of Sylvie when you first saw her?"

"Well, hell no, I didn't. Leda has the same body type as Sylvie, but so do millions of other women. I've seen Sylvie's type countless times. And Céleste, she has the same coloring as Sylvie, some of the same facial features, but so do millions of other women. You just don't automatically make all those connections to one woman, especially a woman you haven't seen in over two decades."

"But to 'look like' someone, that's different."

"Yeah," he conceded. Amado was right. "I don't know why I didn't see it. Maybe the deformity was too much of a distraction."

Amado studied him through a fresh billow of smoke. "What was it like sketching her?"

He thought a moment. "She changed shapes."

Amado was startled.

"One moment she was simply a normal, beautiful young woman. The next she was

. . . surreal. And, oddly, the two views often metamorphosed right in front of me. What I saw as I moved around her changed, and sometimes it caught me by surprise. Which surprised me."

Amado nodded, listening. "And so you're going to explore this, is that it?"

"Look, there are genuine aesthetic considerations here," he said, a little irritated that Amado was pushing him and a little uncomfortable with himself too for feeling as though he had to defend his decision, something he had stoically refused to do for years.

"Aesthetic considerations?"

"Yeah," he insisted, "things like our attitudes about beauty . . . and repulsion. How does Leda live with both of those things in the same body? How do *we* live with it? How does society deal with a person whose appearance is dramatically different from the norm? Do we make it impossible for them to be happy? What are the limits of society's requirements for acceptance? Hell, I don't know, Amado. Aren't these questions worth examining?"

"You've managed to avoid exploring them for thirty years."

"What the hell is this? I seem to remember a few times over the years when you've pointed out to me that I was too quick to take the easy road — and the good money — that I didn't take my talent seriously, that I didn't wrestle with my demons."

"First of all," Amado said stiffly, "I never discussed anything like that with you unless you asked my opinion. And then I answered you honestly."

"But isn't this exactly the sort of thing you were talking about, seriously confronting the hard questions of aesthetics and art?"

Amado stared back at him, the smoke from the cigar twisting between them.

"That could be argued," he said, "but do you think that's really what you're doing here?"

"Why the hell wouldn't it be?"

"This doesn't sound like you, Ross. I think you're reaching for a reason to do this. These 'questions' you want to examine, you know very well these things can't be addressed in a single sculpture. What are you thinking about? Maybe if you'd devoted your career to these questions; maybe a lifetime of sculptural works dedicated to these issues . . . maybe then it would make sense to talk like this. But to do this with a single work? Come on . . . what are you trying to do here?"

Amado's voice was softly scornful, and Ross was secretly embarrassed. He felt like he'd been caught trying to run a con. Amado let him off the hook.

"What about Céleste?" Amado asked.

"Céleste? You mean, have I found her as beguiling as you did?"

"I think you've already answered that question, although I don't believe you've realized it yet."

He felt a twinge of discomfort, caught in another deception.

"You know what this reminds me of?" Amado mused, nodding to himself as if this idea exactly fit their present discussion. "There's a quote by Flaubert, I can't remember if it's from a letter or what, but I think it describes the way you think about women. He said" — Amado tilted his face toward the darkness, remembering — " 'The contemplation of a naked woman makes me think of her skeleton.' " He dropped his eyes to Ross and raised his eyebrows. "Make sense to you?"

"Not the least bit. Does it make sense to you?"

"Ross, you are being deliberately evasive. Look, you and I approach women in very different ways," Amado went on. "I react immediately, emotionally. You have a more cerebral approach. I'm swept away by the beauty or the special indefinable something of a particular woman. You're curious. I see sexuality. You see anatomy." He squinted in thought. "You work from the outside in, I think, like Flaubert."

"Is that what he does?"

"Flaubert didn't say that when he saw a naked woman he thought of romance or of stardust or of the secrets of her soft places . . . he thought of her *skeleton*."

"I don't know what to say about that."

"He doesn't intuit a woman, he figures her out, like a mathematical problem."

"Okay . . ."

"So here you are faced with this extraordinary young woman — with both of these extraordinary women — and you've already turned it into an analytical exercise. You're going to figure them out, beginning with their bodies first. That's what you see when you see a woman, a mathematical problem."

"Fine. What's wrong with that?"

"Wrong? It's not a matter of wrong. The thing is, there is the woman you see, and then there is the woman you don't see, *la mujer al dentro*, the woman within. This is the woman who keeps the secret of who she is. You have always concentrated on the woman you see, but it's the woman you don't see who holds the magic. Magic doesn't make sense. Mathematics is not magic."

"Bullshit, Amado. And what do you see when you first look at a woman?"

"I can assure you, when I first saw Céleste I did *not* think of her skeleton."

He suddenly didn't want to hear Amado's emotional — or visceral — responses upon first seeing Céleste.

"What's the point here?"

Amado looked around, caught the eye of one of the waitresses across the patio, raised his empty bottle of Pacifico, and gestured that they both wanted another. Then he turned back to answer the question.

"I'm only trying to say, really, that I think . . . your usual way of doing things with women is the wrong way of doing things with *this* woman."

Amado paused and nursed his cigar.

Sometimes Ross lost his patience with Amado's amorphous, intuitive approach to life, but he had to admit that he felt in his gut that Amado was right about Céleste. He also had to admit that for whatever reasons, and he really couldn't put his finger on anything in particular, he didn't want to talk about her anymore.

"Let's let it go, Amado," he said.

Amado gave him a deferential nod, studying him for a moment before he looked away to survey the crowd in the courtyard.

Neither of them spoke for a little while as they waited on their drinks, which came shortly, brought by a young Mexican waitress with a face too thick, a lower jaw too heavy. She was fond of Amado and treated him with special respect, wiping up the little circle of condensation where his empty beer bottle had sat, putting his new sweating bottle on a square white napkin instead of the rustic blotter-board coasters, brushing away imaginary ashes and nonexistent crumbs from his side of the table. She emptied his ashtray, which held only a single, neat cylinder of ash. He thanked her with equal politeness and respect. He never spoke of her solicitous attention, nor once gave Ross a knowing wink or made light of the girl's regard for him, nor did he ever flirt with her. Actually, both he and the waitress behaved with a rather grand gravity in light of what was — or wasn't — passing between them.

"Ross," Amado said, and held up his bottle, reaching across the table. They chinked the necks of the bottles together as Amado said, *"Salud,"* and a kind of truce was settled between them.

Amado studied him from behind his

cigar. He had returned to his habitual, languid posture, the vantage point from which he most often regarded the world. He put on his best nonjudgmental face.

"Well," he said softly and with an air of melancholy, "this will be interesting."

Ross lay in bed, the lights out, the sheets thrown back, a breeze floating across him. Nearby in the woods a little screech owl punctuated the night sounds with his gentle rising and falling quaver. He thought of Leda's unexpected relish in posing nude for him. The sketching sessions would not be an ordeal for her, at least not in the ordinary sense. He thought of Céleste's puzzling anxiety about the night they had spent together. What was she seeing in all of this that was causing her so much apprehension?

Maybe there was something after all in Amado's overdrawn observations about the way he understood women. What if he was lying here sleepless in the darkness, baffled by Céleste's behavior, because in fact he had spent his life immersed in only the flesh and clay of women, never bothering to understand anything else? Was he really blind to everything except that which he could touch? He couldn't believe it . . . but he was beginning to wonder.

Chapter 16

When Leda arrived the second morning she was carrying a pastry box from Kirchner's Bakery on the river.

"I thought we should start with some almond croissants," she said snappily, plopping the box down on one of the workbenches.

"Did they ask you if you were bringing them to me?" he said, coming over with his cup of coffee.

"No, why?"

"I'm their single greatest buyer of almond croissants."

"You're kidding." She dropped her purse on the modeling platform.

He opened the box, which was still warm, and the yeasty odors rose to meet him. "God, I love these things."

"Any more of that?" she asked, nodding at his coffee.

"Yeah, in the thermos back there." He nodded toward the corner at the rear of the studio as he took one of the soft croissants from the box. "There are some cups on the shelf above it."

"Any of these cups are okay?" she called to him.

"Sure. They'll be dusty. Rinse them out."

"Oh," she gasped. "They're filthy."

He heard water running in the sink, and then after a minute she came back with a cup of coffee and got a warm croissant from the box, too. They sat on the platform, eating the cream-filled pastries.

"Oh, this is heavenly," she said through a mouthful of croissant. "How do you feel about it now, the morning after?"

He looked at her.

"The drawings," she said. "They'll be helpful?"

"Oh, sure. It's a good start."

"So what do we do today?"

"Same thing. Over and over."

"And that's the way it goes?"

"That's the way it goes."

"Good coffee, too," she said. "In spite of the cup."

After they finished their croissants, they sat for a moment, sipping coffee. Leda had worn a loose shift that buttoned up the front, as had the dress the previous day. It was probably the easiest design for her to deal with. When they were ready to get started, he got his sketchbook and pencils while she went up on the platform, unbuttoned the shift, and slipped it off. This time there were no panties. The shift was all she'd worn.

He began sketching, and they worked steadily for the better part of an hour as he circled around her. She became more adept at choosing poses that she could hold comfortably, and only occasionally did he need to ask her to move an arm or leg or shift her weight. It went very well, but he noticed that she tired easily in those positions in which she could not easily counterbalance the massive hump.

Every model, professional or not, who poses without her clothes has her own particular way of making herself comfortable with being stared at intently. Some maintain total silence and lose themselves in a private inner world, others want music. Others need to talk. Leda quickly sensed and accommodated his preference for working in silence and found her own silent way to occupy her mind. He even thought that she, too, fell under the spell of the summer sounds that floated in through the windows, the inescapable drone of cicadas, the somnolent purl of mourning doves, and the loopy vocal flights of mockingbirds.

But eventually Leda wanted to stop and smoke. And talk.

"What do you think of Céleste?" she asked, reclining on the red damask-covered bed. He was learning that she wasn't having trouble being naked at all. Once again, she was using her protuberant back as a prop. It was an odd thing to see, as if he were visiting with a Minotaur at rest.

"I think she surprised the hell out of me yesterday." He was working on one of the sketches. He looked up. Leda was waiting with an expression of curious expectancy.

"Really?" There was a brittle edge in her voice.

"She told me who you were."

"She *did?*"

"You didn't know she was going to do that?"

"No."

"What were you going to do, just keep it a secret?"

"I don't know. Maybe."

"You two are full of surprises, aren't you?"

"At the rate we're going we won't be much longer," she said testily.

Céleste wasn't the only sister who preferred to hide more than she revealed. God, they sure as hell shared that with Sylvie.

"You didn't answer my question about Céleste," she said.

"It's a wide-open question."

"Oh, give it a go," she said with mock goodwill.

"I try to keep my opinions about people to myself."

"Do you really? Are you always successful?"

"Generally."

Leda smoked. "She hasn't had it easy, you know, these last few years."

"Her husband?"

"Yes," she said sourly. "Lacan."

"What's his story?"

"I have *no* idea. When Céleste 'inherited' me, she and Lacan were already through. She was leaving."

She stopped and smoked, regarding him with calculating eyes as if she were weighing the wisdom of going on. She seemed to assume that he already knew about Céleste's guardianship.

"I'll bet you wonder why she puts up with it, don't you?"

"What, the bad marriage? Sure . . ."

"No, not *just* the marriage." Pause. "I'd be stupid if I didn't think you've seen as much of her body as you've seen of mine."

He stopped fiddling with the sketch and looked at her.

"This is something you want to talk

about?" he asked, crossing his arms.

"No. None of my business," she said, shifting on the bed, "but don't pretend you haven't seen the bruises."

He didn't answer.

"Yes, I thought so," she said. "Well, that's what I'm referring to . . . why she puts up with *that*."

He waited. Damn right he wondered, but he didn't want to play this game with her. On the other hand, he did want to hear what she had to say.

"You see," Leda said, "I'm at a bit of a disadvantage here. You and Céleste have had a lot of time to talk. I imagine she's told you a fair amount about me, hasn't she?"

"I'd bet a lot of money that it's less than you think."

She laughed. It was a beautiful laugh, and her face was radiant in laughter.

"Well, all right, then." She put out her cigarette, and he thought she was ready to get back to the sketching. Instead she reached for another one and lighted it. "But she told you, I'm sure, about how Eva died and left this trust for her to oversee, dole out the money to me."

Once again he waited in silence, without confirming her assumptions. She smiled hugely at his reticence, and he had the feeling she found him amusingly predictable.

"The truth is, Eva had gone through every cent of it when she died," Leda said, her tone going bitter. "Every . . . cent . . . of . . . it." She smoked, watching him. "Of course, she had failed to tell either of us that. So, she and her money exited together. As usual, her timing was impeccable. Céleste is 'administering' thin air. The only money she handles is an insultingly generous stipend that Lacan gives us."

"And that's why she stays with him?"

"Right."

"Jesus Christ."

"But" — Leda smiled cynically — "there's more to it." She arched a lovely dark eyebrow. "There's always more to it, isn't there?" Pause. "It's not just a matter of . . . being 'kept.' When Céleste inherited me, she inherited . . . a few complications."

She sat up awkwardly on the side of the bed, as if her back were hurting her, though, too, as if it were something she was used to.

"I'm going to need some operations," she said. "Expensive ones. And I have ongoing medical expenses." She tried to smile wryly, but it didn't work very well. "I'm an expensive woman to keep. Monsieur Lacan most graciously agreed to absorb all the medical

163

bills, and provide us with an allowance. Most graciously."

"In exchange for . . ."

"Yes. And then he developed this . . . this *aberrant* taste. . . ." She stopped. Silence. She stared into space, preoccupied.

He waited, watching her, and she remained that way for so long that it began to seem like truly strange behavior. Minutes passed. The sounds from outside drifted into the studio, and she remained fixed. He was tantalized by this sudden and complete catatonia, and then a sense of discomfort gripped him as he began to fear that her immobility really was a kind of genuine paralysis, a peculiar sort of seizure.

Just as he was about to say something, she sighed smoothly and slowly and stirred, seeming to recover in increments, and stood wearily.

"Well," she said hoarsely, "gaze at me some more, Mr. Marteau. Feast your eyes."

Leda had related her sordid story about Céleste and Lacan with an effortless mien that gave the horrible story a creepy aftertaste. The more he thought about it, the more awful it became.

Before they could get started, the telephone rang. The remainder of the partial shipment of limestone blocks that had been delivered two days before was at the front gate. They wanted to know where to unload the stones.

"This is going to take at least half an hour," he told Leda, who was sitting naked on the daybed. "You might as well get dressed. We've done enough, anyway."

"One thing," she said from the bed, stopping him as he started out of the studio. "I'm always saying more than I should. I'm much more impetuous than Céleste, as you must have noticed. What I told you a while ago, well, she would consider that way out of line. She would be horribly ashamed to know that you knew about it."

She looked at him from the bed, a kind of sibyl, as strange as the mythic Sphinx herself.

"Don't let her know I've told you. If you want to talk to her about it, it's none of my business. But don't bring me into it." Pause. "And, please, be clever about it."

This last was said with a tone of condescension that seemed almost impertinent. Leda, he was learning, was quite capable of that and never suffered any pangs of conscience about it, either. It said a lot about her and about the kind of life she had had. It said a lot, but it didn't say nearly enough. His growing curiosity about the two sisters

165

was gradually shouldering aside his concentration on the Beach commission.

"I won't say anything," he said, and turned and walked out of the studio, leaving her alone on the bed.

He walked through the woods to the house and then up the drive to the gates. He told the driver that he wanted to check the load before he maneuvered his truck all the way to the back of the property, and he climbed up on the side rails and looked in. The blocks were the wrong size. The blocks he ordered were an odd size, and the yard foremen at the quarry were always trying to send him a near size that was also a common size used for building construction.

Frustrated, the driver climbed out, and they measured the blocks. The mistake confirmed, the driver climbed back into the truck, radioed the quarry, and had an argument with the yard foreman. Then in disgust he slammed the truck in gear and pulled out onto Las Lomitas and headed down the hill again. Ross started back to the studio.

He took a shortcut through the woods and came up on the studio from the side of the kiln rather than from the path that led to the front of the studio from the house. As he passed the front of the kiln, his eye caught the unmistakable flash of a mirror's reflection on the deep sill of one of the tall windows.

Recognizing the flash for what it was, he instinctively slowed his pace. Mirrors? The flash had been too big to have come from a hand mirror that Leda might have kept in her purse. The only mirror in the studio was in the bathroom . . . and, yes, there were two old full-length mirrors on rickety wooden stands next to the back wall of the studio, not too far from the rear of the modeling stand.

He impulsively gave in to an adolescent curiosity to spy on her. He crossed in front of the building and went to the windows opposite the side where he saw the reflection. He knew which window he could look into without being seen from the position of the mirrors.

Feeling every bit as foolish as he would have appeared if he'd been caught, he nevertheless gave in to curiosity and carefully approached the open windows.

Leda was not difficult to find in the dim interior. She had angled the two mirrors so that one of them picked up the sunlight from a nearby window and threw a spotlight of hyperbrilliance onto her still-naked body, causing her to stand out in the dim interior of the studio as if she were caught by lasers. She had positioned the mirrors so that she could see her reflection in both panels at once, one presenting her front, one her back. Though her reflection was bright, she saw herself through a chalky, speckled haze of grime and dust that covered the long-neglected mirrors.

She stood in front of herself, motionless, her eyes moving over the beautiful and strange terrain of her body as if she were studying a map of fascinating interest. She was intent and serene, much as she had been earlier during her catatonic episode. But he was sure that he and she were not seeing the same images in those reflections.

After a few moments of this singular concentration, she raised her arms and reached straight back and gripped the hump on her back with both hands. She held it with spread fingers, and he could see the pressure she was applying to her back as her fingers bent and buckled with the effort, becoming angular claws.

Just as he thought she was about to bury her fingernails into her own flesh, she released herself with an upward jerk of her arms, which she then held high over her head, hands stretched upward, out of the laser light and into the shadows so that she appeared truncated, her arms missing above her elbows. She studied herself.

Then she lowered her arms slowly and turned so that she observed herself in profile. Slowly she bent forward, crossing her arms and tucking them under her, once again creating an image that was truncated, limbless. The hump on her shoulders rose up in sharp profile and blended into the rest of her back all the way to the crevice of her buttocks. Now her calm gave way to a nervous but contained excitement, and he could see her eyes darting about her body, devouring her image as she assayed the unidentifiable shape that she had become by this contorted posturing.

As he looked at her she reminded him of nothing so much as a monstrous, humpbacked, black fly, stopped in the sunlight, mindless, hardly even an insect. Her face, framed by her jet hair, was unrecognizable, her features having been washed away to nothing by the brilliant light. As she held this posture, straining, her concentration on herself exceeding obsession, she lost all human resemblance. She became a stooping, faceless thing that defied any phylum of identity.

Appalled, he turned away.

Chapter 17

"I'd like to meet her," Amado said. "When would be a good time?"

"Leda?"

"Yes, Leda."

He hadn't expected this, and he hesitated, frowning at the distant summer sky above the valley that fell away in front of them.

They were sitting at an outside table at La Residencia, the health spa on the eastern slope of the hills overlooking San Rafael. Amado had suggested they meet there for lunch instead of at Graber's because he was picking up a friend there at three o'clock.

Ross didn't like the place much. It was the fanciest commercial operation in San Rafael, and even though from the outside it blended in with the laid-back ethos of the town, inside its grounds it dripped ostentatious indulgence. If he couldn't be critical of the indulgence — he was guilty of his own varieties of it — he sure as hell objected to the peacockery of it all.

The spa complex was large. Behind the main hacienda, which was flanked on both sides by a score of secluded bungalows tucked into the wooded hillside, was a central sprawling lawn that descended in gentle terraces that overlooked San Rafael and the valley below the town. Small patios were scattered along the terraces, each accommodating one or two tables shaded by arbors and palms and umbrellas. Meals were served on the patios twenty-four hours a day.

"What's the matter?" Amado asked.

Ross had finished his lunch, but Amado was still eating the last of a mango torte and sipping coffee.

"I don't know how she'd feel about that," he said.

"Oh."

He heard the quick retreat in Amado's monosyllable. This was different. Amado was alert.

"I don't know her well enough to know how she feels about meeting people."

"Is she reclusive?"

"I've just met her, Amado."

Amado pushed away the last few bites of the torte and pulled his coffee closer. "Then, this . . . thing, this *is* her life."

"I think so. But you're never really sure with her."

"What's she like?"

"Mercurial. Moody. Likable. But she can

be mean." And unbelievably strange, he thought to himself. He was still troubled by what he had seen a few hours before.

He watched the clouds drifting northwestward over the valley. The day had the look of summer. Spring was relinquishing her delicate moments to the longer, sterner hours of a more serious season.

"It's hard to explain," he said as if he were making an admission. "To be honest, I've found Leda's appearance more . . . disconcerting than I'd imagined."

"What do you mean?"

"Well, when she first took off her clothes, I thought, Oh, this isn't so extraordinary. I can do this. But, actually, the . . . oddness of her body increases with exposure. Sometimes I'm looking at her, sketching, studying an angle, and suddenly it's as if . . . as if I don't recognize the shape at all. It's like seeing a common word while you're reading and all of a sudden it doesn't look right . . . it looks as if it might be spelled wrong . . . and then it looks only remotely familiar."

Amado didn't say anything for a moment. Then he finished his coffee.

"Well, maybe later," he said. "Maybe something will seem natural to you later, and I can meet her."

"Yeah, give us a little time."

The truth was he couldn't be at all sure what Leda might say in Amado's presence, or even do. Céleste could be trusted to be discreet, but Leda was unpredictable. He and Amado had talked about women over the years, but they had never talked about the women with whom they were living, not of their intimacies, anyway.

But now he found himself not wanting to reveal anything at all about his deepening involvement with Leda and Céleste. There was a distinct sense in which he felt that these two women were living on the edge of something, something slightly foreboding. He couldn't explain why, but there was even a feeling of the illicit in his dealings with them. He could always walk away, he told himself, but not just yet. In the meantime, whatever it was that was happening between himself and these two strange women, he wanted to keep it among the three of them.

"What about Céleste? What's she like?"

"Tough. Insightful." He looked at Amado. "Guarded. And barely holding things together."

"Ah, now that's what I would be afraid of."

"I think 'tough' trumps that last observation," he said. "If she's just barely holding

173

things together, she also seems to be quite capable of doing it indefinitely."

"No, that's not what I meant," Amado said, shaking his head. "I meant I would be afraid of whatever the things *are* that she's trying to hold together."

Chapter 18

When he got home from La Residencia he changed into old jeans and a threadbare khaki shirt and walked down the path to the kiln shed next to the studio. He wanted to think about the conversation he had just had with Amado.

It was nearly four o'clock when he finally got to the shed. It was approaching the hottest part of the day, but the kiln faced east so that the front of it, where he had to work, was already in the shade.

The kiln was a hulking brick affair next to the studio, the two buildings being separated by a shed where there were worktables and where he did much of his stone carving. It was here that he fired his smaller maquettes and where Marian had fired her pottery, including the turquoise vase she had shattered in Paris a few months ago. Cleaning out a kiln was a job that's always there to do, like taking out the garbage. When he left for Paris over a year ago, it was already past its cleaning time. Now was as good a time as any to get it done.

The kiln had been specially made for him

with a section of rail that ran into it the length of its interior and extended out its door an additional ten feet. An iron flatbed cart sat on the rail and could be rolled completely out of the kiln and loaded with its cargo, a maquette or pottery, and then rolled back into the center of the kiln so that the door could be closed and locked down for firing. Firing was a messy process that threw off debris, necessitating the frequent cleanings.

He had worked for nearly two hours and was just finishing when he looked up from closing the kiln door one last time and saw Céleste. She was sitting on the massive millstone that lay in the shade of a palm at the edge of the woods twenty yards away. Her legs were extended out in front of her, ankles crossed, her arms straight down at her sides, hands braced on the surface of the stone. Her sandaled feet emerged from the shade into the sun.

Neither of them spoke as they looked at each other. Sweat was pouring down his face. He had shed his shirt and was covered with dust and cinder streaked with sweat.

"How long have you been here?" he asked. She seemed preoccupied, as if she had been watching him only because he was in front of her.

"Only a little while," she said. "Go ahead and finish."

"That was the last of it," he said. "I'm through." He reached for his shirt, which was hanging on a corner of the kiln, and glanced at her as he wiped his face with it. Something told him she hadn't come by just to look at the sketches he'd made of Leda that morning.

"Let's go to the house, and I'll clean up," he said, walking over to her. "I'll make some iced tea."

He bathed in the outdoor shower and put on clean clothes. When he went into the kitchen Céleste was already there, and two glasses of iced tea with lime slices floating in them were sitting in front of her on the table. She was cutting up one of the fat peaches and putting the small wedges on a saucer of brightly painted Mexican pottery.

"These looked good," she said.

She pushed the saucer toward him as he sat down, and they ate the peach together in a silence broken only by the smooth cooing of a mourning dove that floated through the screen door. Whatever her intentions, he was going to let her do it however she wished. He wasn't going to initiate the conversation. He watched her putting the half-moon slices into her mouth, her eyes

177

dwelling absently on the colorful pattern on the little plate. She seemed to belong there, sitting across the table from him as if they had done this a thousand afternoons together. Despite her preoccupation, she appeared to be relaxed; the disquiet of the previous afternoon had disappeared. But she had brought a solemnity with her, too, and he was eager to know what it meant.

When they had eaten the last of the peach, she got up and rinsed the saucer and knife and left them on the draining board beside the sink, then washed her hands. He watched her back, her stomach against the sink, as she gazed out the window, drying her hands.

"Could we sit outside, under the arbor?" she asked, turning to him.

They took their glasses of iced tea and went out the screened door to the courtyard.

The arbor bench was dappled in shade, and he leaned against one of the stone pillars that supported the arbor beams and crossed his legs. Céleste sat near the next pillar, her profile to him, outlined against the stones. The ice sounded friendly and cold when they drank from their glasses.

"I wasn't sure I wanted to see you again," she said after a moment. She was holding her glass in her lap, her eyes fixed on a clay pot of geraniums near the edge of the sun.

He was surprised. Had his remark been that devastating to her? "What do you mean?"

She didn't say anything.

"Céleste?"

"I think we've got ahead of ourselves," she said, starting to run a middle finger around the rim of her glass.

"It's all seemed natural enough to me."

"Yes, I'm afraid it's seemed natural to me, too."

" 'Afraid'? I don't understand why you're so . . . I don't know, apprehensive about what's happened. Maybe we shouldn't have done that. I told you, I'm sorry if . . . if it seems wrong to you now, but I don't under—"

"The other night," she said, interrupting him, concentrating on the rim of her glass, her finger going round and round it, "was very strange . . . strange because I began to feel as if I had known you before. It was as if we had been separated for years and years, and finally" — she looked up at him — "we were together . . . again."

It was incredible how similar their feelings about that night had been, how similarly they had reacted to each other.

She returned her eyes to her glass.

179

"It was an incredibly vivid sense," she said, "even disturbingly vivid. I felt disoriented, adrift. When you woke up and found me standing in the dark, by the windows, I was trying to calm down, trying to understand what was going on."

God, he could hardly believe what she was saying.

"But later," she went on, "when I had some time, some distance, from it and had time to reflect, I realized I'd . . . just got carried away, like a schoolgirl. I guess it's been so long since I've felt like that . . . I just didn't recognize what was happening." She paused. "And that's where we got ahead of ourselves. This is a terrible mistake."

"What are you talking about?"

"We're starting something here that's not going to work. Nothing good is going to come of this. It's an illusion."

"I just don't understand why you've got such a dark view of what's going on here," he said, frustrated. "Maybe we got a little ahead of ourselves, should've gone slower. I accept that. We could've done it differently. But I don't understand why you're painting such a grim picture of what did happen. Maybe it was a mistake, happened too fast, but that doesn't make it tragedy."

"Your . . . impulsive question, Ross," she

said, looking at him. "You asked me: 'Do you like it?' and it was out of your mouth before you even knew you were going to say it, wasn't it?"

She didn't want an answer. She was making a point.

"Well, that question is the serpent in the garden," she went on. "It's never going to go away, and it will eventually destroy this illusion. This has been unusual from the beginning, wonderful, but strange. But now it's going to be even more complicated . . . because you're not going to be able to forget these bruises . . . or how I got them. You're going to find that impossible to live with. And I'm going to find *that* impossible to live with."

He knew she was right. But he didn't want to believe it.

"It doesn't have to be like that," he said. "It's not inevitable, for God's sake."

She shook her head and stared at the ground. When she spoke, the tone of fatalism in her voice was chilling.

"You don't know anything," she said, "about what's inevitable in my life. Or even in yours."

It was a statement of clarity that shocked him and cut through the obfuscation that had been gradually affecting his own thinking during the last ten days. It made him aware that somehow he had actually been losing sight of his own vaunted cynicism. They were both too practical to believe in romantic notions that offered cloudy explanations for whatever it was that was happening between them, but neither of them could deny that something was happening. They just understood it in dramatically different ways.

He hesitated, didn't know what to say.

She gave him a knowing look and turned away, staring at the shadows stretching out from the arbor into the courtyard.

"It doesn't matter how I met him," she began. "At an exhibition. This was a few months before Eva died. I'd never been married. It was never a consideration. Then the car crash, and I took on the responsibility of Leda, and . . . there was . . . everything changed dramatically and quickly. I simply didn't see him for what he was. I wasn't an inexperienced girl. . . ."

She shrugged.

"It was never a marriage, not from the first week, even. I won't go into it. His money comes from an inherited family industry, construction materials of some sort. He has no real involvement himself. Proxies run everything for him. He simply spends the money."

She sipped her iced tea as if to give herself time to think.

"He travels incessantly. He owns a home in Antibes and another in Strasbourg. I live in the home in Paris. He lives in a hotel in Paris. I see him, maybe, once every three weeks. It's irregular. I never know when he'll show up. He just appears. When we were first married, and I was still stupid enough to think there was some hope of normalcy, I used to try to keep up with him. Was he in Antibes? In Paris? But he got furious with me. . . .

"It's embarrassing, to have been such a fool. . . ." She stopped again and swallowed. "You know, I don't . . . I thought I could talk about this, I wanted to, for your sake, to help you understand, and maybe accept. But I can't. I just . . . can't do this."

"Why in the hell don't you leave him?"

She turned to him. "Ross, no, let's don't."

"You started this, Céleste."

The tormented look on her face was wrenching and stopped him. She was right, he *did* want her to talk about it. The thought of Lacan inflicting those bruises, the whole scene in his mind, her submission, all of it was excruciating to him. He wanted to probe the abscess of that sick arrangement until it was lanced of all its poison and destruction and Céleste could see her way to be free of it. But the look on her face told him that the words that would take them through that grueling discussion were too mean and too many. He didn't have the heart to do that to her.

They were both silent, looking at each other. The long shadows of late afternoon were beginning to blend together in the surrounding woods, and the bench under the arbor was drawn into a deeper shade. The sun had set, but the sky was rich in its reflected glow and threw a blush onto the rear of the stone house. Céleste's face caught the last moments of the faint, fading color.

"When will you see him again?" he asked.

Her eyes glittered suddenly with a dense, fierce emotion.

"You must never — ever — ask me that again."

He said nothing, but he agreed, and in that moment the serpent glided silently between them and stopped, comfortable in their warmth, content in their weakness.

For a time they continued in silence as the evening surrounded them, each trying to calm the turmoil within. They knew the night would be over soon, and they wanted to stem the tension, to dissolve the distance between them before it turned to regret.

After a while he got up and went inside

and mixed a gin and tonic for each of them and returned. They took off their shoes and leaned back against the rock pillars and stretched their legs toward each other on the arbor bench, their feet almost touching.

They began to talk, and after a while the awkwardness between them melted in the warm night. The feeling of old familiarity that was so new to them returned as easily as their own breathing and seemed as natural to them as the crickets in the darkness.

A lopsided moon, three-quarters full, rose over the tile roof of the house, and the limestone pavers in the patio glowed in the pale light. It was even bright enough for them to distinguish the cerise color of the bougainvillea.

Céleste pulled her dress into her lap and drew up her legs, her feet on the cushions of the bench. Moonlight fell through the arbor, casting webby shadows over them, and through this dark net he could see a luminous brush stroke of her white panties between her legs.

The pauses between their conversation lengthened as the night grew later.

"Would you lie down with me?" she asked.

They lay together on the wide cushioned bench, and she curled up to him and pulled his arm around her and held it. He couldn't get enough of the feel of her, and of the gentle movement of her breathing. Whatever she needed from him at that moment, she wanted in silence. They listened to the loping rhythm of the crickets and stared up through the bougainvillea at the broken moon.

Chapter 19

Leda arrived with her pastry box of almond croissants, which they again shared with coffee. He toyed with the idea of asking her more about Céleste's reluctance to tell him why she remained with Lacan, but he didn't want to start the sketching session on that note, so he let it go.

She wore a regular dress instead of the shift, and again she wore underwear. This time when she undressed she left the panties on.

"I want you to do a series of sketches of me removing my panties," she announced.

"Why?"

"It's a problem of balance," she said unconvincingly. She removed the panties to demonstrate her point. Naturally there was a problem of balance, but not one that seemed to him to be worthy of a series of sketches. Though, in truth, it didn't matter. Anything she did would be helpful to him.

For half an hour she posed for him in varying stages of the process of removing her panties. And again he had the uncomfortable sense of seeing her as two completely different women. Though the protrusion on her back was the focal point of difficulty in almost every pose, there were rare angles when the hump played no role at all, and Leda became the most stunning model he had ever drawn.

He doubted that she was even aware of this phenomenon of the disappearing hump. She had been obsessed with her condition for so many years that he suspected she couldn't look at herself without seeing it. And he guessed, too, that sometimes when she looked at herself she saw nothing but the hump, so that her personality and all that she was disappeared underneath that cartilaginous monstrosity until she became, only, the Deformity.

When she took her break, Leda collapsed on the bed and lighted her first cigarette. The panty-removing poses had, understandably, exhausted her. While he continued to fine-tune the last sketch, he asked her — he tried to make it sound offhanded, incidental — if Céleste was doing anything to extricate herself from the situation with Lacan. What, in the long run, was she going to do?

"Ah, that again," Leda said with bored indifference, blowing smoke into the air. "Well, I suppose she's doing what she's going to do. What's the matter, are you finding it . . . disgusting . . . to have to rub against Lacan's snail trails every time you make love to her?"

It was an unexpectedly brutal question made all the more repellent by the grain of truthful insight that it contained. Had he been younger, he would have lashed back at her with his own bit of civilized cruelty. But he let it go, more saddened for both of them than angry.

She must have seen how it affected him and regretted it. Her tone changed, but what she said next was even more shocking.

"We've talked of killing him."

He looked up from the sketchbook but couldn't think of anything to say.

"Really," she said, looking at him with blank innocence. "Actually, Céleste has talked about it."

Was she joking?

"She's talked of *ways* of doing it," Leda added.

"What? You're kidding."

"No, I'm not."

"When?" He didn't believe her.

"What, when did she talk about it? Or when did she talk about doing it?"

He shook his head.

"Often, off and on. Any time."

He got up from the far edge of the model's platform where he had been sitting, tossed down the sketchbook, and walked toward the nearest window and looked out, hands in his pockets.

"You're surprised?" she said as if *she* were surprised that he was surprised. "Really, are you? Wouldn't you think about killing him too if you were in her situation?"

He turned around. "When did you last talk about this with her?"

"Oh, relax. Maybe it's more accurate to say that we fantasized about it together."

What the hell was this? Was she telling the truth or what? Or was she wildly exaggerating just to provoke him?

"It's only talk, Ross," she said dismissively. "I'm showing off. I wouldn't have told you if I'd thought it would *immobilize* you."

She looked at him, finishing her cigarette. Then she mashed it out in the ashtray. He could tell that his silence was having its own sort of effect on her, just as her brutal words affected him. He waited to see what she would say next.

"We should get started," she said, and she straightened up on the bed and swung her feet to the floor. "Look, I was just jabbering away. For Christ's sake, don't tell Céleste I said anything about this. We were fantasizing, just messing around. Céleste is a very burdened woman. Fragile, even, in her own way. She would die if she knew I'd told you this."

With some effort she stood. He had noticed that she grew increasingly stiff during the course of their sessions.

"The truth is," she went on, "we don't share all that much with each other. When she does confide in me, even if it's a silly fantasy, well, I don't want her to think she can't do that without me blabbing to someone about it."

She paused, cutting her eyes around at him.

"You see what I mean, don't you?" She thought a moment. "Actually, the same thing applies with you and me. I'd like to think I could talk to you, tell you things that, well, like that . . . that are personal. And I'd like to think that we could keep them just between ourselves. Everyone needs someone to talk to in that way. Céleste and I, we're rarely — almost never — open to each other like that."

She walked over to the sketchbook lying on the edge of the platform and looked down at the last drawing he had made.

"Demons," she said, not to him, not to

anyone. "Everyone has demons." She twisted her head to see the drawing better. "Every single person. Céleste has memories from Lacan. Lacan, his own sick mind. Me, well . . ." She looked up at him. "And, you . . ."

He didn't say anything.

"Really?" She pretended confusion. "You don't know? Or maybe you believe that nothing is stalking you? We're all stalked by something, don't you think? Something we're born with, maybe. Something inside us."

She looked down at the drawing again and studied it a moment.

"We have to struggle with them," she went on in a distracted fashion, almost inaudible, "incessantly. If we don't, they will gnaw at us and gnaw at us . . ."

She slid one leg forward, and with her toe she moved the sketchbook around so that she could see the drawing of herself from another angle. She studied it.

"The only thing more dangerous than our demons," she said pensively, nearly whispering, "is refusing to believe that we have them."

There was silence in the studio except for the throaty buzzing of cicadas outside in the morning heat. She stood with her hands on the back side of her hips, fingers down, staring at the drawing.

Again, as she had done the day before, she grew weirdly still. He noticed and watched her with new interest. Her complete immobility was something he sensed as much as he actually observed. He stared at her rib cage, wanting to see the rise and fall of her breathing. There was none. Frustratingly, he wasn't in a position to see her face, but her rigidity was more than an absence of physical motion. It was as if her mind had stopped, not as if her thoughts were elsewhere, but as if the hummock-burdened body before him *had* no mind.

By the time he decided to go over to her, she began to recover. She did so in minute increments, not all at once as if she were "snapping" out of it. A finger on her hip moved a little, a twitch, then a shoulder returned to life, and then her rib cage began a measured rise and fall, shallow, not energetically as if she had been holding her breath. Her face was the last to return to animation, and she turned to him.

"Do you have mirrors here?"

She showed no signs of knowing, or at least acknowledging, that she had been "absent."

"Yeah," he said, "a couple."

193

"I want to use them for the next series of poses."

"Now?"

"No? You don't want me to?"

"No, that's fine," he said. "Let me get them." At this point he was curious.

He went to the two mirrors she had used the previous day — she had pushed them back in place — and hauled them out from the corner and set them up on the platform. Leda helped him adjust them at particular angles to the bed. When they had been positioned as she wanted, she said that she was ready to begin the second session.

He stepped off the platform, got his sketchbook and pencils, and they began.

By this time, sketching Leda had become secondary to his immediate interest. He didn't know whether Leda was acting more peculiarly now than she had at the beginning or whether he simply had begun to be more aware of her eccentricities as time went by. Whatever the reasons, he was increasingly intrigued by her unpredictable behavior.

As soon as she began to "pose" in front of the mirrors, a major change took place in the dynamics of the session. Now that she was confronted with the contemplation of her own reflection, Leda largely forgot about him. As she went about the business of positioning herself on the bed in relation to her own view of her reflection, she moved with a tai chi grace and concentration. Just as quickly, and thoroughly, as she had lost herself in her queer cataleptic departures, she now flew away into the world of her own reflection.

As she gazed at her smutched image through the begrimed and dusty double lenses of the old mirrors, she was transported to another place. Ross quickly began sketching, but it was rather less an academic exercise than it was a futile effort to capture the dazzling transformation of a chrysalis.

Leda vamped for her own reflection as if she were dancing before Herod. It was an immoderate performance. Ignoring any pretense of posing for the purpose of benefiting his sketching, she struck seductive and erotic postures, her eyes sometimes locked on to her own eyes, sometimes rolling this way and that on the bed with lupine restlessness. Abruptly she shifted to deliberately crude postures, attitudes that she held — completely still — for minutes at a time despite their obvious difficulty for her, and which, performed by a woman of such extraordinary beauty, seemed grotesque in the extreme. And then just as quickly she assumed clinical positions, even gynecological contortions, postures that must surely have echoed the medical examinations she had had to endure since she was a child.

All of this was done with an earnestness that had been entirely absent in her poses before. It was a performance that seemed to be for no one so much as the other two women who looked back at her from the grime-glazed mirrors. For approximately half an hour she focused on herself with an intensity that was remarkable, and which disregarded him completely. When she finally managed to break her concentration and stopped and turned to him, she was glistening with perspiration.

When she did that, and he had stopped, too, he realized that he had covered page after page in his sketchbook with fast, furious drawings, many of them reflecting the energy she had invested in her fierce interaction with her own image. Both of them were drained.

Chapter 20

In the afternoon he drove down the hill to Rinser's Cellars on Bodet, a steeply sloping street that ran into Buena Vista above the river. He was looking for another case of a particular red wine from a small château near St.-Émilion that Rinser had got for him a few months earlier.

While Rinser and his owlish son disappeared into their maze of passages dug into the hillside to check their inventory, he leaned against the counter in the front room and looked out the windows to the river.

"Ross Marteau."

He recognized her voice instantly, but before he could even turn around, Anita Beaton slipped her arm through his and held him.

"Is it true what I hear?" she asked, standing beside him as if they were two strollers, arm in arm. She reeked of gardenias, a perfume he detested. Anita had a genius for irritating him. He guessed that even the kind of underwear she wore and the kind of breakfast cereal she ate were precisely the style and kind he would find ridiculous.

"I seriously doubt it," he said. He had no idea why he bothered being polite to her.

She grinned, her thin lips peeling back from her teeth in an unintended fleer. "I'm hearing that you're quite good friends with Céleste Lacan's sister, Leda."

He looked at her, astonished, and she saw it in his face.

"Jesus," he said, shaking his head in annoyance.

He pulled away from her and turned and leaned back against the walnut counter, his elbows resting on the dark wood. He had had the impression, obviously the wrong impression, that Leda kept very much to herself.

"Oh, really, Ross," she said, "what do you expect? If you weren't so . . . reserved — I didn't say reclusive — maybe people wouldn't wonder what in the hell you were doing all the time. And then you start something with a woman like that . . . such a strange girl, and you're *surprised* that people know about it. Surely not." She leaned her long, angular frame back from her waist, regarding him skeptically. "Surely not."

She was trolling. She had suspicions, but she didn't really know anything. In a moment of weakness he wondered how accurate her information was. She was studying him with a vague smile.

"What do you mean, 'start something'?" he asked.

"Life in this town is absurdly simple," she said with the condescending tone of a cosmopolitan. "The maid of a friend of mine was in Kirchner's the other morning when Leda was in there. They both left about the same time. Naturally the maid noticed her. When the maid drove away it happened that Leda followed her in her own car. The maid works for a woman who lives past you on Las Lomitas, farther up in the hills. In her rearview mirror the maid saw Leda turn into your gates. Naturally I got a phone call about that. And then the exact same thing happened again this morning."

"She's come to see me a few times," he said, "and you conclude I've 'started something' with her?"

"Maybe my phrasing could have been refined a little."

"It could have been refined a lot."

She glanced back toward the passages, past the stacks of wine and racks of liquor, as if to make sure they weren't being overheard.

"Céleste created something of a stir when she first arrived," she said, "but she didn't cause *this* much talk. I hear she has an extraordinarily beautiful face."

He didn't say anything.

"Did you know those two women in Paris?"

"No."

She looked at him, trying to sense if he was lying.

"You know," she said, "a friend of mine in Paris gave Céleste my name. When she came to see me I thought she was captivating. She could be aloof, though, which was a little off-putting to some people. But then when she did pay attention to you, when she did turn her eyes and mind on you, you felt so special that all was instantly forgiven her.

"I saw right away that she wasn't really the social sort at all," Anita said, looking around the store. "Which was odd, I mean, why did she come to me? I tried to introduce her to people I thought she would find interesting. I gave her plenty of opportunities to branch out. But she didn't seem to particularly want to. I know she turned down a number of invitations to dinner parties.

"You know" — she looked down at a case of wine beside her and bent to examine the label of a green bottle in a bed of straw — "you're the first person she's had anything to do with at all. She just sort of went right straight to you, didn't she?"

"I wouldn't say that. She'd been here more than a month before I got back."

"She's quite attractive, Céleste is, but there's nothing rare about being handsome these days. What's different about Céleste's beauty is that it's a beauty . . . of its own kind. Nothing else quite like it in this age of dreadful sameness."

He didn't say anything.

"I imagine you like that about her."

He glanced toward the passages. Where the hell was Rinser?

"You have to admit, Ross, that it's all happened very quickly between you and these two women. That's why I wondered if you'd known them in Paris."

Again she studied him, but he didn't say anything.

"In the first couple of weeks Céleste was here," Anita continued, "she and I spent a good bit of time together. I took her on a grand tour of San Rafael, you know, pointing out the homes of famous people. She asked, quite innocently, it seemed, 'Doesn't the sculptor Ross Marteau live here?' And we drove by your place. I didn't think anything about it at the time."

He didn't much like the flavor of this. It sounded as if she were piecing together the movements of the suspects in a murder plot.

"I think you're working too hard on this one, Anita."

"It's all very fascinating," she said. "Have they commissioned you to do something?"

"No."

"Just friends."

"That's right."

Anita stepped over to another opened crate of wine displayed in straw with plastic grapes.

"I contacted my friend in Paris. You know, just to get a little background on Céleste."

She examined the labels again. He noted her choreography, the casual segue into the point of her story. She looked up at him.

"It turned out," she concluded with a little lift of her shoulders and raised eyebrows, "that she didn't really know anything about her. She was doing a favor for a friend of a friend, too. It seems Céleste's connection is so far removed from any of us that no one really knows where she came from."

"Nope. No more. I'm sorry." Rinser was standing with his hands on hips, his smudged glasses a little crooked on his nose, the tuft of his widow's peak out of control. "You got the absolute last case of it, Ross."

"Well, it was good stuff," he said. "Too bad."

"Karl is on the Internet," Rinser added. "If something turns up, I'll call you, okay?"

"That'll be fine."

Rinser looked at Anita and dusted his hands together.

"Oh, no thanks," she said, sliding toward the door. "I was just . . . looking around." She glared at Ross. "It was good chatting with you."

Chapter 21

The days fell into a pattern. In the mornings Leda arrived with her almond croissants, which they ate while sitting on the modeling platform, drinking coffee from the thermos that he brought from the house. The sketching sessions themselves were increasingly experimental affairs.

Leda's remarkable performance with the mirrors was not repeated again, at least not in precisely that same way. She continued to use the mirrors, but her repertoire of poses was more selective, fewer at each session, though often no less outrageous. She held the poses longer, gazing at herself to the point of distraction, lost in self-fascination. He often had to remind her to change positions. Leda, it became evident, had a fetish for her own reflection.

One day he brought out some glass cleaner from the storeroom in the back of the studio with the intention of cleaning the mirrors. She quickly stopped him, very agitated. She did *not* want the mirrors cleaned. And so the sessions continued as before while she communicated with herself in her own strange way through the blotchy haze of neglect.

During their breaks they continued to talk about whatever was on Leda's mind, and in these conversations her mercurial nature was increasingly evident. She was moody, sometimes euphoric, sometimes depressed, alternately loquacious and taciturn.

He wanted to use these opportunities to learn more about Céleste, but Leda was far too clever to be finessed into discussing her sister. No matter how innocent the approach, any query about Céleste would provoke a sharp response from Leda, often one that took a nasty turn toward cruelty. He learned that Leda considered questions about Céleste to be distractions from Leda's rightful ownership of these few hours with him and during which she felt that all of his attention should be focused on her. During these few hours every day she wanted his world to contain only her. Everything else should be insignificant.

Increasingly Leda would sit down after their sessions and study his sketchbook. As was his habit, the better he got to know his model's body, the more effort he put into the sketches, adding shading and texture, isolating small details of anatomy, and working them thoroughly, incorporating subtleties.

As the drawings became more refined and began to look more "real" to her, Leda grew more serious about studying them. For the most part, he had left the length of the sketching sessions up to her. He learned that she tired easily, so he let her set the pace. As she became more interested in what he was producing, she grew less patient with posing. By now he had filled several notebooks with drawings of her, and after she had finished posing for the day she would take one of these sketchbooks and go to a corner of the studio and settle in to look at it for another half hour before she dressed and left. She began to take the whole exercise of the drawing sessions more seriously.

Though he continued to ask her to stay for a light lunch, she never accepted his invitations. Their relationship remained, at Leda's insistence, that of artist and model, limited to the confines of his studio. He never saw her in any other context. And he certainly never saw her with her sister again after that day Céleste had brought her to meet him for the first time.

The afternoons belonged to Céleste.

She didn't come every day, but she came most days, arriving late when the bright summer light was just beginning to soften. She, too, wanted to look at his latest renderings of Leda, and they often went over the sketches together in the studio while sharing a bottle of wine. She would ask questions: Why did he focus on this part of the anatomy with such fine rendering? Why did he choose to study so many instances of foreshortening? The questions were detailed, and she listened carefully to his explanations.

But Céleste didn't come to see him in the afternoons in order to ask him questions about his progress on Leda's drawings. She came because they couldn't get enough of each other's company. Sometimes they made love in the studio, but they always ended up in his bed, and she always stayed the night.

From the beginning, his interest in Céleste had been as unusual in its progression as he had felt she was unusual in her appearance and behavior. For him, at least, it was an association permeated as much with what was absent as with what was present.

He was powerfully attracted to her, but more than that, he felt an equally powerful kinship. This was a different ingredient, one that had not been present in any of his other relationships with women. In the past the women with whom he had become seriously involved had personalities and natures that were complementary to his own by virtue of their disparity. They most often possessed attributes that counterbalanced his own personality: white to his black, yin to his yang, light to his shadow, smooth to his rough, quick to his slow. They were, in effect, women who provided opposition to his own essential qualities, enabling their relationship to achieve a degree of equilibrium.

But Céleste, far from being his opposite, was like him in so many respects that it was magnetic being with her, as if his personality, in confronting hers, met no significant resistance at all. He didn't have to make allowances for her, nor did she seem to make any for him. She was, of course, a mystery to him, the way one human being is always a mystery to another. But at the same time they were kindred souls, and it didn't take either of them long to recognize this. It wasn't dissimilarity that drew them together, but a preternatural understanding of each other that was almost umbilical in its intuition.

While Leda seemed to be retreating deeper within herself as his drawings of her became more realistic, his relationship with Céleste deepened in another way altogether.

It grew richer, and her arrival nearly every day became the central event of his life, the one thing around which everything else revolved. He was content only when she was there with him, and the time when she wasn't with him became little more than time in transition, that which happened in between her departures and her arrivals.

And for the time being, they tacitly agreed to ignore the presence of dread. They neither spoke of it nor even acknowledged its silent patience in the wings.

Chapter 22

It was dusk, and he was sitting alone at the kitchen table, eating dinner. Looking out through the screen door into the patio, he watched as the indigo light of evening deepened and the arbor and the clay pots scattered about the courtyard were gradually swallowed by the hungering shadows. He was listening to Antonio Carlos Jobim's "Insensatez" on the CD.

It had been several days since he had seen Céleste, and even Leda hadn't shown up for her sketching sessions the last two days. They were the first sessions she had missed. He wanted to call them to see if they were all right, but it seemed somehow inappropriate. The strict separation between himself and the two sisters was something they seemed to have wanted, and he was reluctant to breach intent. He didn't have to have it spelled out for him. If they wanted it that way, he didn't feel compelled to disrupt their logic.

Still, he missed Céleste, and he was curious why she hadn't called him. As he was thinking about this, the telephone rang. He got up and went to the counter and answered.

"Ross! Ross!" It was Leda. "God! . . . God!"

A cold wave washed over his face.

"Leda? What's the matter?" He could hear her trying to get her breath. Was she crying?

"My God, Ross . . . come . . . please . . . Oh, God!"

"Listen . . . Leda, listen to me!"

"Oh . . . oh . . ."

"Leda! Stop!" He could hear her weeping hysterically, and he knew that she wasn't listening to him, that no matter what he said to her she wasn't going to hear him. Suddenly he panicked, thinking of Céleste. Why wasn't Céleste on the telephone?

"Leda . . . listen to me . . . Leda, are you . . . is Céleste hurt?!" He was suddenly furious with her for being hysterical. Goddamn her!

Suddenly Céleste was on the telephone.

"Ross." Her voice was flat, chillingly calm. "Get over here. Now."

The telephone went dead.

He started to dial back, then something told him not to do it, and he grabbed the Jeep keys off a hook by the telephone and ran out the front door to the driveway. In moments he was roaring down the gravel drive and then out onto Las Lomitas, turning down the hill toward the river.

San Rafael was not a busy place at night, but the streets were far from empty. As he negotiated the crooked course that fell toward the river, he imagined catastrophes. Leda had cut herself. Or it was something horrible like a hemorrhage, something to do with her physical condition. But why was Leda talking to him herself? And why were they calling him instead of an ambulance? He told himself to slow down. Be careful. No police. Why?

He crossed the river at Los Ciprés bridge and followed Rio Encinal to Rambach's Mill, where he turned up into the foothills on the other side of the valley. He was in Palm Heights within minutes, pulling up to the front of the old Victorian home that sat slightly above him off the street.

He yanked the emergency brake and clambered out of the Jeep, taking the steps two at a time as he came to them on the rising sidewalk. The lights were out in the house, at least in the front rooms, except in the entry and the living room. He bounded up the front steps to the porch, and just as he reached for the doorknob the door opened, and he was inside.

It was the first time he'd ever been in the

house. The owners, whoever they were, had restored the place immaculately. But he was only subliminally aware of this and only instantly. After that, the shock of seeing the two sisters obliterated everything else.

"Jesus Christ," he said.

Both women were in their dressing gowns. Leda sat on an upholstered bench in the entry hall, her feet and knees together submissively, looking at him from under a Medusa-like tangle of jet hair. Céleste had backed away from the door and was leaning against the framed opening into the living room, her arms crossed over her stomach, her shoulders huddled. Both were smeared and spattered with blood. Leda hadn't even tried to wipe it off, the spatters still dotting her face like scarlet freckles, the front of her gown blotched with what appeared to be spurts of it. Céleste at least had wiped her face and gotten much of it off, but she'd managed mostly to smear it. If anything, her gown seemed to have more blood on it than Leda's.

His eyes stopped on Céleste.

"We're okay," she said hypnotically. "We're not hurt."

Leda lurched to her feet and flung herself at Ross, embracing him, weeping, distraught. He looked at Céleste for an explanation, but she simply stared back at him, nothing in her face. Leda's bloody face was buried in his neck as she wept, and he could feel tears and mucus against his neck. Reflexively he started to put his hand on her head to comfort her when his eyes caught something in her hair just inches from his face. It was a grape-size gobbet of viscous, near fleshy something tangled in the snarl of strands. It no longer glistened but was now going smoky, congealing.

He jerked his face back — he couldn't help it — and gasped, swore. Leda yanked her head up in surprise, saw his face, and shrieked, pushing, stumbling away from him screaming, shaking her bent head in a wild jig, flinging herself about clumsily like a crazed buffalo-thing, slapping at her tangles in a frenzy.

Instantly Céleste was grabbing her, holding her, calming her. Wrestling with Leda, she threw a look at him.

"Upstairs — my room — end of the hall." And with her arms around Leda, they went down the entry hall, he guessed to a bathroom, Leda weeping, whooping in a queer, silly way.

Wanting to get away from them, away from the out-of-control feeling of them, he turned quickly toward the stairs that ascended to his right off the hallway. They were wooden stairs, the wall and banisters painted white. A carpet runner covered the dark, wood-stained treads. When he put his hand on the newel to start up, he put it in something sticky. Blood. Jesus. He looked, and it was everywhere, against the sides of the wall, on the white balusters, smeared, streaked. Swirled palm prints. Tracky finger drags.

He froze, unable to imagine what she was sending him up the stairs to see. Looking up the stairwell ahead of him, he took his handkerchief out of his pocket and wiped his hands. Then he started up, deciding in an instant to get it over with. He couldn't imagine . . . he couldn't imagine . . . he couldn't imagine what was up there.

At the landing the banister that overlooked the entry hall below was on his left, and on the right were two closed doors that he supposed led to other bedrooms. At the end of the hall in front of him, he saw an opened door to a dark room.

He went straight for it, the shortest trip of his life, and suddenly he was reaching around the door into the darkness, groping for the light switch on the wall.

The lights.

The bedroom was large. The bed was in

the center of the far wall, and everything in the room led to it or came from it: bed-clothes streaming off the bed toward him, strewn underwear, a container of spilled powder spattered away from it, a stipple of red black blood sprayed through the powder, an upturned slipper pointing toward the bed, a leather belt stretched out like a dead snake, buckle toward him. The body was on the bed, a man, and even his legs pointed toward the door, the soles of his feet fish-belly white, exposed in a visual alignment with his doughy buttocks.

He went straight to the bed.

All he could think of was that the blood was excessive. Gratuitous. Plethoric.

The white sheets were coiled about the man in a hasty manner that revealed his naked body in spiraled strips, his putty gray flesh visible between the angled ropes of twisted material. His head was completely swaddled in sheeting that was supersaturated, spongy with blood. The shape of one ear was visible through the material. His shoulders were bare. And hairy. A strip of sheet went around his midriff and under him. His buttocks were bare. Black hair crawled up his inner thighs and into the crevice of his anus. A strip of sheet went under one leg, over the other. His lower legs were bare. As he looked at this dead flesh with an uninvited gaze, he realized that nothing he saw gave him any clue to what this man looked like. He could have been any man. Everyman. Humanity.

In Céleste's bed. He retched, fought it, held it. He was grief-stricken. Appalled. Sickened. Above the headboard of the bed a spurt of blood had hit the wall and squirted upward. Then the stuff had dripped down of its own weight. Chairs were overturned. Only the chair where the man had put his clothes was upright. A bedside radio was on the floor. A picture frame was facedown on the floor, as was a whiskey glass. The room smelled puggy, and he could taste the rancid sweetness of copious blood.

He felt the nausea begin deep in his bowels, a twisting, folding sensation that crept up through him. Afraid of vomiting, he stood there like a little boy, dreading it. Just when he thought he was going to be sick, he coughed up bile. That was all. It stung his throat. He swallowed and began to perspire. He stared at the body.

The man was repulsive. It was Michel Lacan, he knew. He was slightly overweight. There were gentle bulges on his sides above his hips. He hated the look of the guy's buttocks, but he was grateful that he was on his stomach. He would have hated it worse to see his face and his penis.

He turned around and looked out of the room from the foot of the bed. The strew of debris — it had been possessions before this, things belonging to Lacan or Céleste, but now, in this postchaotic wake, it was just debris — looked different from this angle. The opened door and the long empty hallway brought back the nausea, and he felt his bowels crawling again. Christ, he did *not* want to vomit.

He walked out of the room as fast as he could, not looking at anything but his feet, swallowing, swallowing the rising in his stomach, wiping his damp face with his hand, hating the feel of cold sweat around his mouth.

The descent down the stairs was very near an out-of-body experience. His life had changed. He saw himself, face drawn, going down into a different world from the one from which he had ascended. This was not something that would happen to him. He didn't know people who got involved in things like this, or who did things like this, or who suffered things like this. This was not his métier. This was not his world. Yet here he was. Or here was someone very much like him.

The sense of dread weighed on him with such oppressive density that he thought he might black out from his inability to draw enough breath. He gripped the banister with his right hand and concentrated on getting air, forgetting the blood that he smeared along behind him.

Chapter 23

When he reached the bottom of the stairs, Céleste and Leda had returned to the same places they had been when he'd first entered the house, Leda sitting on the upholstered bench in a taut, mindless daze; Céleste standing in the doorway to the living room, her arms folded across her stomach as if she had a stomachache.

"What in the hell happened?" he asked hoarsely, looking at Céleste. There was a kind of crazy vibration in his sternum, a submerged excitement.

"He just . . . two days ago . . . showed up at the door."

"That's Lacan."

She nodded.

He waited. She looked at him, her eyes reddening. She couldn't go on.

"Goddamn it, Céleste, what *happened?*"

Leda's head snapped up.

"I killed him," she said. "I couldn't stand it . . . not another minute, not another . . . not anymore. I went in there . . . while . . . while . . ."

Céleste turned toward the living room,

her back to them, still leaning against the doorway frame.

"And . . . and . . . I hit him . . ." Leda paused. "And I hit him, I hit him, hit him, hit him, hit him . . ." She spoke with the cadence of a metronome, then stopped, her mouth sagging. "Killed him . . . forever."

He was incredulous. "What did you hit him with?"

"A piece of iron. I don't know."

"Where is it?"

"I don't know . . . I guess up there. . . ."

He looked at Céleste. She had bent her head forward and was holding her forehead in one hand. He couldn't see if she was crying. Leda wiped a damp hank of hair out of her face. They must have tried to wash it out, whatever it was. She looked frightening, her hump twisting her body eerily, blood and damp matting her hair.

"Look at me," Leda said. Her face crumpled as she looked down at herself. She began to cry. "The bastard," she said, sobbing. "The bastard."

She began to wail, her face buried in her hands, a pathetic sight. He was numb.

"I've got to call the police," he said. He wasn't speaking to either of them. He was just thinking out loud.

Leda stopped wailing, looked at him in shock.

"No!" It wasn't a rebuke, but an expression of disbelief.

Céleste turned around, her face rigid.

He looked at them, both women gaping at him.

"We've got to call the police," he said again as if asking for confirmation. They *did* know that, didn't they, that they had to call the police?

"That's insane," Leda said.

"Leda, there's a dead man up there."

Silence. The two sisters stared.

"You don't think we're *not* going to call the police, do you?" he said.

"It'll be the end of . . . my life," Leda said. "He deserved to die. It's not right."

"They'll come to that conclusion, too," he said, not having thought it through. "There're mitigating circumstances. . . ."

" 'Mitigating circumstances,' " Leda repeated. "I don't know . . . he wasn't threatening me . . . I didn't . . . I just killed him. I *killed* him . . . just like that, just did it."

Céleste hadn't moved. She was focused on Leda, watching her intently. She looked wild in her blood-splattered gown, her hair disheveled, her dark eyes beautiful in the way they beheld the insanity of her circumstance.

Leda got to her feet. Her hump looked even more freakish as she began to pace about the wide entry, the back of her gown hiked up higher than the front because of the distortion on her back.

"Well," Leda said, rubbing her arm nervously as she moved this way and that, looking out in front of her at some spot on the floor. "Well, this won't do . . . God, no, it won't do. No, it won't."

She was in her own world, a vastly different world from his, he suddenly realized. They definitely were not going to see this in the same way, not the deed, not the resolution. Céleste was staring at him, waiting for him to do something.

He understood now that he had been brought here to "fix" this disaster, and the two sisters did not consider calling the police an option.

Leda stopped pacing and stood in front of him, rubbing her arm, looking up at him with an attitude and tilt of her head that reminded him of a panicked cat.

"What about you?" she blurted. "If you call the police . . . what about you?"

He hadn't thought of what about him.

"No? You don't know? What do you think

this is going to do to you? A murder scandal. You . . . you've been having an affair" — she glanced at Céleste, then back to him — "with a woman who was being sadistically abused . . . enslaved by her husband. Yes, right. And you *knew* it. Uh? Yes. And what did you do about that, Mr. Famous Sculptor? Anything? Anything!? How sick is that? When you think about it. Yeah, think about that. How sick is that? When it all comes out . . . all of it . . . and it will . . . what a mess . . . the magazines . . . the newspapers . . . your haute clientele . . . your media-finicky clients will disappear like . . . roaches." She rolled open her gorgeous eyes. "Where will they be then? Where will *you* be then? When it all comes out . . . and it will . . . you *know* it will."

He was dumbfounded. Jesus Christ. This . . . Leda was threatening him. It was a horrible moment. He was staggered by her anger, at how clearly and viciously she had stated the brutal reality of her own situation, and his. Worse, he knew she was right. He knew very well how his affair with Céleste would look when it was taken apart and picked over in the media.

Leda moved in to shore up her case.

"My God, Ross, the man was garbage," she wrangled. "Do I deserve to spend the rest of my life in prison because of that . . . that dead thing up there?"

She was boring into him with her eyes and with the question. She was wound tightly, and it showed in her face, the muscles of which were rigid to a degree that almost transformed her.

"You asked me," she continued, "how could I go on letting Céleste . . . do this for me . . . for my sake. Well, I couldn't . . . I *couldn't!*"

Leda didn't have to elaborate on her argument for him to see his situation in light of her reasoning. In fact, if she hadn't brought it to his attention, he would have thought of it himself anyway as reality began to trickle back into his predicament with the passing hours. All the more reason not to decide anything too quickly.

With every passing moment the old house took on a different reality. The very fact that he hadn't already picked up the telephone to call the police meant that the events were beginning to swallow him. The very fact that he was even thinking this, that he was equivocating, stalling, meant that the moral light of these moments was changing, taking on hues of doubt and calculation.

"For Christ's sake!" he blurted to no one. He was anguished, even as a cowardly weakness gained ground within him with embarrassing haste.

"You've got to get cleaned up, both of you," he barked. It wasn't a solution, he didn't have a solution.

They just stared at him.

"Another bedroom? Damn it. Can't you go to another bedroom, clean up?"

The sight of them repulsed him. It wasn't only a visceral reaction, but a moral one as well, their spattered nightgowns, the blood still in their hair, in the creases of their fingers, on a jaw, a neck, every drop, every smutch of it, was a moral indictment, a harrowing admission of guilt, of complicity, of God knew what else.

Céleste finally seemed to come to her senses.

"Yes, of course." She turned and went to Leda and took her by the arm, and they started toward the stairs.

He followed them, and they didn't ask why.

Leda was first, but Céleste was one step behind, her hand on Leda's back as if to say "I'm here, it's okay. I'm here." Leda clung to the banister, snuffling, moving more slowly than he imagined was necessary, her mind not focused on the job of climbing the stairs.

They went into the first bedroom on the

right, near the head of the stairs, just past the landing. He followed them in, and again they didn't question why he was there. Céleste turned on the light in the bathroom, and they went in while he remained a few steps away in the darkened bedroom.

Leda stood with her back to him. When she made no move to undress, Céleste began helping her with her gown, the blood-crusty chemise having to be worked over her hump and her head. For an instant she was naked from her high waist down, her upper torso hidden under the gathered gown, and then she was naked, still facing away from him. Céleste tossed the soiled gown into the doorway, knowing what he was waiting for.

Then she began removing her own gown, crossing her arms in front of her and gathering it to her waist, then pulling it over her head. Again, for an instant she too was naked from the waist down, her head shrouded. Why he thought of an angel he could not imagine, but he did, an angel with momentarily shrouded wings, only her earthly beauty showing.

Céleste stood there, looking at him. Then he saw the bruises, fresh ones, and there were places he thought looked like cigarette burns. She refused to hide her wounds or modestly turn to hide her sex. She let him look, and God help him, he did look, hungry for her and ashamed of it. She saw it in his face, and he was abashed. She should have seen something else, a world of other emotions, none of which should have had at their heart the selfishness that she had seen.

As she stood there before him in stunning self-abasement, giving him the opportunity by some as yet unimagined act or word to redeem himself and to give her some reason not to despair, he bent down, picked up the gowns, and turned and walked out of the room.

Chapter 24

He didn't have a plan. How could he? How the hell could he? He acted by instinct, unaware of any design or objective.

Carrying the gowns, he returned to Céleste's bedroom and dropped them on the floor near the door. He stood a moment and looked at the body on the bed. The first time he saw it he had been in shock. Now he was offended, angered by the dumb lump of inert flesh. He thought of Céleste's new bruises, of the burns. He imagined Céleste allowing him to do it. He imagined Leda, alone in another room, knowing what was happening and why.

He stepped up to the bed. Part of the covers were hanging off on the floor. With the tips of his fingers he picked up a fold of the sheet and pulled it, dragging it away from the bed, tugging at it until it wouldn't come anymore. Then he tugged at another fold, pulling it this way and that, working it away from the body. He kept at this for a while, a kind of dainty fiddling that wasn't getting him anywhere because the sheets were coiled around Lacan so thoroughly that after a certain amount of give nothing more could be done.

Pissed off, he grabbed Lacan by the ankles and pulled him around straight on the bed, moving him almost completely off the spot where he had been lying. There was a shallow depression the length of the body, sogged with coagulating seepage. How long had he been here? Protruding from under Lacan's chest, as if coming out of his armpit, was the end of a pipe.

He took a clean section of the sheet and used it like gloves to grab Lacan by his left shoulder. He pulled him back, rolled him over. Lacan's head remained wrapped in the blackening shroud, a relief, but now that he was on his back his penis was exposed. It was purple with lividity, circumcised, twisted awkwardly because it had been bent when death came. Leda had said that she had come into the bedroom and hit him "while . . . while . . ." Here it was now, twisted and preparing to rot, and probably rot quickly because of the blood that had settled in it, an ironic presence in the absence of arousal.

He threw the sheet over Lacan's groin and reached down and picked up the pipe. It was common, galvanized plumbing pipe, a section about three feet long with a blunt elbow fitting, the end that Leda had used to pound Lacan's head.

He walked out of the room with the pipe, down the hall, and down the stairs. In the entry he turned right, guessing that the hall would lead to the back of the house. It did. He passed the large kitchen on his right and went out the back door to the porch. He stepped out on the back porch. In the night he could see a broad yard that fell back to tall hedges. To the right Céleste's rental car sat in the driveway in front of the garage.

It was an old clapboard garage with a gravel floor and smelled of age and oil and must. He didn't even look for a light switch because he didn't want to attract the attention of neighbors. He stood for a few minutes in the middle of the garage, his hands down by his sides, holding the pipe and waiting for his eyes to adjust.

Luckily there were several small-paned windows on the left side of the garage over a long workbench about waist high. A pale blue light came in through the windows, bright enough to allow him to distinguish the pots and potting tools on the workbench. At the back of the garage was another set of windows and another workbench, this one with a sink. He went to the sink and turned on the water.

He washed the bloody elbow fitting, running the water through the pipe from the opposite end and putting his fingers inside the elbow to clean the threads. He left the pipe in the sink to drain and returned to the house.

As he came along the sidewalk to the back porch, he saw the lights on in the kitchen window, and when he came in the back door he found Leda and Céleste waiting there for him. They had dressed hastily, their hair still wet. Leda was sitting in one of the kitchen chairs. Céleste stood near the sink, the back of her hips resting against the counter. There was an awkward moment as he stood in the doorway.

"What were you doing out there?" Leda asked, clearly suspicious.

"I found the pipe. I was washing it."

Silence. There. They knew.

Céleste turned and took a glass out of the cabinet and filled it with water from the sink faucet. He and Leda watched her. No one spoke while Céleste was drinking from the glass, her back to them. Then she turned around, one hand on her stomach, appearing to be nauseated, her eyes on the floor.

"What do we do now?" Leda asked.

He stepped into the room and pulled out

one of the kitchen chairs and sat down opposite Leda.

"What happens when he doesn't show up?" he asked, looking back and forth between the two sisters.

Céleste looked up. "Doesn't show up? Where?"

"Anywhere. You tell me."

She realized what he was getting at.

"I don't know. I don't know where he might have been going when he left here . . . if anyone was expecting him."

"You said you never knew when he was coming."

"Yes. But I don't know if . . ."

"Well, what's your guess?"

"He's rich," Leda interjected. "Rich people do what they want to do, don't they?"

"For Christ's sake," he snapped. "Tell me who's going to be the first to miss him."

"His accountant would be the first to ask questions," Céleste said. "That's what I would guess. The hotel, the staff at his home in Antibes, the home in Strasbourg, I think they would just wait for him indefinitely. But his accountant, he'll want to get in touch with him eventually."

"Who would know that he came here?"

Leda and Céleste looked at each other.

"No one, probably," Leda said. "He likes being alone except when . . . he wants something. He has strange friends . . . other women . . ."

Céleste flushed.

"But you're his wife," he said to Céleste. "Wouldn't you miss him first?"

"Eventually . . ." She hesitated. "That's . . . that's the way it ought to work, of course. That's what people would expect . . . but it's not how it would happen in our situation."

"Does his accountant know about you? I mean, about the way your marriage works? Not the intimate part of it, but the arrangement."

"I doubt it. Michel kept his lives separated. People knew him in isolation, only in their own contexts."

Mentally he took a deep breath before asking the next question.

"Do you inherit any money if he dies?"

Céleste was suddenly rigid, embarrassed.

"The bastard leaves her only a small stipend," Leda interjected. "A token. The allowance she gets now, that's all there is. That's all he'd ever let her have."

"Nothing?" He looked at Céleste. "You get essentially . . . nothing?"

"That's right," Leda answered for her.

"When he dies, that's the end of it?" he asked Céleste.

"A pittance," Leda said with disgust. "Nothing."

He continued to address Céleste.

"Then . . . financially, you have nothing to gain, everything to lose, by his death."

Céleste and Leda stared at him. They began to understand the point of his questions.

"If . . . if we do this," he said, "then . . . we just let happen whatever happens . . . go on as if nothing . . ."

He stopped, his mind stumbling ahead.

"Céleste is right about the accountant," he continued, "he's not going to fork over the money indefinitely — to the estates in Antibes and Strasbourg, your allowance, whatever else — without some contact with Lacan at some point."

"I'm sure Michel sees him on a regular schedule," Céleste said. "When Michel misses one of those meetings, that's when the accountant will start asking questions."

"Okay." He leaned back and crossed his legs, resting one elbow on the kitchen table as he thought, looking at Céleste. "What you do is, you just go on as always. When they come to you — whoever 'they' are, the accountant, the police, whoever — you tell them the truth. You haven't seen him since the last time you saw him . . . as if this time didn't happen. You haven't seen him since the *last* time. Okay?"

Céleste nodded.

"Explain everything to them about how irregularly you see him. They have to understand that randomness with this guy is the norm. Even . . . even the abuse. Don't mention the fact that you don't get anything from Lacan's will. It'll be less suspicious if they discover it for themselves. You . . . you'll be shocked to learn that he's missing, and that you may eventually lose your allowance."

There was a visible change in the sisters' demeanor as they slowly realized that their situation might not be entirely desperate.

"No, on second thought," he said to Céleste, "don't tell them of the abuse. That would be a mistake. It would be a motive for wanting him dead. Instead, just let them slowly realize, as they question you, that your marriage is simply a mercenary arrangement on your part. Lacan has other women. You don't give a damn as long as he keeps providing you with a generous allowance."

"God . . ." Céleste turned her head. It was humiliating. It seemed to him that her role in this whole sick enterprise had always been a humiliating one.

"This could work." Leda was suddenly animated, her depression fading. "Yes, this could be done, couldn't it?"

He looked at Céleste. "Are you all right?"

"No."

"There's a lot to do," he said.

No one spoke for a moment. He looked at each of them.

"You know that we've got to clean up this place. Every . . . inch of it. It has to be immaculate."

Céleste set her glass on the cabinet and crossed her arms over her stomach again. No one spoke as they thought of the massive undertaking.

"Do either of you," Céleste asked, her voice taking on a new gravity, "*realize* what we're talking about doing?"

He studied her. "Do you want to call the police? That's the only other alternative."

Her face was unreadable. She threw a look at Leda, hung her head, shook it.

"Okay, then, we've got to talk about this. It has to be methodical . . . it has to be —"

"What about . . . *him?*" Leda interrupted. "It's not that easy, to get rid —"

"Leda, shut up!" Céleste glared at her, furious.

"I'll take care of it," he said.

"The kiln," Leda blurted. It was almost too quick, almost as if she had been waiting for this moment.

He and Céleste looked at her, stunned.

Silence.

"Let's talk about how we're going to clean this up," he said.

Chapter 25

Céleste and Leda picked up everything off the floor between the bed and the door to the bedroom. The rest they could deal with later.

He had pulled on a pair of yellow rubber dishwashing gloves he'd gotten from the kitchen and was standing by the bed, looking at Lacan. The two sisters were on the other side of the bed. Leda was mesmerized by Lacan's body, staring at it with a curiosity that he found indecent for reasons he didn't even understand. Céleste would look at the bed, but not at the body, a reaction he found more understandable, and palatable, than Leda's unabashed fascination.

He took a sheet from the linen closet in Céleste's bathroom and spread it out on the floor beside the bed. Then he unfolded another sheet and laid it on top of that one.

While Leda and Céleste stood by, he grabbed Lacan's rubbery body and began wrestling it toward the edge of the bed. It was a process at once repulsive and ridiculous. He got blood all over his clothes, so much that he wondered why he bothered continuing with the gloves. But he did. He didn't want to inadvertently paw Lacan's bare flesh.

When the body finally fell off the bed onto the sheets, the density of its own weight forced gas from its diaphragm, and a grotesque *whoosh* burst from Lacan's mouth through the blood-saturated wrapping on his head. They all staggered back from the corpse.

Céleste spun around and ran into her bathroom and started vomiting.

"Christ!" He quickly gathered his wits and immediately started wrapping the body in the sheets onto which it had fallen. Leda stood, transfixed, watching him.

With a good deal of struggling, he managed finally to wrap the body in both sheets. He removed the shoestrings from a pair of shoes in Céleste's closet and tied the top and bottom of the sheets. Then he took the belt from Lacan's trousers that had been thrown over a chair and buckled it around the middle of the body to keep the bundle from spreading open.

Céleste's vomiting didn't last long, but she didn't come out of the bathroom until he had dragged the weird bag out through the bedroom and into the upper hallway.

When he came back into the room, Céleste had righted one of the overturned chairs and was sitting down. Leda was sitting in a chair near a window on the far side of the room. She was also pale, her fascination gone, as if the adrenaline deficit had suddenly hit her.

Both women looked at him. He was hot and sweaty.

"Any more sheets in there?" he asked Céleste.

She went back into the bathroom and returned with two more folded sheets. As before, he spread both of them on the floor. He pulled everything off the bed, the pillows, the bottom sheet, the pad underneath it, and — to his great relief — the plastic covering underneath the pad. He had been worried about how to dispose of the blood-soaked mattress. Now he didn't have to.

He threw everything onto the sheets that was cloth and had blood on it. The old house had polished hardwood floors with area rugs scattered throughout. There were several around Céleste's bed, and these too went into the pile on the sheets.

When he had gotten everything he could think of, he tied the four corners of the sheets together and dragged this bundle out into the hallway, too.

He walked back into the bedroom.

"Leda, go down the stairs ahead of us and

pull all the rugs out of the way. We're going out the back door."

She was still looking weak, but she struggled out of the chair and went out the door without saying a word.

He looked at Céleste.

"How're you doing?"

"I'm fine. I'll drag the bundle, right?"

"Can you?"

She nodded.

They went out into the hallway. Grabbing one end of Lacan's shroud, he pulled, sliding the cocoon easily along on the polished wood. Céleste followed, doing the same thing with the bundle of linen. When he got to the head of the stairs, he went around to the other end of the cocoon and pushed until most of the body was off the top step, and then gravity took over. All he had to do was hold on to regulate the rate of its descent down the two flights of stairs.

When he reached the bottom and pulled the body away from the last step, he looked back. Céleste was standing at the landing.

"Just push it off," he said. "It won't come untied, and it's not heavy enough to hurt anything."

She did as he said, and the bundle of bloody clothes and sheets and rugs lumbered down the two flights of stairs in efficient silence.

Leda had shoved all the rugs to one side of the entry hall, and Lacan's cocoon whispered smoothly over the polished wood to the back door. Here everything became more difficult.

Céleste pulled the rental car into the garage while he went out the front door and brought the Jeep around and parked it behind the car. Even though the car would have provided more concealment for transporting the body than the Jeep, he would have had to worry about getting blood on the upholstery. He guessed that Lacan's cocoon was going to start leaking. Even though he seemed to have spilled every drop he had in bed, when Lacan's heart stopped beating it stopped pumping blood out through his wounds. The odds were that there was still plenty in him to leak out, and the Jeep could easily be hosed down.

He parked close to the sidewalk that led to the back porch, opened the tailgate, and by the time he came up the steps to the back door, his fear about the blood had already proved true. The end of Lacan's cocoon that covered his head had become a spreading dark stain that had left behind a streaked smear of rusty red.

"Shit," he said, standing over the body.

Leda looked at him. "What's the matter?"

"This polished floor's going to clean up okay," he said, "but if we get blood in the split grain of this old porch, you'll never get it all out. Same for the sidewalk. They'll find it. I'll have to carry him out to the Jeep."

He knew it was going to be awkward, and he could tell from dragging the body that Lacan was going to be heavy. It would have been easier if he could have dragged him out to the steps of the porch so that he could pick up the body from a lower position, but as he had already decided, that was out of the question.

It took all of his strength to lift the frustratingly pliant cocoon a little at a time until he could get his right shoulder under the body. The corpse was maddeningly limp, making it difficult to maneuver. But finally he got it over his shoulder and slowly, straining, got to his feet. The body, uneasily balanced, was hell to hold on to, but he managed to adjust the weight as Leda opened the door to the porch.

The steps off the porch were nearly too much to negotiate, and even though he was used to fairly hard work, the trip to the driveway seemed to take forever, each step a herculean feat. Finally he dropped the body

down on the tailgate of the Jeep with a jar-
ring *whump*. Then, like a wasp dragging a
spider to its nest, he wrestled Lacan length-
wise in the Jeep, front to back, between the
seats. By the time he finished he was
drenched with sweat and covered in more
blood than he wanted to think about.

He sat on the tailgate to catch his breath
while Leda and Céleste brought out the
bundle of bloody linen and dropped it at his
feet. No one spoke. His heart was driving
like a piston. The night was hot. Not a single
leaf stirred in all of San Rafael.

"You have to start here," he said after a
moment, still sitting on the tailgate, his
voice sounding conspiratorial in the darkness. "He may have dripped some . . . along
the way. Check the sidewalk. The porch.
Just go over every inch of our path from the
bedroom."

They said nothing.

"In the bedroom. Do it this way: Think of
the room as a box, six sides. You can forget
the ceiling. It's too high to have mattered.
Start at the left wall as you enter the door.
Examine it. Clean it. Use a light bleach solution. Move around the room one wall at a
time, floor to ceiling until you've cleaned all
four walls. Then the floor. Same in the bathroom. You have to do it that way, methodi-

cally, or it won't be any good. You'll miss too much."

Silence. He felt a little queasy. Then very queasy. The heat, the strain, all of it. He was getting a headache. He didn't dare stop to think about what he was doing, about the big picture, that he was disposing of the body of a man who had been murdered. It was too . . . it was beyond bizarre . . . there wasn't any word for it.

"The bed frame," he went on. "Imagine the blood, clean where you imagine it might be. It splattered. Think about that and clean where your imagination takes you. Don't forget —"

"Christ, Ross," Leda snapped, "we'll do it. We'll clean the place."

He was looking at their silhouettes. That's all they were to him, talking silhouettes, smudges in the darkness.

"What are you going to do . . ." Céleste stopped.

"Don't worry about it," he said. "I'll take care of it."

Chapter 26

He threw the bundle of linens on top of Lacan's cocoon, making sure it covered the bloody end. Then he unwrapped some tools that he kept in a roll of canvas and tossed the canvas on top of the exposed end of the shroud, anchoring it with the tools. The canvas top of the Jeep would provide some visual protection, even though the sides and back were open.

"That's it," he said to the two dark figures on the sidewalk. "I'll get back to you as soon as I can."

He backed out of the drive and had just started down the slope to the street when he stopped, shifted into low gear again, and went back up the drive to the garage. Leda and Céleste were already at the back steps of the porch. He left the Jeep idling and went into the garage, got the pipe out of the sink, and threw it onto the floor of the Jeep on the passenger's side. The sisters didn't say a word as they watched him from the back porch. Again he backed down the drive and out into the street.

He felt stupid as well as nauseated. He

was numb. From within the event, each moment seemed to have its own logic, one small decision led reasonably to the next. But when he backed away from the discrete judgments and thought of them as a whole . . . yes, even as a headline — SCULPTOR ROSS MARTEAU INDICTED IN MURDER SCANDAL — he grew light-headed. The sense that this was really happening began to bleed away, and the weird episode took on an illusional quality.

On the other hand, it was all too real. He knew that if he were stopped by the police, his life would be over. He had never been stopped by the police in San Rafael, never, not in twenty years, but as he drove down the wooded, winding streets from Palm Heights, he thought that being stopped by them now was almost an inevitability. A pall of resignation settled over him, and then a great sadness that it had to end like this, with the stench of scandal that was not at all typical of his life. It would stain the idea of Ross Marteau, and he would forever be the sculptor of the murder scandal rather than, simply, the sculptor. His work would become a footnote to his life rather than the point of it.

He was surprised to find himself at the bottom of Santa Elena Drive and rounding the corner at Rambach's Mill again. Between there and Los Ciprés bridge upstream, the river flowed at its deepest until after it left San Rafael.

The old mill sat on a small promontory where the Rio Encinal narrowed and the water ran swift as it rushed between two opposing bluffs. Long ago the mill had been turned into a small inn and restaurant, its approach from the drive obscured by a stand of maples.

In his mind's eye he had imagined that he could pull into the parking area of the inn and make his way along a path that ran down below the mill and the restaurant. There, out of sight of the diners in the restaurant above, whose view from the windows overlooked the fast water and the town on the hillside across the river, he would toss the pipe into the river.

Now, as he sat across the road from Rambach's and looked across at the mill, he felt like an idiot. What was he going to do, leave the body in the Jeep for everyone to see while he went on his errand? And what was he going to do if he encountered someone on the path while he still had the pipe in his hand? It was an inn, for Christ's sake, and the view from the path was beautiful, and people often strolled there.

He hadn't been thinking. Or he hadn't been thinking straight, which scared the hell out of him. Jesus, he had a corpse crammed down on the floor of the Jeep, its bloody head rubbing against his calf every time he shifted gears and pressed on the accelerator. Rubbing. Rubbing. Rubbing. And he had blood all over him which anyone could see on even a cursory inspection.

Just get off the damn streets.

He pulled out onto Riverside and made his way along the serpentine course. He met a few cars, let a pickup pass him. It was his advantage that the few street lamps in San Rafael were old, with low-wattage incandescent lights, and were located only on the busiest main streets. Los Ciprés bridge seemed miles and miles away.

But finally he was there, crossing the river. He looked downstream toward Rambach's Mill, the convivial glow of its lanterns painfully innocent and inviting. For the first time he felt alien from all that, from the cozy pleasures of San Rafael that he had taken for granted for so many years now. To his left the cypresses that overshadowed the river upstream loomed like knowing giants, accusatory and darker than the night itself. Underneath them, offering a glittering escape from the nightmare, were the little collection of restaurants and bars that had built up downstream from Graber's, throwing their colored lights across the water. God, how he wished this were just another night at Graber's.

He crossed the river and headed downstream on Buena Vista, hugging the river on its east side now, the pecan trees of the long and narrow Denegre Park separating him from the water. He could see Rambach's Mill almost straight across from him and behind the mill the sprinkling of dim lights that climbed up the hillsides into Palm Heights . . . Palm Heights and the grisly chores under way at 1722 Santa Elena Boulevard.

He was sweating profusely, from the heat and the struggle with the body, but mostly from the panicked flush of the thought that he just might make it without being stopped after all. He watched his speedometer. He used his turning signals when he switched lanes, an absurdity on these small, sparsely traveled streets. He was the epitome of responsibility, the soul of driving rectitude. An oddity. And what attracted more attention than an oddity? He quit signaling.

He turned up into the hills. While he was driving by the river the odors of the water predominated in the warm night, but here the fragrance of cedar quickly filled the air, and once again, even over the noise of the Jeep motor, he could hear the throbbing of cicadas and crickets in the darkness. Soon the Jeep's headlights picked up the front wall to his property and then the opened wrought-iron gates.

Giddy with relief, he turned into the drive and stopped just inside the gates. Usually he left the gates open, but now he reached into the glove box and pushed the remote control. While the gates slowly swung shut, he hopped out of the Jeep and went to a little roofed box behind one of the stone gate pillars. He took out a chain and padlock and wrapped them around the adjacent rails of the two wings of the gates and locked them with the padlock.

Driving slowly, he was halfway around the drive when he turned off into the woods onto a barely visible track. His headlights panned across the close brush and illuminated a narrow tunnel of visibility as he meandered his way around the house until his lights picked up the kiln shed and the studio. Quickly cutting the headlights, he shifted into low gear, slowed to a crawl, and eased up to the front of the kiln shed.

Leaving the Jeep idling, he got out and went to a light pole that anchored the front left corner of the shed. He opened an electrical box and flipped a switch, turning on a low-wattage light that threw a slightly jaundiced glow over a small area at the front of the kiln. He often used the kiln at nights to avoid having to fire it up during the heat of the day and had designed a lighting system to be invisible beyond the walls of his compound.

Just under the shed, nearly adjacent with the front of the kiln, was a butane tank and a control panel for the kiln. He hadn't fired the kiln in a year, but he had made sure the butane tank was filled before he returned to San Rafael. Focusing on an analogue dial on a line that led from the tank to the kiln, he hurriedly turned a brass valve handle.

Immediately he heard the familiar *ping* of butane plunging through the lines, and at the same time the needle on the dial kicked over with a jerk. It continued to climb as he opened the valve all the way until it hit the maximum pressure number on the dial.

He went to the Jeep and backed it around to the track that extended out of the front door of the kiln. He cut the motor and walked back to the kiln, where he turned the large wheel latch on the heavy iron door and swung it open. Then he punched a red button below the light switch, and the heavy iron gurney that ran along the track into the belly of the kiln began groaning. When the gurney had emerged all the way out of the kiln, he released the button and locked the gurney in place almost up against the rear of the Jeep.

He went around to the control panel and studied the instruments. He pushed a few buttons, flicked a toggle switch . . . and waited. *Whoosh!* The kiln ignited. He tweaked a couple of dials and could hear the burners roaring on the other side of the thick brick wall. He studied the panel a few minutes, and when he was satisfied, he came back around to the front and looked through the tempered-glass window to one side of the door. The flames were blue and steady and powerful, and he could hear them blowing.

Without looking at the Jeep, he turned and started up the path to the house. There wasn't much light, but he had walked it a million times and didn't even have to think about it. He crossed the patio and went through the back door into the kitchen, through the kitchen to the dining room, where he opened the liquor cabinet and took out a green bottle of Glenfiddich.

He broke the seal on the bottle of Scotch while he was walking back to the kiln on the dark path, and by the time he got to the Jeep again he was taking his first swig. It was a poor substitute for real courage, and he was ashamed of falling back on liquid fortitude, but at this point in the ordeal it was the least of the things he was ashamed of. He didn't give a damn. It was the only way he was going to be able to get through the things he had to do next.

Chapter 27

For a while — he had no idea how long — he leaned on the fender of the Jeep, sipping the Scotch. He stared dreamily at the tempered-glass window next to the kiln door through which he could see the blue flame. He waited, watching the evolution of its colors as the heat in the kiln gradually built to the temperatures he wanted.

When he began to feel the Scotch, he screwed the top back on the bottle, put the bottle on the fender of the Jeep, and took a deep breath. After unsnapping the canvas top of the Jeep, he yanked it off the frame and threw it on the ground, then took off the frame and tossed it on top of the canvas. Then he removed his shirt and draped it over the steering wheel.

Standing in the back of the Jeep, he lifted the bundle of bloody linen off Lacan's body and threw it onto the ground beside the track and gurney. Then he made the revolting discovery that the body had indeed seeped more blood, and an astonishing amount of it glazed the floor of the Jeep. How the hell much blood could the bastard hold? He grabbed the soggy bundle and began wrestling it off the floor, slipping in the sauce of Lacan's death, breathing its muggy odor as he embraced the body in his struggle to keep his footing and control the grub worm–ish sac.

He was sweating profusely again by the time he got the cocoon onto the gurney and steadied it in place. He jumped down and picked up the bundle of linen and placed it on the front of the gurney, which had been constructed to take a full-size sculpture and so had just enough room for both the body and the bundle.

Again he went to the fender of the Jeep and took several more swigs of Scotch. The kiln was roaring now, a dull rumble that sounded powerful and hellish.

Suddenly he remembered his clothes. He grabbed his shirt from the steering wheel, pulled off his trousers, pulled off his underwear, and slipped out of his socks and shoes. Everything went on top of the bundle, along with the pipe he had also gotten from the floor of the Jeep. He took another drink of Scotch and told himself he could do this. Told himself he was doing the right thing. Told himself he was thinking straight.

He went around the Jeep and into the shed, where he took a long leather apron off a nail and a pair of leather gloves from a shelf and put them on as he walked back to the kiln. He screwed open the wheel latch and pulled back the heavy iron door, backing away and using the door as a shield from the kiln opening. Then he went to the light pole, flipped a toggle switch, and pushed the red button again. The gurney jerked into motion and moved steadily along the track and into the kiln with the bundle of bloody linen and Lacan's cocoon.

When it was well inside, the gurney bumped to a stop, and he slammed closed the door and spun the wheel latch until it locked in place. He scrambled over the track and looked inside the tempered window to the left side of the kiln door.

The bundle was already aflame with a bright orange flare all around it like a halo, and the shroud around Lacan's body was gone, heavy ashes dancing up in a rush from his blackened body, which was already crusted over like a marshmallow. He knew what was going to happen next. And it did. Lacan, black as tar, began to move, rising slowly from his waist, until he was sitting up in an equestrian posture, his arms outstretched as if holding the reins of a bridle, his legs drawn up as if they were in the stirrups of a saddle. Sitting like this, his mouth agape, he suddenly burst into a coruscating blaze, riding like a demon into hell, flames shooting up from his head.

Ross spun away from the window and staggered to the edge of the woods, where he vomited . . . and vomited . . . and vomited.

When he finally regained control of his stomach, he realized he was still wearing the heavy leather gloves and apron. He took them off and returned them to the shed. Then he went back and sat on the millstone, which was about knee high and felt cold against his naked buttocks. The furnace was roaring with such exuberance that he could feel its reverberation.

But he didn't sit long. Again he made his way into the darkness along the path to the house. From the laundry room he took a bottle of bleach and a long-handled scrub brush. He didn't put on any clothes because they would just be contaminated by the splashing from the cleaning process.

He returned to the kiln, then got into the Jeep and backed it into the woods near the millstone. There was a water hydrant at the millstone and a garden hose with a spray nozzle. He stood inside the Jeep and splashed the bleach all over the floor, front and back, emptying the whole jug. Then he turned on the water full blast and hosed down the Jeep, not bothering to be too neat about it, concerned more about getting rid of all the blood.

Doing the job at the edge of the darkness was frustrating. The weak bulb in front of the kiln shed was of little help to him here, and he had forgotten to get a flashlight from the house. Still, he washed and washed until he couldn't imagine anything being left.

He got up on the millstone to get out of the mud, removed the sprayer nozzle, held the hose overhead, and washed himself. He would bathe properly later, but right now he wanted to feel washed.

Finishing this, he stepped off the stone and walked to the kiln shed, where he kept several tarpaulins on shelves. He took one of them and went over to the edge of the courtyard in front of the studio and unfolded it on the ground. He went back to the front of the shed, where he found the bottle of Glenfiddich he'd thrown off the Jeep, turned off the low-wattage light, and took the Scotch back to the tarpaulin and sat down.

Exhausted, he looked at his watch. At nearly 1,800 degrees Fahrenheit he thought it would take, maybe, three hours for the kiln to do its work. That would be a little after three o'clock. He would check through the kiln window then, but he wasn't going to look before that.

Shit. He stretched out on his side and opened the bottle and took another drink. It was done. Whatever happened now, he was in for the ride. He couldn't get out now no matter how desperately he wanted to. It wasn't a dream, not a nightmare. This was as real as anything could ever get.

Another drink.

He thought of the two sisters and what they were going through. At least he didn't have to do the endless scrubbing, room after room of reminders of what they all had done. Whenever he began to feel weak about what he was doing, he forced himself to think of Lacan and what Lacan had done. If Ross had broken the law, fine, then he had, but he didn't think he'd broken the spirit of the law.

Leda had taken the law into her own hands, and that was wrong. And he had helped her cover it up, and that was wrong. But if they had called the police, and if the legal system could have been convinced that in Leda's state of mind she believed her only recourse for deliverance from this man was what she did . . . *if* they could be convinced of that, wouldn't, in the end, it all have re-solved itself in the same way? More than likely, if he was thinking about it soberly, she would have gotten a probated sentence. But the damage to his life, to their lives, would have been so much greater. The media would have done what the media did best: sensationalize.

He took another drink.

No doubt about it, he had violated the statutes of the criminal legal system. But he wasn't going to let himself believe he was guilty under a moral law.

He thought about that. And for a moment he felt justified. Yes, he could live with that. He felt justified.

Then, in the next instant, he knew deep down that he had done what he had done not out of moral indignation, not out of a moral sense of justice, but out of a deep desire to save his ass from disaster, to save his image and his career. He had done it to save himself from indignities and from embarrassment. Good God, was he that shallow?

Yes, he was.

Again he was beginning to feel the Scotch. He lay naked on the stiff canvas, resting on his elbow as he watched the light from the kiln window reflect a peach glow off the huge millstone and the front of the Jeep. The light flickered. Normally it didn't.

When he was firing a maquette or a statue there was nothing to consume. Now there was. So it flickered.

Watching it made him nauseated again. He lay on his back and looked up at the sky. Stars were visible, but not a sea of them. Still, he could see enough of them to want to stare at them and wonder.

It didn't matter whether all of this was resolved in a court of law or not. He knew that everything had changed anyway. Everything. He wasn't the same man. Well, maybe he was the same man, but he was more than the same man, too. And less. When you did what he had just done, you were both more and less. More of a coward, more of an outcast, more of an outsider. Less worthy, less stable, less comprehensible. More unpredictable. Less acceptable.

He drank some Scotch.

The kiln roared like a dragon, and he realized that never before had the sound of that conflagration sounded sinister to him. Always before it had meant the culmination of a creative process of which he was proud. The firing of the modeled clay was the christening of a creative act.

But now, goddamn it, he was in the process of burning a man to cinders, and the sound of the fire was as appalling to him as the sound of his own thinking, the sound of the hard work of his own thoughts trying to justify what he had done and what he had become.

Chapter 28

He didn't sleep, but he wasn't exactly conscious, either. Rather, he floated through a twilight of dreadful images that too much resembled scenes in Goya's *Caprichos*: "He sees Céleste's stricken face"; "A naked body in bloody sheets"; "Leda explains the murder"; "A corpse is hard to handle"; "Lacan rides flaming into hell."

When he woke at dawn, he was stiff and thickheaded from the Scotch. The only sound he heard was the rumble of the kiln, the far-off thunder of fire. The surface of the tarpaulin was glazed with dew, and his hair was damp with it, and he was chilled.

Unsteadily he sat up, waited a moment to recover his equilibrium, and then got to his feet. He made his way to the small window in the kiln, where the radiant heat was so intense that he had to turn aside to approach the glass. He looked in. The gurney was empty, except for a long scattering of white flaky crumbles where Lacan had laid.

He went to the control box at the front of the shed and turned off the burners. The

265

roar subsided. He folded the tarpaulin and returned it to its shelf. He picked up the Scotch bottle, tightened the cap, and started down the path to the house.

The whole time he showered and shaved and dressed he thought about Céleste and Leda and what they were doing. A breeze drifted through the screened panels of his bedroom, and the mourning doves were already moaning in the morning shade. How could everything be so unchanged? Everything should be different. Everything should be . . . less so. For some inexplicable reason, the fact that nothing had changed saddened him. It made him feel as if he had been cut off from all the beauty of the place, that he had been separated from it by what he had done, and it was going on without him. It was as if he had died and nothing had changed.

He made coffee and a couple pieces of toast, which had no flavor. Even though he really didn't want it, he ate a peach. He poured another mug of coffee and walked out of the house and back to the kiln. It had been only an hour and it was still as hot as if it had never been turned off.

He walked over to the Jeep and looked at it. He didn't know what he expected to see, but he didn't see anything different except that the damn thing was cleaner than it had been in years. He got in, started the motor, and drove back around the house to the front drive and on to the front gate. He unlocked it and drove away, leaving the gates open as always.

Céleste answered the door. She looked exhausted, but she had bathed and wore a fresh, crisp sundress. She pushed open the screen door, and he went inside. They stood awkwardly in the entry hall.

"Where's Leda?"

"Upstairs in her bedroom, asleep."

"You finished?" he asked, looking past her.

"Yes. About four-thirty." She paused. "Go ahead. Look around," she said wearily.

He couldn't help it. He did.

He walked through the entire house, at least that part of it where there had been blood, and everything looked bright and clean. He could smell the bleach. Windows were open everywhere, and morning light came in through thin curtains that lifted pleasantly now and then on the soft breeze. The place looked innocent.

When he returned to the front door, Céleste was sitting on a sofa in the living room. He went in and sat on the other end from her.

"What did you do with him?" she asked.

"The kiln. There's nothing left."

She didn't react. She was sitting in the corner of the sofa with one leg folded underneath her, her elbow on the arm of the sofa, her head tilted to the side, resting in her hand. She was so tired that she looked weak. He wanted to put his arms around her and hold her, but he didn't know if they could ever do that again. He didn't know how any of this was going to affect anything.

"We had a chance to do it differently," she said as if she knew what he was thinking.

"None of us wanted to pay the price."

"No, we didn't." She stared at the floor. "Do you really think this is going to work?"

"It'd better."

"The question was: Do you think this is going to work?"

"I don't know." But that wasn't what she wanted to hear. He knew he needed to do better than that. "It can," he said. "Yeah, it can work. The hardest part now will be going on as usual. As if last night never happened. We'll have to do that."

" 'As usual,' " she said to herself. "Nothing will ever be 'as usual' again . . . ever."

"We'd sure as hell better act like it is. I'll be through over there by the end of the day. Let's wait another day. Let the adrenaline subside."

"And then?"

"Business as usual. Leda comes back to the studio. We pick up where we left off." He paused. "She can do this?"

"You'll have more trouble with it than she will," Céleste said bluntly.

"What do you mean?"

"I mean you will have more trouble with it than she will."

"Well, can you elaborate on that?"

"She's not exactly a weakling, Ross. You know that by now, don't you?"

"Are you trying to tell me something?"

"No. Nothing more than what I've said."

For some reason he didn't quite buy that, but he didn't know why.

"You mean she's not as shaken by this as she seemed?"

"No, she was shaken. She just wasn't damaged."

He was beginning to feel funny about the conversation, as if maybe he should be reading between the lines.

"You think I've been damaged?" he asked.

She looked at him. "*I've* been damaged, Ross. And I hope you have been, too."

A tingling crept along the top of his shoulders. He didn't know what the hell was going on here, but it seemed to be more than he was understanding.

The lazy sounds of palm fronds rustling in the breeze wafted in through the opened windows from Santa Elena Boulevard in front of the house. The odor of bleach that stirred through the rooms suddenly seemed as nauseous to him as something rotten. The large old house seemed achingly lonely, and he had an adolescent desire to be somewhere else with Céleste, somewhere away from everything that had brought them together, away from the ghastliness of the last twelve hours.

She was looking at him, and he thought he saw in her face that she knew what he was thinking. Maybe it showed in his face, too. As they looked at each other, they seemed to understand that the distance between them was growing with the imperceptible and inexorable swing of an hour hand. He didn't see tears in her eyes, but he saw anguish, and it made him afraid. This time he was not afraid of the disaster that would befall them if this weak fabric they had woven began to unravel. Rather, he was afraid that what he and Céleste had begun they would not be allowed to finish.

★ ★ ★

When he got back he went to the kiln and rolled out the gurney. Only gray crumbles of Lacan's bones were still there, not entirely consumed. He pulverized them easily with the end of a small log from the woodpile. He used a flat shovel to scoop up the drab ash and then scattered it in the brush behind the kiln. Lacan was gone.

He lay in his bed, his arms behind his head, his eyes dreaming at the ceiling. Outside, the hard-driving drone of cicadas lifted him from the bed, and the warm afternoon breeze flowed around him.

He had left Céleste sitting on the sofa. The day was odd. The way he felt, he had never felt before.

Chapter 29

"What's this? Something different?"

She was standing in the opened doorway of the studio. It was two days later.

"Yeah, something different," he said. It was the first time they had spoken since the night of Lacan's death. He was standing at one of the workbenches where he had set up a modeling stand and was beginning to lay out his tools, which he kept in drawers and shelves underneath the benches.

"A maquette?" she asked, coming into the studio. "Is that it? You're going to be doing clay?"

He turned around and looked at her. He had barely been able to keep food in his stomach for two days, and although he knew they had to get on with their routine, he hardly expected a perky attitude to be part of it.

She came up and leaned her forearms on the opposite end of the workbench to watch him. Her face, her incredible face, was as fresh as if her life had been carefree and blessed. She wore a yellow sundress, cut low in front, an undeniably sexy style. The lump of her back was shockingly discordant.

"A rough maquette," he said. "I'm just going to experiment."

"But it's what you usually do, isn't it?" She reached across and picked up one of his rosewood modeling tools and began toying with it.

"I guess. For the most part."

He bent down and pulled a five-pound box of Colorado Red terra-cotta clay off the shelf, hoisted it onto the bench, and began pulling out chunks of clay from the plastic bag inside.

While he prepared the armature on the modeling stand to take the clay, Leda wandered over to the opened windows. She stood at one of them and looked outside, at the kiln shed. She said nothing, but he was afraid she would. She stared at the kiln a long time. He kept working.

"We ought to talk about it," she said, still staring out the window, tapping the smooth, curved end of the tool against her lips.

"No, we ought not to talk about it." He stayed busy, not looking at her.

"Why?"

"Dumb question, Leda."

She turned around to look at him. "Maybe dumb to you, but I need to deal with this."

She sounded embarrassingly insincere, as if she were quoting from a pop psychology advice column on "closure."

"You seem to be dealing with it quite well as it is," he said.

"Do you believe that things are always the way they 'seem'?"

"Aren't you and Céleste sick of it by now?"

"What do you know about it? Nothing. We haven't said a single sentence to each other about it."

"Why?" He found that hard to believe.

"She won't. I've tried. She won't."

"Well, I won't, either, so it looks like you're out of luck." He looked at her. "You'd better get your clothes off."

"Yes. Céleste told me that was our big plan, 'business as usual.' Sounds like a shrewd scheme to me."

He ignored her sarcasm as she went to the modeling platform and began to undress.

"Get comfortable," he said, "this'll take longer than the sketching poses. You'll be there awhile."

She tried several positions, then settled into one, and he began to work. After anchoring a ball of clay to the armature for the core of the figure, he flattened a pad for the base and rolled lengths of clay between his hands to get the solid coils for the legs.

He worked in silence, and though Leda honored it, he could tell from her face that she was doing plenty of thinking. He didn't care. He wasn't going to tell her that he was still too shaken to continue sketching. Drawing required a kind and degree of concentration that he couldn't muster anymore. He didn't know how to analyze it, he just knew that the thought of drawing was unnerving. At least modeling clay had a therapeutic quality to it.

Time passed quickly. Leda was stoic, but after a while he noticed her trembling slightly, and he knew he had taken her as far as she could go without a break.

"Smoke a cigarette," he said, standing and going to the sink at the back of the studio. He washed the clay off his hands, dampened a rag, returned with it, and draped it over the developing maquette.

"What's the matter?" she asked, lighting a cigarette.

"I'm just keeping the clay wet. You want to see it?"

She shrugged. "Sure."

She came off the platform with her cigarette, as comfortable without clothes as she had always been. He didn't know why that was unsettling to him, but it was. Should she be more modest now that she had clubbed a man to death? What was the protocol for behavior after such a thing?

He took the damp rag off the maquette, and she stood beside him and looked at it, smoking. She moved around to the other side of the worktable and looked at it. She went to the other end of the bench and looked, and then she came back on the other side of him and stood close to him. She was very close. Closer than she needed to be. He moved over a step. She moved closer to him again, bending to one side to look at the maquette. He could smell her, the fragrance of her, despite the cigarette.

She put out the cigarette on the rough corner of the workbench and turned to him, letting the last wisps of smoke snake out of her parted lips.

They looked at each other, and she reached down and took his hand. She took the damp rag out of it and put his hand on one of her breasts. He recognized the shape of it, knew it, the perfect, conical shape of the Esquiline Venus.

She was staring at him so hard that all he saw was her face, nothing else. He examined every angle of it, every rise and fall of its small planes, every subtle blue vein that floated just below the surface of her youthful skin.

She guided his hand over her breast, lightly, softly, so that he could feel the change of texture when it passed over her nipple. He concentrated on the planes of her cheekbones as she took his hand lower, circled his fingers around her navel so that he felt the smooth gradations of the muscles of her abdomen, floated them over the contour that fell toward her pubis so that he felt the line of her groin reaching in from her hip. He studied her brow, her temple, the margins of her hair, as she took his hand between her legs.

She tucked it there, held it with her thighs, and then she put her own hand on his crotch. Her smile confirmed what she thought she would find there.

There was a moment when he didn't know what was happening, didn't allow himself to recognize what he was feeling.

Suddenly she spun around. Instinctively he raised his arm, and in an instant he found himself embracing the swollen, cartilaginous hump, a feeling so unnatural, so far beyond his experience, that he couldn't react at all. He stood there, holding Leda in an embrace that pressed his face against a form of anatomy that he never in his life imagined he would see, much less touch, much less embrace.

He didn't know what made him do it, or rather not do it, but he didn't recoil. In that moment he knew that that was exactly what she had expected him to do. He knew that she had tried to seduce him, but only so that she could shock him, to repulse him, and to have him experience all those emotions in the turning of a few seconds.

But he just stood there holding her. She began to laugh, thinking he was stunned, too stunned to move. He continued to hold her. Her laughter started to build, then faltered. The longer he held her, the less sure she was of what was happening. His shock should have been quickly followed by a recoil, but it wasn't. Her laughter died in the silence of his refusal to release her.

What was he doing? He didn't know. They stood there in stupid silence, he refusing to withdraw his awkward embrace, she suddenly discombobulated, her cruel intentions baffled by his unwillingness to behave predictably.

Suddenly he was astonished at the intensity and the nature of his emotions, as his embrace became an enfolding act of compassion. He had recognized her derisive laughter, had felt her uncertain reaction to his immobility, had understood her withering confusion. And now, in an unbelievable reversal of everything either of them had expected, he found himself holding her because he wanted to comfort her, to comfort the anguished child who had watched in horror as her body began to swell like some unimaginable creature in a cruel fairy tale, to comfort the young woman who dreaded the recoil in the eyes of men and who must have lived with a sense of isolation that was far beyond anything he could even have understood.

She began to weep. In silence at first, then softly, then openly, then uncontrollably.

He had no idea what made him hold her in that way, what compelled him to commiserate with her, but he did. He did.

She seemed to weep forever. He stood there, holding this naked, strange, beautiful, undeniably unattractive woman while she cried as he had never heard another woman cry in all his life.

And then she ferociously tore herself away from him. She ran — staggered — to the modeling platform and stumbled onto it and grabbed her dress off the chair, her face averted. She pulled on the dress, struggling, fumbling unsuccessfully, sounds coming from her that he could compare only to squeals. She fought the dress with such futility that he was about to go up and help her when she finally got it on in some fashion of disarray, and then she left the platform, avoiding the steps — and him — by crouching down and sitting on the edge of it and finding the floor with her feet as she held the dress on her with her hands and arms.

Stifling sobs and clutching awkwardly at her dress, she fled, bumping into workbenches as she contorted her body to keep her face turned away from him. She disappeared through the door into the sunlight.

He stood alone next to the workbench like a slow-witted adolescent who has just misunderstood an encounter with a woman. Yet he did understand, all too well, profoundly, deep within himself.

Chapter 30

He wasn't able to keep his mind on anything at all in the afternoon, and the empty minutes piled up against each other in drifts.

He stared out the windows; he stared at the walls; he stared at the ceiling; but most of all he stared at Leda's unfinished maquette. He wondered why in the hell she had done that. Was it a reaction to the maquette? Had she planned it before she came? Why, to either question? If yes to the first: Then she must have been disturbed by the appearance of the maquette. If yes to the second: Then . . . then what?

His mind rammed up against the question again and again, but each time it was repelled by his own lack of insight. He wasn't even sure that he was involved in what she had done at all, except as a convenient tool for her assault on her abyss of frustrations. Did she want to know if she could arouse him sexually? She had. Then why the cruelty that followed? Maybe she sensed that he wasn't going to allow it to go beyond that point. Or was she angry at herself for not having the guts to push it all the way and find out?

Maybe it was for all of those reasons. And for far more than he would ever know or could understand.

He waited for Céleste all through the hot afternoon. Sunset turned the summer clouds bloody orange and laced their margins with gold. Then the shadows crept in, and dusk sucked away the color until it was dark.

When the telephone rang it woke him. The second and third rings echoed in the high ceiling of the studio.

"Hello." He knew it was going to be Céleste.

"How about a Pacifico at Graber's?"

"Amado."

"Yes."

He didn't want to. He really didn't want to. "Okay," he said. "When?"

"I'm walking out the door right now."

He started to take the Mercedes. He already had the keys in his hands before he stopped. The Mercedes? He wouldn't do that. Why was he avoiding the Jeep? Shit. That's how easy it was. Just like that. He went back and got the Jeep keys and drove off.

He stopped at the bar — he didn't want to, but that's what he always did — and got a

Pacifico from Nata, who said that Amado was already waiting in the patio.

The place was full. He didn't look at anyone as he made his way through the tables to Amado, who was already smoking a fresh cigar. He liked the smell of it. But he didn't look forward to the conversation. He just wasn't up to it. He didn't want to do it.

"So you've been busy, then?" Amado asked with unsuspicious cheerfulness as he sat down.

"Why?"

"It's been a couple of weeks."

"Oh, yeah. Yeah, I've been busy."

"How's the commission going?"

It was an innocent question . . . and it wasn't. Amado knew damn well he was working with Leda. Why did he pretend he'd forgotten that? What was it about someone acting innocent that gave them away? Was Amado being too casual? And how did one describe too casual? It was all in the infinitesimal degrees of subtlety. If he had to write it out in a paragraph, describe what he saw in Amado's demeanor, it would be impossible to express.

"What do you think?"

Amado looked guilty. "Really, then. You're still working with Leda?"

"Did you think I wouldn't be?"

"I didn't know."

"Do you think I'd change my mind?"

Amado didn't say anything.

"Did you think I *should* change my mind?"

"Ross —"

"Why didn't you just ask me?"

"Ross, I could tell you felt strangely about it."

"Oh. You were being careful with me?"

"Well, yes, damn it, I was," Amado said, almost losing his equanimity.

He cringed inside. He wasn't acting right. Already he was acting "different."

"Are you still seeing Céleste?" Amado asked.

"Not in a while."

Amado nodded and pulled on his cigar. He wasn't going to follow up on that one, and Ross was glad.

"What about the sketching, then? How is that going?"

He did his best to talk about Leda's sketches as he usually talked about his work with Amado. It required unbelievable discipline. If Amado was too casual, Ross couldn't be casual enough. He didn't know *how* to act, and he was afraid his confusion was all too clear to Amado. And normally Amado would have been curious about everything having to do with so unusual a project. He would have been overflowing with questions. Specific questions, detailed questions about Leda's appearance. He never stinted or gave short shrift to his curiosity.

But now he listened to Ross with an expression that told Ross he wasn't going to ask a single one of those questions that were so typical of him. And he didn't.

"Well, it sounds fascinating," Amado said when he stopped. "You seem to be enjoying it."

It was a blatant lie, and this time he was aware of Amado studying him closely. They both knew it was a lie, and Amado wanted to see his reaction to it. For all his understanding of what was going on, he couldn't bring himself to react at all, not with honesty, not with a lame response, not with . . . anything at all.

Silence fell between them. They looked around the patio. He felt oddly detached. He couldn't even muster enough care to pretend with his old friend. His emotions were cauterized, as if a thick scab had grown around his heart.

"Ross."

He looked at Amado.

"I'm going back to London in a few days,"

Amado said. "For a couple of weeks, I think. Have to check in on the house, catch up on some business there. Why don't you come with me? Not for the whole time. Four or five days. We'll look up old friends, dine at our favorite restaurants . . ."

Ross was already shaking his head. "Can't."

"A few days? You're not into the full swing of anything yet. And we haven't done that in a long while."

"I can't, Amado." Did he say that too abruptly? Did he sound impatient? "Look," he added quickly, "I'm . . . just starting a series of maquettes. I've got to keep my mind on that. I just can't leave now."

Amado held up both hands and turned his head, making a calming motion. "*No problema.* I understand that," he said. "Work is work. It was just a thought." He softened his tone, as if he were a humoring physician trying to sound reasonable with an unreasonable patient. "If you want to, if it happens that you could come for a few days later on, then come on. It would be good to have you there."

Ross quickly took a swig of beer to cover his discomfort. He was botching this. Amado knew something was terribly wrong, and what was worse, he wasn't quizzing

Ross about it. Something was telling him to be solicitous, to back away.

Another awkward silence. Ross turned away, pretended to be looking around the patio, but he wasn't seeing anything. His heart was slugging away, and he could feel Amado's eyes on him. Goddamn. He felt transparent, as if his heart and mind were made of cellophane, and Amado could see the cause of his symptoms.

Shit. He had burned a man to cinders in his kiln. How in God's name could that be? How the hell could he have *done* that?

"I don't know . . . ," Amado said.

Ross jerked his head around, gaping at Amado.

"I don't know, but I have to be honest with you, my friend, you seem to me to be under a lot of pressure." He puffed on his cigar. "I know you well enough to know that now is not the time to inquire of your private affairs, Ross, but, you know, I don't have to remind you that I am a man of discretion. I can keep secrets."

He paused.

He stared at Amado in surprise . . . expecting him to say he knew about the murder . . . about the kiln . . . about everything.

"If you want to talk to me, my friend, I will

happily listen." He smiled, a genuine, warm Amado smile, not a tense, not a calculated smile. "And I can give you good, free Mexican advice."

He nodded. He couldn't speak. He drank some beer and nodded while he swallowed.

"Everything's fine," he said, trying to sound grateful, trying to sound genuinely grateful, which he was. "Everything's fine."

He knew that Amado knew it was a lie. And he also knew that Amado understood that that would have to do for now.

Chapter 31

Leda didn't come the next morning.

He forced himself to work on the maquette, which he finished out to the extent that he wanted to develop it. Then he began another. These were not detailed works, but something equivalent to the quick sketches in his notebook. The idea was to get fixed in his head the volume of her body, with the additional complication her slanted pelvis added to the overall irregularity . . . all of which was married to other features that were exemplary in their beauty.

It was no small problem to bring together all these discordant anatomical differences, and the difficulty of it was something that fascinated him in spite of all the other distractions pulling at him.

After a lunch of cold grilled chicken, olives, and onions and a glass of Barbaresco, he returned to the studio and yet another rough maquette.

By four o'clock his mind was wandering to Céleste to the point of distraction, and he was beginning to make stupid mistakes with the clay. He quit, not even bothering to cover the clay to keep it damp, and washed up in the sink. He opened a bottle of Barbaresco from the stash in the wall at the back of the studio, rinsed a glass at the sink, and took both up on the modeling platform. He sat in the chair there, poured the wine, put the bottle on the floor beside him, and propped his feet up on the bed.

From where he sat the three maquettes on the workbench were silhouetted against one of the tall, opened windows. They were strange images, their shapes unfamiliar at first glance, requiring some study to understand. In a queer way they were more difficult to apprehend with a quick look than if they had been pure fantasy creatures. A completely alien form would have been immediately recognizable as such; the mind would immediately comprehend the disconnect from reality. But here, much to his surprise, a partial deformity of the normal was far more difficult to grasp than complete fantasy. He hadn't expected that.

His mind wandered, moved this way and that by the sounds of the doves in the mesquite trees and by the changing light of the summer sun picking up momentum in its descent. As the light failed, the shadows that lived in the corners of the studio began to move out into the open like timid creatures growing bold with time. He had watched this phenomenon so often over the years that the shadows themselves almost acquired personalities. He knew which ones grew longest with the changing seasons and angles of the sun; he knew the darkest ones and where they met as they converged in the dying light.

And then he was aware of someone standing in the opened doorway. He looked around and saw Céleste's silhouette framed in the pale light.

"Ross?"

She didn't see him in the shadowed spaces of the great room. Perversely he didn't answer. She stood in the rectangle of blue light, her posture hesitant, tentative.

"Ross?"

"Where have you been?" he asked.

She looked in his direction, and he could tell by her posture that she was gradually making out his form on the platform. Without responding, she came into the studio, walking toward the platform. When she got to the edge of it, she stopped and they looked at each other, their features now visible to one another in the blue light of evening. Neither of them spoke.

She turned and went to the steps and

came up on the platform and approached him. He put his glass on the floor, and when she got to him he embraced her hips and laid his head against her stomach. She put her hands in his hair and caressed him.

God, he didn't know why, he didn't know what it was about this woman, that made him feel as though he needed her so much. She let him hold her as if she understood and was giving herself to him, letting him get what he could from her. It wasn't something she could explain to him; it wasn't something he wanted her to explain, but he knew by the way she behaved that it was true and that they both knew it.

His hands followed her legs down to the hem of her dress and under, coming up her naked thighs to her hips. He found the ribbed band at the top of her panties and began pulling them down as she shifted her weight to allow them to come away from her, down her long legs to the floor, where she stepped out of them.

He returned one hand to her crotch, and he felt her hips shifting again as her legs parted slightly to accommodate his fingers. She unbuttoned the top of her dress down to her waist, and they let it fall to the floor. He stood, and she slowly helped him take off his clothes.

The light through which he saw her breasts as he kissed them had become a sharp amethyst, a damascene shade that turned the red of the model's bed a saturated purple. His mouth descended to her stomach, past her navel, and he could feel the muscles of her abdomen twitching against his lips and tongue. She opened her legs to him and reclined back on the bed, and he could feel her reaching for the back of the chair to steady herself. He looked up; she was watching.

"Everything's changed," she said.

They were lying on the model's bed, and night was coming in through the tall, opened windows, creating a backdrop of sapphire columns along the dark walls. They had been awake, but quiet, looking toward the windows.

"I know."

"But what we did, that will never change."

"No."

Silence. Only the pulsing of the crickets in the weeds.

"I have so many regrets," she said. "I used to say I didn't, but I do. Even before this, long before this."

He said, "Regrets . . . I don't know . . ."

"Can we . . . do you think we can regret the future?"

"The future? God . . . I think just about anything's possible now."

"We can," she said. "I know we can."

Silence again. He could smell her, that faint sachet that he always wanted more of, its elusiveness being a great part of its poignancy. He had a hand on her stomach, and he could feel her pubic hair with his little finger.

He said, "I thought you weren't going to come back."

She waited. Then, "I almost didn't."

Her words stung him. He realized, and it shocked him to realize it, that it would have killed him if she hadn't.

"But I had to see you, Ross," she said. "I didn't know what was going to happen. Please believe that."

It seemed an odd thing to say, as if she were saying she didn't know that lightning was going to strike or that a gust of breeze would blow out a candle. One couldn't know those things.

He said, "No, of course not. How could you?"

But she didn't answer. Then she said, "What do you think will happen, eventually?"

"I've decided I'd go crazy if I tried to figure it out. So I'm not doing that anymore.

How the hell do you try to figure this out?"

"But you've got to try."

"We can't even figure out what will happen tomorrow . . . or an hour from now."

"But that's a philosophical . . . we don't live like that. We make plans, we speculate . . ."

"I'm going to treat our situation philosophically . . . for now, anyway."

"Why?"

He got up on his elbow and looked at her.

"Because I can't figure out the 'How am I going to live with this?' part of it. I can't even get a grip on that yet. So I'll live tonight . . . tomorrow . . . tomorrow night . . . just as they come to me, one at a time. I don't know how to handle it any differently right now."

She looked up at him, and he thought she was trying to see something, looking for something.

"But, in the meantime," she said, "we're not going to talk about . . . us . . . are we?"

"Should we?"

There was a long silence, and he thought, or did he imagine, he could feel her emotion stirring down the long length of their touching bodies.

"No," she said. "We shouldn't."

She turned her face toward the blue columns of the windows, and he looked at her. In the sapphire light he saw her blink a couple of times, saw glistening in her eyes. And then she closed them.

Chapter 32

Leda came the next morning and acted as if nothing had happened two days before. So did he. She undressed, and he asked her to take a particular pose, helped her to get comfortable with it, and began another maquette. When break time came she lighted a cigarette, and they talked about the maquette. He explained why he had chosen the pose and showed her what he was trying to do. After she finished her cigarette they went back to work. When he noticed her growing tired again, he said he had gone as far as he could for the day. She dressed, took another look at the new changes he had made in the maquette since the break, and left, saying she would be back the next morning.

She had remained perfectly relaxed throughout, never once appearing to be self-conscious. She was genuinely relaxed and genuinely seemed to have no memory of anything unpleasant having happened at their last session.

Céleste didn't come in the afternoon.

In the following days a monotonous routine evolved that Ross found petrifying in its slowly building portention. Leda was an ideal model, no outbursts, cooperative, polite, accommodating. She reined in her tendency toward outrageousness and desire to shock and simply helped him do the best he could with the maquettes.

Céleste didn't come in the afternoons.

Two weeks passed in this way. Ross battled depression, a sense of loss that increased with the coming of each night without Céleste. The afternoons alone seemed interminable, the nights almost unbearable.

"You know what we've never talked about?" Leda asked one morning when she was halfway through the first cigarette of her break.

"No." He was using a modeling tool to redefine the angle of a shoulder. He wasn't much listening to her.

"Sylvie."

He looked up, the end of his wire loop tool just touching the surface of the clay.

Leda was twisted around on the bed, regarding him with an open-faced innocence, knowing damn well she was broaching a subject he wouldn't want to talk about. He lifted the wire loop from the clay and smoothed the place in the clay that he had been about to shave, making a more subtle adjustment than he had intended.

"What was she like back then?" she asked. "Physically. More like Céleste, or more like me . . . I mean, without the hump, naturally."

"You know the answer to that, Leda."

"I knew she was smaller than Céleste, but, well, it was years later when I knew her. She'd had a hard life by then. There wasn't much left of the Sylvie you knew."

She shifted her position, ready to listen. He hesitated, but he really didn't know why. It had been a long time ago. Still, Sylvie was as real to him as Leda. He hadn't forgotten anything about her, good or bad.

"Her eyes were like yours," he remembered, looking at her. "And her mouth was like yours. Breasts too. Neck too. You're taller than she was, but your proportions are the same. Maybe she was a little heavier in the hips."

"She was about the same age then as I am now, wasn't she?"

"Yeah," he said, "I guess she was."

"How else am I like her?"

He studied her. Actually, it was odd that they had never talked about Sylvie. It would seem that she would have been a natural subject for conversation, but she had never even been mentioned since Céleste

299

revealed their relationship.

"The texture of your hair," he said, one memory reviving another. "Sylvie had beautiful hair. Sometimes the way you look at me when you're thinking, not saying what you're thinking, not even going to say, that's like her, quite a lot like her, actually."

"But I talk more than she does."

He thought of Sylvie in his Paris studio of those days and was surprised at how vividly he could resurrect her once he began to remember. She was the first model he'd ever had who posed with complete indifference. Even models who were entirely comfortable with their bodies were at least moderately self-conscious. They cared how they looked. They wanted to look nice, even when that wasn't the point of what you wanted from them.

But Sylvie was completely oblivious of being posed in unflattering positions. Once she took her position to pose, she went into her own world. But besides that, though she was an extraordinarily handsome woman, she possessed no vanity whatsoever, and how other people saw her was irrelevant to her. She put no value in her physical beauty. That was one of the oddest things about her.

"Don't I?"

"What?"

"I talk more than she does."

"Yeah," he said, "Sylvie was a sphinx."

"Tell me about the fight that split the two of you."

"She's already told you. Céleste said she had."

"She told me her side of the story."

He stood and picked up a rag from the workbench and dipped it into a can of water. He wrung it out and draped it over the maquette.

"You were lovers," Leda prompted him.

"We weren't. And then we were. And then we weren't."

"That's not what she said."

"I imagine not."

"She said —"

"Leda, I'm not going to do this. You wanted to know about her physical description. I told you."

"I don't know why we can't talk about the relationship."

"Because I say we can't."

"It was twenty-three years ago."

"That's right. And it was an ugly ending. I don't want to talk about it."

"An ugly ending."

"Yeah."

"Ugly. We haven't talked about ugly, either," she said, mashing out her cigarette as though she had made a decision. She got up like a rhino rising to its feet and took her dress from the chair beside the bed. She hadn't worn any underwear. She steadied herself against the bed and stepped into the dress. She pulled it up over her hips and then slipped her arms into the sleeves as she made a series of little hunching jerks with her shoulders to work it up over the hump. He had watched her do that scores of times now.

She looked down as she buttoned the front of the dress.

"Sometimes," she said, "when I was a girl, I'd catch my mother looking at me when I was dressing. She never said anything, of course, but I could see the disgust."

She buttoned the last button and sat on the edge of the bed.

"Actually, that's not exactly true," she said. "It may have been a subtle look of disgust, but to me, I mean, when you're the object of a *subtle* look of disgust . . . there's no such thing, is there?" She paused, looking down at the floor as she remembered. "She might as well have vomited."

She reached out and smoothed the coverlet on the bed, her hands making slow, stroking motions away from her over the cloth.

"I remember the first time that happened," she said, "the *very* first time. I was twelve. The onset of the kyphosis had begun. They told us it was impossible to know the extent to which it might develop. So we watched its progress with obsessive attention. I'd dream that it became gargantuan, bigger than me, so big that I became *its* appendage. I'd wake up sick . . . I'd actually wake up vomiting. I'd turn on the light and go to the mirror and look at it. A little twelve-year-old girl, looking at the gristly hump on her back in the mirror in the middle of the night."

She paused, watching her hand smoothing the scarlet fabric.

"The damned thing just grew and grew," she said, "until it looked like a mammoth boil that was about to pop. It just got so big neither of us could believe it. It was a horror story."

She paused again.

"I got pubic hair and breasts and a hump all in the same year. And then I began menstruating."

Silence. She stopped smoothing the fabric and looked at him.

"I was already a pretty girl. Boys liked me, and I knew why. I loved beautiful clothes. I flirted. I imagined . . . I imagined a wonderful life, that I would become a beautiful woman. I would charm myself into a beautiful life with my beautiful face and body. I had dreams. Dreams are important in a little girl's life."

She stared into space.

"And then, along with puberty came ugly. I was introduced to ugly. Ugly came and stayed."

She looked at him. "Don't you think . . . that whatever causes ugly is evil?"

He was caught off guard. She saw it in his face and grinned.

"It was just a thought," she said. "Still, it is a thought." She took her hand off the bed and put it in her lap with the other one. Long, pretty fingers.

"Do you know Tiresias?" she asked, going on without waiting for an answer. "The blind seer of Thebes. One day he was walking along a road and came upon two snakes having intercourse. He struck the female on the head and killed her. Instantly he was changed into a woman. Seven years later, as a woman, he again came upon two snakes copulating, and he did the same thing again, and was changed back into a man. Because he had been both man and woman, Zeus and Hera called on him to settle a dispute about which of the sexes enjoyed intercourse more, man or woman. He said woman, nine to one.

"I feel like Tiresias," she went on. "If the gods called on me to settle the dispute: Which is the more powerful, that which is beautiful or that which is ugly? . . ." She paused and looked at him with a sour smile. "I would have to say, in my wisdom that I've acquired from having been both: Ugly, nine to one."

There was a long silence.

"If this weren't true, why doesn't this" — she raised her hands and held them slightly away from either side of her face as though to frame it — "cancel this?" She rolled the hummock of her back to him in profile.

It seemed larger, more gross, than only a few moments before. Then she turned her head to him and smiled flirtatiously over her shoulder.

Chapter 33

By the end of the third week he was getting only a few hours' sleep a night and was beginning to feel the stress of Céleste's absence. After a month of wanting to be constantly within arm's reach of him, she had inexplicably dropped out of sight.

As for Leda, after her blissful behavior during the first session following her crude seduction game, she began to exhibit an increasing agitation. Her mood swings began to look less like quirks of eccentricity than symptoms of instability.

"They look like insects," Leda said. "Beetles." She was smoking, taking a break, sitting on the model's bed, one leg crossed over the other. There were now nearly a dozen small clay maquettes of her, all of them lined up along the workbench where he had set up the armature on which he constructed the models.

"Not to me." He was sitting on his stool, misting the maquette to keep the clay workable.

"What do they look like to you?"

"You," he said, putting down the mister

bottle and looking at her.

Silence. She shifted her eyes from the maquettes to him, and they studied each other in a long stare.

Leda said, "You haven't even tried to call her, have you?"

"I can understand if she needs to be alone."

"What if there's something wrong? Ever think about that?"

"You'd tell me."

"What if she told me not to?"

"Are you saying there's something wrong?"

Pause.

"We should've talked about this, Ross," she said, an edge of uneasiness creeping into her voice. "The three of us. We should've talked about it a lot."

"What's the matter?"

She waggled her dangling foot and regarded him seriously.

"She's been locked in her room." She smoked. "I think she's having some kind of nervous breakdown."

"What?"

"Yeah. We're living in that big old house like a couple of weird sisters. Sometimes I don't see her for several days at a time. We don't eat together. We don't talk."

"Why didn't you say something?"

"You've been acting strange, too. I don't know what you're thinking, what you want."

Strange? Weird? Leda was the only one who didn't seem to be affected at all by what they had done. How strange was that?

Something changed in Leda's face. She put out the cigarette and stood and got her panties from the chair and put them on, steadying herself on the bed. She got her dress from the chair, too, and he watched her awkward struggle with the common task of dressing. She was fighting back tears. Buttoning the dress, she came off the platform, her careful descent, her constant effort not to lose her balance, a poignant maneuver that was as much of her reality as was her beauty.

She came over to the workbench and stood on the other side of it, looking at him across the miniature replications of herself, her eyes sagging with secrets.

"I didn't kill Lacan," she said flatly.

He actually felt his face go rigid.

"She did it. Céleste killed him."

His heart stuttered. He didn't doubt her, and it anguished him that he didn't.

"How . . ."

"He was asleep." She spoke from tightly coiled emotions. "She went out and got the pipe . . . and came back and did it. I heard something. I walked in while she was doing it."

He put his hand on the workbench to steady himself. "Why did you —"

"Because she thought you would insist on going to the police. She thought I'd get more sympathy from them . . . less likely to be convicted . . . in the long run . . . maybe not even charged . . . a better chance . . ."

He swallowed.

She turned away, stopped, then made her way to the old sofa and sat down. The tears had broken now, and she let them spill over her high cheekbones.

"I needed to tell you," she said. "It isn't right for you to hate me for something like that, something I didn't really do. I know she's made sacrifices for me . . . but, God, to ask me to do this . . ."

He felt nauseated.

"And something else." She fought for breath, for control of her voice. "She . . . we . . . came here . . . to get money from you. Neither of us . . . we couldn't endure any more of it. We couldn't . . . We knew you had money."

"Jesus," he said.

"The original plan was . . . that she'd seduce you . . . you'd eventually take Lacan's

309

place. You can't blame her. It was horrible, what was happening. No hope, no end in sight. She made hard choices . . . impossible choices . . . survival choices."

He stood, dumbfounded. His mind faltered. In a fog he went to the modeling platform and sat on the edge of it, facing Leda's profile.

"So, that's . . . what all this has been about?" he asked.

"That's how it began," she said. "I don't know . . . I can't know what's happened between you. Céleste and I don't talk about . . . I told you." She hesitated. "Actually, we hardly know each other."

His mind was tumbling with questions, but he couldn't bring himself to articulate them. They sat there together, Leda looking at him with concerned care. He was staring at some crumbles of clay on the floor underneath the stool where he had been sitting.

"Killing him," he said, not taking his eyes off the crumbs. "She didn't have to do it, then. He wasn't really threatening her at the time. Good God, she just decided to do it. She murdered him."

"I don't know that." Leda squirmed on the settee, her hump looming above her ridiculously. "You know, I think that's what she said. I just can't remember the details.

I'm sure that's what she said, but . . . really, does it matter?"

"What?"

"I mean, just half an hour before, he'd been beating the shit out of her, for God's sake."

Silence.

"I've got to think," he said, his eyes fixed on the floor.

Leda waited. Outside, in the brightness, the grasshoppers and cicadas railed in the noonday heat. She stood laboriously, gripping her purse, and walked out of the studio. He didn't even look up.

He wanted a drink, but he didn't get one. He was suffocating. He went outside and walked to the house, went into his bedroom, and changed into his work clothes. Then he went back to the studio, to the kiln shed. He took off his shirt, grabbed a sledgehammer from the corner of the shed, and began breaking the limestone blocks he was going to use for small carvings.

He didn't fight it. He went about it methodically, paying attention to where he was hitting the blocks, trying to break them evenly, trying, for some inexplicable reason, to be efficient about it, splitting the blocks into smaller blocks rather than crushing them to dust.

Could he believe anything that had happened between him and Céleste? Could she have been that perverse, really? And if she had been, could he have been so gullible, so imperceptive, that he had misread her completely?

He couldn't believe that. He had to trust himself more than that. Whatever Céleste had set out to do, she must have changed her mind as she got to know him. If she had fallen in love with him, then he knew that she was haunted by guilt and shame over her original intentions. He could understand that she would be depressed.

But the murder itself was another issue. Why hadn't she told him the truth about it? And how could she — it seemed so out of character for her — how could she have asked Leda to take the responsibility for it? It was as shocking as Leda asking Céleste to endure the beatings from Lacan on her behalf. God. These sisters. Sylvie. All of them were strange women.

He broke limestone blocks until he couldn't even swing the sledgehammer anymore, couldn't even bring the thing up in the air. He sat on the stones, his arms trembling, his body slick with sweat, his chest sucking the hot summer air for oxygen. The cicadas whined in the brush and in the wild grass that was turning brown in the sun. He itched from the limestone grit and dust that was stuck to the sweat in the hair on his arms and chest.

As he stared out into the bright light of July, he made up his mind that he wasn't going to believe everything Leda had told him — at least, not in exactly the way she had told it. He was going to talk to Céleste. He wanted to hear about it from her own lips.

The night was worse than sleepless. Questions and doubts blew about in his mind like ashes on a whorling wind.

Chapter 34

He overslept the next morning, and as he stood at the kitchen sink waiting for the coffee to finish brewing, he saw Leda come around the edge of the house and start down the path to the studio. It was open, and she would go in and wait for him. He wouldn't be able to work, anyway, not until he talked to Céleste and settled some of the questions eating at him.

He poured the coffee into the thermos and followed her to the studio.

"A lousy night?" she asked as he came into the studio door.

"Yes, it was," he said. He walked past her to the sink at the back of the studio and got two cups off the shelf and poured two cups of coffee. He went back to the modeling platform where Leda was sitting on the edge of the stage and handed her one of the cups.

He stood beside her and took his first sip of coffee, feeling as if he hadn't slept for a week.

"I can't work this morning," he said. "I can't even think until I talk to her." He looked at his watch. "I'm going over there."

Leda gave him a horrified look. "That would be a . . . terrible mistake," she said.

"I don't think so."

"She doesn't want to see you."

"I'll believe that when she tells me."

"If she had wanted to see you, Ross, do you think she would've stayed away for so long?"

"I just want to hear her say it."

Leda stared at him in silence, and then she put her cup on the stage beside her and struggled to her feet. She paused and then took a few steps away from him, then turned and looked at him, the monkey skeleton dangling behind her. She crossed her arms.

"If you do that," she said, "you'll regret it."

They measured each other. He knew she had more to say. "Go ahead," he said.

"Céleste may be the most levelheaded of the three of us," she said, talking about the sisters, "but that doesn't mean there's no limit to her . . . sanity." She stopped, seemed to be having second thoughts about what she wanted to say. Her demeanor was suddenly more brittle, her tone growing edgy. "She's hanging on by a thread, Ross. It won't take much to snap it." She looked as if she were about to snap herself. "*I* don't want to see that happen. She . . . she's the only thing I have left, for God's sake. The only thing . . . I don't want to lose her." She looked at him, her crossed arms pulled in tightly as if she were physically holding herself together. "You understand that, don't you?"

He did understand that. He thought. Maybe that was all he understood.

An odd turn had taken place. Now rather than Céleste looking after Leda's interests, Leda was looking after hers. It was almost as if the two sisters were reinventing themselves right in front of him. And maybe they were. At one time or another each of them had said they were practically strangers. Maybe what he was watching here was the birth of a relationship that even these two women had never believed would be possible. Long separated, they were coming together at last, in spite of themselves, in spite of a nightmare even worse than the ones they already had lived through.

It was his awareness that they, too, must be slowly realizing they had been thrown into an unlikely alliance that prompted his next remark.

"The 'original plan,' " he said.

"What?"

"Yesterday when you were telling me about your conspiracy to have Céleste se-

316

duce me for my money, you said that was your 'original plan.' Has that changed?"

She was instantly flummoxed. Already wound so tight that she was almost trembling, she now literally couldn't find the words to speak. What the hell was this? Something more? Was there something more?

"Leda!"

She flinched. She gathered her courage. Uncharacteristically, there didn't seem to be very much of it now.

"A few days ago . . . ," she said, and stopped. With the delicate fingers of one hand she lightly covered her mouth, touching her cheeks softly as if blotting away the perspiration. She was using the time to compose herself.

Jesus Christ, he thought.

"She was outside, in the garden," she went on, "just sitting there. She goes out sometimes, it's the only place out of the house she goes. I wanted her sewing kit, I had a button coming off . . . it doesn't matter . . . so I went into her room . . . into her closet." Pause. "I found . . . videocameras . . . and tripods . . . three, three of them."

He was stone.

"I found cassettes. I thought Lacan, you

know, had . . . I got one of them and put it in the VCR in her room." She looked as if she had quit breathing. Her voice squeezed to a whisper. "It was you . . . wrestling Lacan's body off the bed, wrapping it in the sheets . . . telling us what to do."

He was struck dumb.

"I think there are others," she said.

He sat on the edge of the platform where she had been earlier. He couldn't think, and he didn't see anything with his eyes. Or he wasn't aware of seeing anything. He started to speak. Couldn't. Swallowed.

"She could've . . . I would've . . . helped her . . . you." He thought he was going to black out, nothing in his lungs. "You *saw* the tape?"

She nodded fast, nervously. "Only a minute . . ." Her voice quavered. "Less than that."

"There were others?"

"I don't know," she said quickly. "I'm guessing . . . the three cameras."

"You said there were cassettes."

"Yes, there were other cassettes."

"I've got to talk to her."

"No!" she almost shrieked. "God, no. She's . . . I don't know how to explain it . . . let her get through another day . . . two days . . . just two days."

318

"What's the matter? What's wrong with her?"

"I don't know." She was fighting tears again. She turned from where she was standing and moved jerkily to one of the shorter stools and sat down. "She's . . . she's stressed, unraveling . . . she *killed* a man, for God's sake. She —"

"Shit!" he exploded. "*She's* stressed! She *taped* me. . . . What am I . . . what am I supposed to think about that? Stressed! What was she doing? What is this? . . ."

Leda was crying, breathing in heaves, her face reflecting a frantic mind. "Please, let her . . . she's got to have some time . . . get control . . . she's, I think she's suicidal."

"Goddamn it, Leda. What do you expect me to do?"

"Give me a few days," she pleaded. "A week. No, three days. Give me four days to get her. . . . I'll find out about the tapes . . . confront her. Find out what's really going on. But if I do it too soon . . . I have to be careful."

He was incredulous. He couldn't believe this. He couldn't believe how quickly everything had begun to fly apart. And Leda didn't seem to be in any shape at all to help anyone.

That night when the fireflies came out and the brush around the house was filled with their glimmering, he took a glass of Scotch and made his way shirtless and barefoot to the kiln. He lighted the kiln, opened its door, and sat back against the cool millstone. No good reason for it, he just did it.

While the kiln slowly grew to a shuddering roar, he stared into its opened belly where it had digested Lacan and went over the painful conversations with Leda as if he were picking pox scabs. Then he replayed every distressing conversation or incident that he had experienced with Céleste and Leda, examining every nuance and implication again and again. If there were answers to any of this, he believed, he would find them in the pain. Anything of fondness he avoided. He didn't want to be reminded, and most of all he didn't want to be deluded by the saccharine emotion of fond memory. He sought clarity of thought staring into the thudding roar of the fire.

The following days were barren. He slept so little at night that by dawn he collapsed into a comatose slumber from which he did not recover until noon. He ate and then went straight to the studio and plunged into another maquette of Leda. During these hours of intense concentration the panic subsided and his mind worked in a mostly coherent fashion. He could think of Céleste then, but not without anguish, not without an aching wish for the lies to be undone, for the truth to be different. He worked through dusk and into the night and exhaustion.

He didn't stop to think why he would obey Leda's demented request to stay away from Céleste. He didn't wonder how cowardly it was not to hurry to her and help her get through whatever it was she needed to get through. He didn't admit to himself that he didn't really have the guts to ask the questions he needed to ask and to listen to the answers he needed to hear.

Four days passed in this way, an undulating and seamless passage of nights and days. He lost track.

The ringing was part of a dream, and then the dream dissolved, and he was left staring at the ceiling, feeling as heavy as lead. The ringing belonged to the telephone on the nightstand beside his bed.

He wallowed on the sweat-stained sheets and picked up the telephone, dropped it, and picked it up again.

His throat wouldn't produce a voice. He whispered, "Yes."

"Were you asleep?" It was Amado.

"Yes."

"Christ, it's two in the afternoon there.

Are you all right?"

"Yes."

"You don't sound too good."

"Are you back?"

"I'm still in London, but listen, I have some interesting news for you, about Céleste and Leda."

He listened, couldn't speak.

"I've been doing a little investigating over here," Amado said.

He waited.

"Ross? You hear me?"

"Yes."

"Okay, Céleste lived in London for so many years that I thought if I asked around in the right places, I'd find people who knew her. So I did. And I did."

"Okay." He was concentrating mightily, trying to comprehend what Amado was saying.

"You're in for a surprise, my friend. It's a small thing, but a big thing, too."

"What is it?"

"Well, Céleste and Sylvie were indeed sisters, it seems. They are indeed part Mexican and part Scot. And I even met a man who had known their mother, Eva. She was an amazing woman — stunning, he said, and as batty as hell."

"Okay."

"This man knew Eva when she died. In a car crash, yes, in Switzerland, yes, but that was about ten years ago, not three. Most important, though — and this fellow swears he knew her well enough to know — Eva had only *two* daughters. He never heard of anyone named Leda."

Chapter 35

Lying on his back, Ross stared down the length of his naked body to his feet. The top of his feet. He thought of the bottom of Lacan's feet, the first thing he had seen when he walked into Céleste's blood-strewn bedroom. The bottom of Lacan's cold, waxy feet.

He had let his hand go limp, and the telephone dangled from his fingers a few inches from his ear, and he could hear Amado's voice, far away and tinny: "Ross! Ross . . . Ross!"

Suddenly he sat up and flung the telephone as hard as he could, sending the whole thing clanging across the foot of his bed, jerking the cord out of the wall. He sat there, thickheaded, clear thinking, livid.

He rolled over and got stiffly to his feet. His neck was tight from having slept on it crooked and from having worked for so many long hours on the endless string of maquettes. With great effort he made his way into his bathroom and through the back door to the outdoor shower. He turned on the water and stood there, sullen and aching under the spray.

He didn't bother to shave. He dressed quickly, and with his hair still wet he went out and got into the Jeep and drove away. His anger did more to clear his head than a dozen cups of coffee. He was furious at the two women for their elaborate deceptions, and he was furious at himself for his own feckless self-deception. He had made it easy for them, and he was aghast at his own stupidity. But most of all he was furious because he still didn't know what it was all about. Why had he been through what he had just been through?

He didn't stop at the front of the house on Santa Elena but pulled into the driveway and up the incline to the back of the house and the garage. Céleste's car was not in the driveway, and the garage door was closed. He jumped out of the Jeep and went around to the side of the garage and looked in the window over the workbench. No car.

He took the steps on the back porch two at a time, then started banging on the back door. He could see the length of the entry hall all the way to the front door. He could see part of the kitchen to his left. Nothing.

Without thinking, he took off his shirt, wrapped it around his fist, broke the glass in the top half of the door, and reached in and turned the dead bolt. He put his shirt on without bothering to button it and went inside.

He didn't call their names; he just went looking for them. Stalking down the hall, he glanced into the living room, then turned right and started up the stairs. When he got to the head of the stairs he could see down the length of the landing to Céleste's door. It was open. The bed was made; the room was immaculate: The sun was streaming in from the windows. His heart sank.

He found nothing in the closets, nothing in the bathroom, nothing in the drawers of the chests.

He stood in the middle of the sunny room. The windows were closed, and there was no breeze now to lift the thin curtains. The house reverberated with silence. It was a thing instantly understood. Nothing. He waited. The house creaked. He could smell the oldness of the wood. As he looked out the door of the room, he could see the upper hallway shining, the glint from the brightness where he stood gliding all the way to the landing where the stairs dropped off. The emptiness in the house and the emptiness within him resonated each with the other, and the two voids harmonized.

He stood there a long time.

He looked into the garage again on his way to the Jeep. A Realtor's sign was leaning upside down against the wall.

He drove to Fielding's Real Estate Agency on Romero Canyon Road. The agent he talked to said, no, he didn't know the residents on Santa Elena had left, but the agency leased that particular summer home on a quarterly basis, and the clients had paid in full in advance. It would have been helpful, he said, to have known they were leaving nearly two weeks before the end of their lease — that was unusual, sure, that they had left without saying anything — but he was sure that their deposit would cover any maintenance problems the agency might encounter.

No, he couldn't give Ross their home address. That was confidential. With their clientele, well, that was just standard agency practice. Sorry.

He drove home and called Amado in London.

"They just moved away without saying *anything?*" Amado was shocked.

"Yeah. We'd . . . we'd had a fight," he lied. "Céleste and I. I hadn't seen her in a couple of weeks."

"A serious disagreement," Amado said

327

cautiously. He didn't sound convinced.

"Yeah."

"How did Leda react to that? She was mad to have the sculpture done, wasn't she? Did she go crazy?"

"I don't know. I didn't talk to her either during those weeks. She quit coming, too."

Jesus, did that make sense? He had to think about it. Yes, that would have worked. He had to make sure his lies would hold together. But why would she have quit coming to their sessions because Ross and Céleste had had a fight? Had Céleste forbidden it? That wouldn't have happened. You didn't forbid much to Leda. He panicked, trying to come up with reasons to back up the lie. There was a momentary silence from London. Amado wasn't going to pursue it. Maybe because the lie was transparent, and he didn't want to embarrass Ross by putting him on the spot. He didn't know. But he was just grateful for Amado's restraint.

"Okay, my friend," Amado said at last, a sad tone of resignation in his voice. "I'll see what I can do. It's a long shot."

"Sure, I know that." He was desperate. "But I want to try to find her. I need to."

"I understand."

"Don't bother to call me if nothing turns up. Just let me know if you get something."

The conversation was cryptic. When the call was over, he played it back in his head. He had been too abrupt. Amado hadn't bought anything but the truth: that Céleste and Leda had left San Rafael. The rest, well, the rest he knew was bullshit.

He sat at the kitchen table and stared out the screened door to the patio. The bougainvillea was brilliant on the arbor, so bright in the noon sun that he had to squint to look at them.

He couldn't escape the feeling that Leda hadn't told him entirely everything about Céleste's situation. Or that maybe she had even been deceptive about her own situation. After all that had passed between him and Céleste, he couldn't bring himself to believe that she had been a part of the wild scheme that Leda had described. Or, even if she had been, he couldn't believe that she would have voluntarily left San Rafael without talking to him. Unless, of course, she was as distressed as Leda had described. Or unless Leda was, in fact, forced to make Céleste's decisions for her. Even then, though, why would they have left without even contacting him? One of them, anyway. And what about the sculpture?

And the videotapes . . . what about them, for God's sake?

329

He could only surmise that he was going to be blackmailed. If Leda had managed to get her hands on them, wouldn't she have let him know? But then, why should he believe that? He didn't even know who the hell she really was. What in God's name had made him believe her? What had made him trust her?

As it turned out, he had believed both women, each at different times, even when their stories eventually turned into contradictions, even when they both reversed themselves and very likely were lying about each other. Or, worse, if they were in collusion and not lying about each other, but rather were playing out a byzantine plan of coordinated deception, he had even believed them then, too.

Why had he not permitted himself to be forewarned by all these signs during these last strange weeks? When he thought about it, it reminded him of an incident that had happened to him years ago.

He was staying at a friend's ranch and had walked out into a small pasture to bring in an old saddle horse. It was in the spring, and a thunderstorm was rolling in. The rain caught him while he was still on his way out. When he finally got to the horse in a far corner of the pasture, he was soaked and a wild lightning storm was moving in over the near hills. The horse was waiting for him, standing still in the downpour, watching him. The horse could hear the bridle jangling in his hand, but he was waiting anyway.

Then, as Ross approached the old horse carefully and was within an arm's reach of him, he felt an inexplicable thrill of menace. His body tingled, there was a sense of excitement in his chest, his wet hair began to crawl and coil on his head. The horse had felt it, too. He threw up his head, his eyes walled in puzzled wonder. But he didn't bolt; he didn't run. They looked at each other, waiting. Then there was a sickening explosion.

When Ross woke up he was lying in the mud, his clothes smoking, and he was covered in black, smoldering shreds of horseflesh.

They both had felt it coming, he and the horse, that eerily heightened intoxication preceding the lightning, but neither of them had bolted. Thinking back on it, he realized now that they were held by a disturbing seductiveness that they felt in the wild sensations of that ominous moment before the blast. They were riveted by their own horrible curiosity.

And so it was with those rare days with Céleste and Leda. Maybe he could have turned away from it all, but for some reason he didn't. Maybe it was a dark curiosity. He couldn't really explain why he hadn't. Nor could he explain what had happened.

Chapter 36

The following days didn't lend themselves to work. The maquettes remained right where they were. He didn't touch them. He didn't work on the Beach commission, either. He didn't work at all.

He milled around the studio, unable to think of anything but Céleste and Leda and the events of the last two months. What in God's name had those two women tried to do? Or had they already done it? If they had actually intended to get at his money, why had Leda told him about it? Why hadn't they just gone through with it? Or had Leda been lying about that? If she had been lying, why? And why were they pretending to be sisters? What was the point of it? And who the hell was Leda?

These questions tormented him, apart from the genuine heartache of confronting the possibility that Céleste's affections might not have been genuine. That was the question he pondered most of all, and which caused him the most agony.

But it was the existence of the videotapes that filled him with dread. As long as

Céleste and Leda were in possession of those tapes, they decided whether or not he had a future. And he could imagine that the videotapes would always exist; he would never be free of it. They owned him. But he didn't have the slightest clue why they wanted to.

A week passed in this way, and then a second, and then a third.

When the telephone rang he was sitting on a wooden workbench in the kiln shed, chipping away at a small limestone block, carving a cicada. He couldn't concentrate on anything of significance, but it made him restless not to be using his hands for any extended length of time. Every day, even if only for an hour, he had to do something with his hands; he had to make something. It provided him with a means of continuity, a link between his mind and the reality around him.

He started to ignore the ringing, then decided to go ahead and answer the telephone. He took off the leather apron he was wearing and tossed it down, grabbed a damp rag from the end of the bench, and headed for the front door of the studio, wiping his hands as he went.

The answering machine was already

taking the call when he reached the telephone. He picked up the receiver just as the
caller was beginning to talk.

"Hello, this is Ross."

"Mr. Marteau?"

"Yes."

"I'm Cecil Reisner, San Rafael Community Bank."

"Yes."

"Mr. Marteau, you know a Ms. Leda
Verret, I believe?"

He hesitated. What the hell was this? Shit,
he shouldn't have hesitated.

"I'm sorry," he said, and cleared his
throat as if something there had caused his
hesitation. "Yes, I know her."

"Well, a couple of months ago Ms. Verret
made arrangements with us to call you on
this date and notify you that she has left
something for you in a safety deposit box
here. If you'll bring some identification with
you, I'll be happy to give you access to the
box whenever you want."

He paused again. He couldn't help it. The
videotapes? She had left him the videotapes?

"You said, that was a couple of months
ago?"

"Yes, uh . . ." He seemed to be referring to
something in front of him. "As a matter of

fact, exactly two months ago."

He couldn't be sure, but he thought that was before she had even told him the videotapes existed. It couldn't be the tapes. Unless . . . Christ . . .

"Thank you," he said, trying to sound as dispassionate as Mr. Reisner himself. "I'll probably be down there later in the day."

"Any time, Mr. Marteau."

He put down the telephone. The light coming into the studio had gone harsh, sharpening the shadows. He looked at the scarlet cover on the model's bed. His eyes drifted over to the workbench; Leda's last maquette was still on the modeling stand, the others were still lined up along the back side of the bench. She had said they looked like insects, beetles, to her. Not to me, he'd said. What do they look like to you? she'd asked. You, he'd said.

Cecil Reisner wore a dapper navy blue summer wool suit with faint chalk stripes, white shirt, and powder blue silk tie with a cross-woven pyramid pattern. He was probably in his early fifties. Avuncular. A high forehead with thin brown hair. A sharp nose, thin lips. He was a nice guy.

"Ms. Verret was an unusual woman," he said pleasantly as he pulled forms and seals out of the drawers of his desk. That was all he said about it, and he said it in a pleasant way, without the intention of probing or implying anything. He got Ross's driver's license number and recorded it, had him sign something, had him sign something else.

He pulled a key from a tray of keys inside the top left-hand drawer of his desk and gave it to Ross.

"Okay," he said, standing, and Ross followed him to the back of the bank through several secured doors to a small room where the walls were filled with mahogany-veneered drawers and compartments. "Okay," he said again. "Two zero seven . . ." He walked along the wall on the right side of the room, "Two zero seven . . . here it is."

He put his key into the top hole and turned.

"You can put your box on one of those tables over there," he said, motioning to a couple of stand-up tables, and then he turned and walked out of the room, closing the door behind him.

He opened the mahogany door of the bank drawer using his key in the bottom keyhole. He removed the black metal box from inside. It was light. It actually felt empty. He set it on the nearest of the two tables and looked at it. He should have been able to feel the weight of the videocassettes. He looked at the box a moment before he reached out and lifted its top, which was hinged at the back.

He was stunned to see that the box was empty. At first glance. Then he saw a single slip of paper lying in the bottom, like something forgotten. He saw writing on it. He picked up the slip of paper, straightened it out. He recognized Leda's handwriting, in blue ink.

He wasn't dead! And you didn't even bother to check. You killed him yourself. You burned him alive.

He was stunned at his stupidity. He *hadn't* checked to see if Lacan was alive, by God, he really hadn't. How could he *not* have checked? But the man had to have been dead. He remembered the darkening, coagulating blood. The wrapped head. And he had seen no movement, no reaction of any kind at being wrestled around, wrapped up, carted, no grunt or gurgle, no gasp or groan. Drugged? Was that it? The man was drugged into a coma?

But he could've died. How would Leda have known, really? She might have known he was alive just before he arrived, but a lot of time had passed before he had actually put Lacan into the kiln. And Leda had come nowhere near him. If he had died during that time, she would never have known.

And there was a second jolt: Neither Leda nor Céleste had cautioned him that Lacan might still be alive. They'd let him go ahead and put Lacan in the kiln! And then Leda — had Céleste been involved, too? — as far back as two months ago, had decided to reveal this to him in this particular way, two months into the future from that time. The timing could only have been an act of deliberate cruelty.

Why?

He couldn't imagine. He could *not* imagine.

Had Céleste known about the note waiting for him in the bank drawer? He would not believe that. In fact, now he was beginning to think that maybe Leda had been lying about Céleste and the videotapes. Leda's underlying talent for cruelty that he had seen flare up from time to time in the studio — and now in the premeditated note — made him see such a contorted device as the secret taping as more in keeping with Leda's character than Céleste's.

God, why didn't he understand more

about them? The way he had handled the two sisters — the two women — had been nothing short of stupid. For whatever reason, they had decided not to spend time with him together. He was either with Céleste or Leda, but never with both of them. That is, not until the night of the killing, and then it was too late. And even after Lacan's death — he still couldn't bring himself to think of it as murder — when they most needed to talk, they reverted to their former pattern. And he let it happen, even encouraged it. He didn't want to talk about it, either.

No drinking. He was afraid to drink. But again the sleepless nights ate into the days, and the days folded into the nights until he was exhausted, and the divisions of time melted together in a marginless sweep of darkness and light.

When Amado returned from London he brought Ross up-to-date on all the people he had met who had known Eva and Sylvie and Céleste. Almost all of them had lost touch with the two sisters after Eva's death.

In turn, he told Amado a cobbled-together, lie-ridden story about his last few weeks with Céleste and Leda, leaving out completely, of course, the recent bizarre turn of Leda's sick sense of irony. As on the telephone from London, Amado saw through the distortions but was a gentleman about it and let the stories stand. The look of feigned acceptance on his face was painful to see.

The truth was, Ross was scared witless and wanted someone to talk to even though he couldn't have the conversation he needed to have. In the worst way he wanted to spill his guts to Amado, but it would have been a selfish indulgence. To tell Amado what had really happened would drag him into an affair in which, if given a choice, he would certainly have had no desire to be involved.

It was a hot night in Graber's garden. Amado sat across from him in a baggy white linen shirt, studying him with a grave countenance as he nursed his maduro cigar and took slow drinks from his bottle of Pacifico. He knew Ross was in trouble, some kind of trouble, and Ross felt like a heel for being coy and cryptic with him. Still, by being so, he knew that Amado understood the trouble was serious.

"Do you see any end in sight for this?" Amado asked softly, as if he were cutting through the layers of vague explanations that Ross had piled on over the last few weeks.

"This what?"

"I don't know. Whatever it is."

He took a drink of beer to cover his reluctance. But he had to answer.

"No."

"Good God, man!" Amado stared at him with a mixture of sadness and incredulity. "How bad can it be?"

Ross hesitated. "Grim," he said.

"And what I'm looking at" — Amado nodded at him — "this is the new Ross Marteau? This morose, brooding man?"

"Come on, Amado," he said, "what am I supposed to say to a question like that?"

"I don't know. I don't even know what questions to ask. What's right? What's not right? What's appropriate?" He smoked, squinting at Ross. "I'll tell you this, my friend, if you don't do something about this — I don't know what you must do because I don't know what in the hell is going on — but if you don't do something about this, you're going to go mad. Huh? That's right. A man can't live the way you're living for very long. Something inside him breaks. And when that happens to you, your life *has* changed forever."

"I told you, I'm already past those kinds of warnings."

"What kind of fatalism is this?" Amado asked, sitting back in his chair again. "I don't understand this kind of talk from you."

"It's not fatalism, Amado. I didn't say I was ruined. I just said . . . things have changed for me. It's not ever going to be the same."

"Your life is over?"

"It's different," he said stiffly. "That's all. I don't know what else to say. There's nothing else I can say about it."

"Are you working again?"

"Yeah, I'm working again. There's nothing I can do about what's already happened. I've got to get back to . . . what's left."

Amado's eyes were fixed on him. Ross could smell the rich, dark tobacco of his cigar, which seemed to be the perfect incense for his dilemma. As he looked at Amado, in the corners of his peripheral view he could see the pools of the amber lanterns in the patio disappearing into a vague infinity and, closer, in the near shadows the fronds of the palms, their deep green on the verge of darkness, their feathered patterns forming a contemplative background for Amado's puzzled melancholy.

"I've always said you've had bad luck with women," Amado observed. "But there's bad luck, and then there's tragedy."

Chapter 37

Summer entered its harshest season. The flourishing and bright green vegetation that had been born in the wake of the spring rains had long since deepened into summer shades, then dried and slowly turned brown in the daily, rainless scorch of August. In the Hill Country September was often nothing more than a lengthening August, autumn a distant wish. Grasshoppers flicked about in the dry grass, and the heat was so intense that it pulled the resin from the cedars and their fragrance hung in the sweltering heat and glare of cloudless afternoons.

He was walking back from the mailbox, which sat just outside the front wall near the pillars of the gate, and was listlessly flipping through the catalogs and magazines and correspondence, none of which he bothered reading anymore. All of it piled up in an armchair in his living room where he tossed it every day when he returned from the mailbox. Bills and checks alike went unopened.

He flipped past it at first, the words registering late. Then he stopped in the middle of the cinder drive, and his thumb retreated back through the envelopes. There it was. Typed. Addressed to him. A return address in Paris.

Everything but the envelope fell in a fluttering shambles at his feet, and he stood there looking at the return address with an alternating and wavering sense of trepidation and hope. He tore it open.

It was a single sheet, a photocopied document in French. He couldn't read French well, but he scanned it for recognizable words, something that would convey its meaning and content:

Certificat de Mort . . . Morgue Municipal de Paris de 16th Arrondisement . . . Madame Célestine Denise Lacan . . . Suicide . . .

The days stumbled by. He didn't know how many. He didn't even bother to dress or bathe or shave anymore and wandered back and forth between the house and the studio in his underwear, leaving the doors open at both places, coming and going like an animal traveling between dens. He came into the shade to get out of the sun, but that was about all he had the presence of mind to do. He ate very little, and what he did eat he carried around with him, leaving parts of it strewn around the grounds whenever and wherever he lost interest in it. He left Scotch bottles the same way, sometimes discovering a formerly abandoned and partially consumed bottle, which he would pick up and carry with him until he absently mislaid it again.

One afternoon he woke up under the spray of the outdoor shower. He must've tried to wake himself and had passed out again. Once the morning sun woke him. He was lying in the tall muhly grass near the front gate, his head in the gravel drive. One day at dusk he fled from Lacan's charred, flame-spewing body and fell against a shovel in the kiln shed, gashing his forehead. He passed out. When he woke his hair and clothes were saturated and stiffening with caking blood. He made it to the shower again and lectured himself as he leaned back against the tile bench in the pelting water.

He sat at an isolated table at the far back of Graber's patio. It was late, nearly closing time. People had drifted away. He didn't see the waitresses eyeing him from the back door. Nata came out and looked at him awhile and then went back inside and made a telephone call.

He was a sober drunk. He didn't slur his

speech or fumble, but his reactions were slow, and he sometimes turned acerbic.

Amado didn't turn acerbic. Amado didn't get drunk, though. And he always looked nice. Always dressed handsomely. Always had impeccable manners. Amado smiled a lot because it was an expression that suited him and looked handsome on him and because it was his nature.

"*¿Tú eres borracho?*"

"I think so," he said. Amado was smiling at him, sadly. "Sit down."

Amado pulled out a chair from the other side of the table and sat down. He was smoking a cigar.

"Just luck, you happening in," he said.

"Nata called me."

"Oh. Good."

"It looks like you've been at this a long time."

"Not goddamn long enough."

"Mmmm." Amado nodded at the information and continued looking at him. "You stink, my friend. Who put those filthy clothes on you?"

"Hell, I did."

"Mmmm." Amado seemed to be thinking about something in particular.

"I can't talk about it," he said.

"What's that?"

"I can't figure it out."

"What's that?"

"I'm waiting for the other shoe to drop."

"Really."

"But she's a goddamn millipede . . . I don't know how many shoes . . ." His train of thought drifted.

"What do you expect next?" Amado was patient. Relaxed.

"She's going to ruin me . . . can't fucking figure it out, either."

"Leda?"

"Leda."

"You want to tell me about it?"

"Yeah."

Amado dragged on his cigar, waiting.

"But I can't. No way in hell."

Amado studied him from behind a wreath of smoke.

"What about the Beach commission?" Amado asked.

"What?"

"I got a telephone call from Jack Brewer."

"*You* did?"

"Yeah. He wanted to know where the hell you were. The Beaches have been trying to get in touch with you. Apparently you're not answering your telephone, your e-mail, or responding to written communication, either."

"No. Haven't had time for that."

"Brewer's in a panic. If I were you, I'd let my agent know what I was doing."

"I'm behind on the Beach thing. Way behind. Brewer's going to be pissed."

"He's already pissed. He says you're on the verge of losing the commission."

"Really."

"Yes. And he said you've missed a deadline for a competition for a big Chicago commission, too. You missed the deadline for the entrance sketches."

"I must've. Yeah, I did. I missed that."

Amado smoked. The patio was empty now. The girls were cleaning up, leaning the backs of the chairs forward against the tables as they worked their way through the garden.

"This doesn't look good, Ross," Amado said softly. "You know? You're going to have to resolve this. Your career's taking a beating here. This is killing you."

"That's an odd choice of words."

"You've got to straighten this out," Amado said. "It's like you're deliberately letting the whole thing go up in smoke."

"That's an odd choice of words, too." He sat forward in his chair, suspicious. What was Amado doing?

"What's the matter, are you burned out?" Amado asked.

349

"What . . . you know about something?"

"You're beating yourself bloody here," Amado said, "killing your career. You're burning it up, cremating it. There's not going to be anything left but ashes."

"You son of a bitch."

"You might as well crawl into that kiln of yours and turn on the gas," Amado said. "You know how effective that can be, don't you? Everything's going up in smoke anyway. It's a bloody shame."

Horrified, he tried to get to his feet. The garden tilted and the lanterns flew out to one side and stayed there, hanging upward.

Amado smoked and the smoke drifted laterally, traveling horizontally out of sight.

"Like Lacan," Amado wheezed, "beaten, bloody, sent to hell on a fiery horse, his hair flaming, galloping like a highwayman, straight to hell. And somebody's got to pay for it. You don't burn people alive and go on with your life as if nothing's happened. It doesn't work that way . . . never has, never will. Somebody's got to pay. Burning a man to ashes . . . that's unforgivable."

He put all of his weight on his hands on the top of the table until he felt as if his wrists were going to snap, and he leaned toward Amado, stared him in his dark eyes where the smoke had mixed with the pigment until the pigment was gone. The whites of his eyes, smoky iris, black dot of a pupil. As he stared the irises turned pale, too. The pupil began to smoke, and then the pupil was ash white, too. Jesus Christ, what a horrible sight it was, Amado going ghoul.

Amado laughed at his expression, he threw back his head and laughed. His teeth were black, Jesus, and he could see smoke in Amado's throat, and deep into the smoke there were flames. When he laughed the flames flared and licked at the edges of his mouth, and his throat rumbled like the kiln, howling and hot.

He remembered the doctor coming to the house. Dr. Henry Schein, tall, thin, hawk nosed, and sharp tongued. He had been in San Rafael for a dozen years now, and he saw a lot of rich people destroying themselves with exotic indulgences, and he saw a lot of locals growing old and others having babies. Ross remembered a long, serene sleep, a morning, an evening, a dusk, a night. There were terrible dreams. Then, more serene sleep.

For several days Amado was there, gliding in and out of the bedroom. And a Mexican woman he didn't recognize was there, too, and she brought to him small bowls of bland tortilla soup on a tray with a cluster of bougainvillea. He heard Amado in another room, talking on the telephone.

Time passed. Not a lot of time, but dense time. One day his appetite returned. In a few more days the Mexican woman was gone. Amado stayed a day or two more, cooked simple meals, and they talked. But he never asked about what had happened. They talked as they talked before Céleste and Leda, as if the two sisters had been a time divide that no longer divided them.

Amado never referred to the drinking binge. It was never mentioned. Sometimes he would catch Amado looking at him from across the room, but nothing was ever said. It was worse than if he had lectured him for hours every day. The rebuke of silence cut deeply.

Then late one afternoon they sat on the front porch watching a paisano hunting for lizards in the margins of the dead grass and rocks, and he told Amado about Céleste. He was too preoccupied with his grief even to notice Amado's reaction. He told Amado about the photocopy twice. He told him twice, as if he still couldn't believe it, and Amado listened in silence. He talked about Céleste for nearly two hours, until well after dark and they could no longer see each other's face. He had never been so honest about a woman, and it made him bitter with himself that it had taken her death for him to be able to understand so deeply how he felt and for him finally to be able to say about her all the things that he should have said to her.

In another couple of days Amado moved out, and he was alone and began to regain his equilibrium for solitude. As soon as he was able to think coherently, he got back to his agent. Brewer had already gone into salvage mode with the Beaches, claiming Ross had fallen ill and no one had known about it. But now he was recovered completely and was ready to get to work.

And that was the way it would have played out under normal circumstances. Only these weren't normal circumstances. To Brewer's dismay, Ross pulled out of the Beach project. He talked to Gerald Beach himself and told him he was going to take a year off, pleading exhaustion from having kept such a grueling schedule for so many years. He apologized and told Beach he would be available in a year's time if Beach still wanted him for the project. Beach was more understanding than he had expected, and the parting was amicable.

Chapter 38

For reasons that he deliberately did not stop to analyze, he felt compelled to turn back to Leda's sculpture. Though he didn't realize it at the time, the process of working on the series of maquettes one at a time in rapid succession had given him a renewed enthusiasm for the challenges that had attracted him to the project in the first place. Despite the appalling emotions that were inextricably bound up in the idea of Leda herself, the artistic riddle her body brought to him was impossible to escape. He couldn't forget it, and now he decided that he would no longer even try. He would begin the sculpture.

He plunged into the project, rethinking his original concept on which the maquette had been based and pushing himself from early in the day and on into the night. He worked feverishly, partly because his new ideas for the sculpture were coming quickly and were exciting and partly because he didn't want to think of anything else. But in the back of his mind the silent discoveries to be made in Paris were always there, pending, threatening to unhinge his life.

The guilt of having contributed to Céleste's despairing state of mind was even more difficult to handle. Not even the diversion of a self-imposed, grueling schedule or exhaustion could rid him of it. It wasn't a weight, rather it was an absence of something, a restless emptiness that prevented him from recovering even a small measure of joy in his excitement for the new project.

The temperatures remained in the mid-nineties, and the September rains had not materialized. Two months of record high temperatures without a drop of rain had turned the country into a hard landscape. Grass and brush fires flared up here and there on the Hill Country ranches, and the threat of a major conflagration had everyone nervous.

Along the highways the grasses that extended from the edge of the roadway and into the fields and pastures had withered to a dusty dun. Even some of the rugged cedars were looking parched, and the rolling hillsides were dotted with trees that simply didn't have the stamina to withstand the harsh conditions of a Texas drought and were dropping their leaves as if it were winter. The country was burning up.

He told no one what he was doing. Amado knew he was working on something, but he was sensitive to Ross's reluctance to talk about it, and he asked no questions. He even stopped coming by the studio.

Ross drove himself without stint. There were no more evenings at Graber's, and he stopped working only at night when he was too exhausted to bring his mind to focus or make his hands obey. Time spooled out in an endless string behind him. There were no tomorrows, only the present moment, only the idea and the clay.

One night late he came into his bedroom from the outdoor shower dripping and weary and glanced over to the small desk at the edge of one of the screened panels where he kept his computer and a fax machine. He could see paper in the "in" tray of the fax machine. First he checked his e-mail. Nothing. Then he picked up the paper from the fax tray.

There was a single sheet. It had no return address other than a commercial photocopy shop . . . in Paris.

I have heard from the police. We must talk. Cimetière du Père Lachaise, 8th division, Avenue Feuillant, #68.

There were two dates, one four days away, another a week away. Both for two o'clock in the afternoon. It had begun.

"You're going to see her, is that it?" Amado gave him a look of impatience across the table. Graber's lanterns hung listlessly in the night heat. At this time of the year summer seemed interminable, as if San Rafael were on the equator, locked in a perpetual swelter. Beer was brought to the tables ice cold and sweaty and quickly consumed. The patrons who favored the patio no matter how hot it was wore thin clothes or little clothes at all. By the end of September the nights at Graber's became very bohemian.

"I might see her."

"Come on, Ross. Who are you talking to here?"

Amado guzzled his Pacifico. His white linen shirt was wilted, the sleeves rolled to his elbows, the front sagging open in the heat.

"Blackmail," Amado said. "She's blackmailing you."

"Jesus."

"Jesus indeed."

"Does it matter?"

"Is it something you can ever get away from?"

"No."

"Never?"

"No."

"What can be that embarrassing?"

"If it were only embarrassing, I wouldn't put up with it. I've dealt with embarrassing before."

A dark look of renewed understanding moved under the surface of Amado's impatience.

"Oh, no. What do you mean?"

"I'm not ever going to tell you, Amado. Ever." He paused for emphasis. "And I'm going to expect you to take the little bit that I've just told you to your grave."

Amado leaned forward across the table. "Ross," he said in a hoarse whisper, "this is a *criminal* thing?"

"Blackmailing is criminal."

"No, no. The *thing* she is blackmailing you about . . . it's a criminal thing?"

He drank his beer, staring back at Amado until Amado's face caught up with his thinking and he slumped back in his chair, dismayed.

"What in God's name —"

"It's too damned complex even to begin with it," he said.

"And so you're going to Paris to talk about this?"

He sipped his beer.

"Is she going to ruin you?"

"I don't know. I doubt it. She'd be ruining her livelihood."

"Her livelihood? What about Lacan? Did he kick her out after Céleste's suicide?"

"Something like that, I think. I don't really know anything for sure."

Amado was holding back a flood of questions.

"This . . . thing . . . ," he stammered, "it was . . . while they were here?"

"Of course it was." He was irritated.

"Céleste was in on it, too?"

"I don't know."

Amado shook his head in disbelief. "Goddamn . . . I knew . . . I knew . . ."

"Don't go into that, Amado," he said. "You'll get it wrong, and I'm not going to be able to tell you enough to straighten you out. I won't."

"I've never stayed at your place before when you've been gone . . . why now?"

"Just . . . will you do it or not?"

"Of course I'll do it, but why?"

"I don't want the place empty."

Amado nodded in resignation.

"And I want to keep the studio locked. I don't want . . . anyone in there yet." He paused. "Anyone."

"Christ. I'm not going to look in the

studio," Amado said impatiently. "When are you leaving?"

"Tomorrow, maybe. Or the next day."

Amado nodded again. "This is bizarre," he said.

"I know."

"So, what's . . . what's the long-term situation here?"

"I don't have any idea."

"You're kidding."

"No."

"You've got to know. Good Lord, Ross, if she's blackmailing you about a criminal matter . . . I mean, you've got to know how *serious* a . . . criminal matter."

"You've misunderstood me," he said evenly. He glared across the table. "You realize that, don't you, that you've misunderstood me and you're getting this all wrong."

Amado was confused.

"You need to forget that, Amado. It would be a mistake to speculate."

Neither of them spoke for a while. Amado moved his beer bottle around on the table in a circular motion and looked around the patio. No one was eating outside tonight, everyone was drinking, trying to cool a heat wave that had settled over the Hill Country like the doldrums. Ross wondered about Graber's birds, silent in the black greenness of the palms, where they slept or gazed down sleepily into the lake of lanterns below them. It had been a good while since he had been here in the afternoon to see them in all their gaudy resplendence. At this moment he missed that enormously, as if it were a pleasure of central importance in his life.

He wished it were the afternoon now and that everything that had happened during the past three months had never happened. Almost everything. Céleste he did not wish to lose, not even for the blessing of making all the horror go away. The memories of holding her were more lovely than the horrors were horrible. He did not want to lose the memory of Céleste, even to save himself from whatever distasteful thing was waiting for him in Paris. God, how he had loved her. And how foolishly he had handled everything. It was his fault if the memory of her was all that he had left of her. He could not blame anyone else for that, not even fate or chance.

Chapter 39

Now that he had Amado's commitment to stay in the house while he was gone, he concentrated on trying to make sure he was thinking straight. He had to consider the possibility that Leda and Céleste's trip to San Rafael would eventually come under suspicion in the police investigation of Lacan's disappearance. He didn't know why that might be, but he had to consider it. And if their stay in San Rafael was going to be part of an inquiry, his association with the two women would be discovered immediately. If investigators came by his compound, he wanted to know it. And he wanted to know if they looked around the property. They couldn't do that legally, of course, without a warrant, but they might just walk around the place "out of curiosity" to see the famous sculptor's workplace. If they did, he wanted to know that. Amado would let him know immediately and be discreet about it.

He hoped that the investigation into Lacan's disappearance did not sweep wide enough to include him. If it did, it couldn't reflect well on him that his inability to continue with the Beach commission had coincided with the period of time during which Lacan had vanished. That would seem more than curious, considering his relationship with Céleste. It would seem suspicious.

He booked a flight out of Austin's Bergstrom International, then spent the next two days deliberately concentrating on Leda's new maquette. Refusing to let his mind wander to the meeting in Paris, he refined the drawings for it beyond what was necessary, beyond what he normally would have done. He lost himself in the shadow and light of it, and the days and nights rippled by with time-lapse swiftness. The night before he was to leave, Amado came over and they talked while he packed.

Amado lounged in a leather armchair, his feet on an ottoman, well into a slow-burning maduro. A warm breeze wandered aimlessly through the bedroom, moving back and forth through the screened walls, mixing in its variation the smoke from Amado's cigar.

A large clamshell suitcase was open on the bed, and he was tossing things into it, unable to concentrate well on either the packing or the conversation, which was not much of a conversation anyway. A nightjar called from the darkness with such clarity that it sounded as if it were in the bedroom with them.

"I love those things," Amado said, the first words spoken for the past fifteen minutes. "Which one is it?"

"Poorwill." He tossed a razor into a pile of underwear in the suitcase.

He felt Amado watching him as he made his way from closet to chest to bathroom to bed, grabbing clothes and miscellany in no particular order. He was an indifferent packer, which often meant he'd have to find a pharmacy as soon as he arrived wherever he was going to get the toothpaste or toothbrush or shaving cream he had forgotten.

"How do you think it'll be," Amado asked, blowing a blue stream into the dull light of the bedroom, "seeing her again? How do you behave . . . now?"

"Now?" He stared into the suitcase, hands on his hips.

"Considering . . . what she's doing."

He looked into the suitcase. He wasn't thinking about what he was looking at.

"You know" — he turned and sat on the edge of the bed — "I'm only guessing she's going to blackmail me. It's logical. But she's not a logical woman, so I could be surprised. In fact, she's managed to surprise me more than not. I don't even know why I think I could guess what she's got in mind."

364

He looked at his bare feet on the tile floor. "And, most of the time, she's lied to me."

Amado regarded him. "How do you feel?" he asked. "I mean, are you apprehensive . . . resigned . . . angry?"

Ross looked up at him. Amado was tranquil, his eyes heavy, the way they got when he was thinking way past his questions.

"Yes," he said, "and five or six more adjectives on top of those." He looked toward the sound of the poorwill. "You know, I can't shake the feeling that this . . . well, that it'll be over, that this is something that I'll pass through, come out the other side all right, and then think back on it . . . with whatever attitude survives. But, at the same time, I know that's not realistic."

He listened to the poorwill lilting along in the monotony of his low, crippled piping. Occasionally the breeze would gust through the room, and he could hear it hissing through the screens.

Amado was loyal to him, but Ross could sense his concern that maybe he had gone beyond a point at which a friend ought to be loyal. There was a line one didn't cross. It wasn't a textbook line, it was a heart line. You would know it when you saw it. Only in Amado's case, to know where he stood in relationship to that line made Amado more knowledgeable about the situation than was good for him. In order for him to know for sure, he would have to become a part of it. And that was too late. It was a hell of a position in which to put his friend, he knew, and he was sorry for it.

"It's one of those situations with extenuating circumstances," he said. "I guess they all are, aren't they?"

Amado waited.

"It's not clear-cut." He shook his head. "Once you're into it, you realize it's not something that can be resolved with any real satisfaction."

He stood and went to a chest of drawers and took out some socks and came back and dropped them into the suitcase.

"The thing is," he said, turning to Amado again but looking into the darkness past him, "Céleste . . . she was like Saleh. Once I reached a certain point with her, I wasn't much interested in life without her. With other women, over the years, there was something inherent within them, or within me, that let me know deep down that I wasn't ever going to find any peace with them. I knew that about each of them after a while. Marian's a good example. She was a storm, and I knew all along that we'd never survive the turbulence together. There was an undercurrent of something wild there that I knew in my gut would eventually rip us apart. And it did.

"With Saleh, and then Céleste — it's true, our relationships were doomed, but not because of anything having to do with either of the two women. Or, I think, with me. Saleh had a husband. Her drowning was tragic, but her death didn't separate us any more than reality already had.

"And Céleste . . . she came with so much mystery and history. Too much of it. I didn't realize it then, but I think she did. Her family, her life. It didn't have anything to do with *her*. It was all the baggage of life that she had to drag around with her. Lacan. Her mother. Her sister. Leda, whoever she is and whatever her claim was on Céleste."

He stopped and shifted his eyes at Amado, who was sitting in a cloud of blue smoke that he had just created.

"I forgot where I was going with this," he said.

"I don't think it matters." Amado dropped his feet on either side of the ottoman and leaned forward, resting his forearms on his knees, his cigar in his right hand. He had taken the paper band off his cigar and was folding and unfolding it with his fingers.

"I understand why you're being so . . . enigmatic, Ross," Amado said, "and I appreciate your wanting to keep me at a distance. But, are you sure you're seeing clearly? Are so confident . . ."

"I'm anything but confident."

"What if you're going to walk into a big mistake here?" Amado persisted. "What if, afterward, you say, 'If I'd only said something to Amado . . .' "

"I know, I've thought of that."

"Well, then?"

"You don't know what you're asking."

"Can it *be* that bad?"

He headed for the closet. "Yes."

The poorwill stopped, and Amado looked toward the screened darkness as he came back with a handful of suits. He tossed them on the bed and began taking them off the hangers. The nightjar started again, and they both listened to him in silence as he continued to pack and Amado smoked, thinking.

Ross didn't look at him, but as he packed he knew what Amado was wrestling with. Should he insist that Ross tell him what was going on? Should he volunteer to step into a conspiracy that involved a risk of such magnitude that his best friend chose not to disclose it to him? Suddenly he didn't want

Amado to have to answer the question.

"Amado . . ." He turned to him, holding a suit. "I need you here, and I need you dumb." They looked at each other. "That's what I need most of all. It's the honest truth. You're the only person who can do this for me, and do it in just exactly this way. I've got to have that." He turned back and finished folding the suit. "Any other way, and you wouldn't be any good to me at all."

That was all there was said about that. The hot breeze swelled through the room again, whispering through the screens. The poorwill resumed its odd, arrhythmic fluting. The two men continued in silence, one smoking, keeping his own counsel, the other feeling desperate, as if this warm, companionable evening would be the last of his life that he could spend in just this way. Uncertainty had never seemed so distasteful to him.

Chapter 40

The next morning he got up just before day-light, threw his suitcase into the back of the Jeep, and drove down Lomitas into town. It was still dark as he parked in front of Kirchner's Bakery, its bright storefront window the only place awake on the street. He sat at a window table with an almond croissant and a cup of coffee and watched the gray light rise. In the pale dawn, before the sunrise, Rio Encinal came into view as if in a moody black-and-white photograph, a thin sheet of fog settled over the surface of the water like a visible breath. As the light rose and the gray slowly came to life, revealing faded pastels, the fog on the river turned white, and he could see a subtle movement where the sluggish stream pushed the under-side of the fog along with it.

When the first honey light of sunrise touched the crest of the hills above Palm Heights, he took one more sip of coffee and left.

He drove to the airstrip south of town, where he parked his Jeep in a corner of the hangar where the charter pilot kept his plane, an arrangement he often used, and boarded the small plane for Austin. He was landing at Bergstrom International about an hour later, and then waited another hour before his flight to Paris departed.

Paris

He arrived at the secluded Relais Geneviève in St.-Germain-des-Prés in the evening and checked into a suite. He unpacked, knowing his suits would be a mess, which they were. He hung them in the bathroom. Later, when he returned, he would turn on the hot water and steam up the bathroom and let the wrinkles hang out. But for now, he wanted to walk off the stiffness and lethargy of the long flight. And he wanted to see the Seine and the city before it changed, as everything would change, after the unimaginable events of the next day.

The evening was full of autumn. It was at least thirty degrees cooler than the nights in San Rafael, and the damp in the air coming off the Seine carried the smells of a changing season. As he walked the small streets, working his way toward the quay, he opened himself to the peculiar feelings Paris engendered.

There was always nostalgia for a time that

he would not want to live again even if given the opportunity but which, nevertheless, held the disturbing memories of his self-centered youth, recollections mixed with the contradictory emotions of regret and the undeniable pleasures of a heedless life.

And, always, there was a tender sadness for sentiments forever lost, a separate sort of thing, inexplicable and gratifying in its own paradoxical way, for time past and times past, for faces and voices and moments never to be known again.

He had intended to walk from Pont Neuf to Pont de l'Archeveché, but turned back at Petit Pont, his self-indulgent reverie turning cold and misbegotten in the chilly night. His heart wasn't in it. There was too much to resurrect. In years past, sorrowful reveries were a nice evening's sentimental amusement. Regardless of how dispirited he might become, he knew he could always escape the doleful aftertaste by looking to the ever-hopeful future, where, no doubt, new memories were waiting to be lived.

But time was out of balance now. The past weighed heavy on the scales, and the future was so light that it hardly made itself felt at all. And what future there was, Leda held ransomed, and Céleste's death made him question whether it was even worth redeeming.

On Rue Christine he stepped into a brasserie for dinner. He was the only one in the brasserie eating alone, and he hardly tasted the food. He was desolate. This was the last time he would come to Paris. He couldn't do it anymore. If he could make it through the night and tomorrow's meeting, he would never return.

He walked back to Relais Geneviève and let himself into his darkened room. He went to the windows and looked out. There were trees along the sidewalks and a small café on the other side. He could see a few tables, a few patrons. It had gotten damper, and the streets were glistening.

Turning away, he went into the bath and turned on the hot water, then came back into the room and took his time unpacking the rest of the suitcase. When he was through, he went back to the bathroom, which was now filled with churning clouds of steam. He checked the suits, pulled the pocket flaps out of the pockets, smoothed the drape of the jackets. He turned off the water and left the suits where they were.

Later, in bed, he watched the splayed shadows on the windowpanes. It was a quiet street, not even the swishing sound of passing cars or the occasional voice to accompany him to unconsciousness. The sheets smelled lightly of Geneviève. Her room, her bed, her sheets. He imagined her. He turned over on his side, facing the windows. Behind him he could hear her moving about in the room, tending to the small personal things, combing her hair a few strokes, lotion, a fragrant cream. Soon he would feel the bed move ever so slightly as she crawled between her sheets and drew next to him. She could comfort, she could soothe, and she was generous with all she had to offer.

He slept hardly at all until just before dawn, when he slipped into a dark unconsciousness. Then he slept late.

It was a bright, crisp morning. After a croissant and coffee in a small café off Rue de Buci, he headed for the antique shops on Rue Jacob. He was desperate not to think about the meeting with Leda. If he went to a museum, he would lose track of time. Besides, he didn't want to concentrate; he wanted distraction. Thus Rue Jacob, where he could divert his mind with just the right amount of preoccupation to carry him through the long minutes of the next few hours.

The time passed quickly. At one o'clock he hailed a taxi and headed across the Seine to Cimetière du Père Lachaise.

He left the taxi at the Boulevard de Ménilmontant entrance of the cemetery and walked in through the imposing gates of the Avenue Principale. He knew the layout of this famous and beautiful cemetery where for two hundred years the famous and beautiful people, the great and obscure, had been buried. Death's judicious hand had gathered a strange mélange, Balzac and Chopin, Jim Morrison and Edith Piaf, Proust, Bernhardt, Oscar Wilde, Simone Signoret, and Yves Montand. Many of the avenues were completely canopied by the gilded leaves of maples and chestnuts and lindens in full autumn color. The cinder paths and lanes were littered with fallen gold.

He was early. He thought he would locate the meeting place and then retreat a little distance to watch Leda arrive. That appealed to him, watching her from a distance, watching her come and wait and fret when he was late.

But something stronger pulled at him. Knowing Leda, the location to which she had directed him was not an accident. He wanted to see Céleste's grave.

He meandered among the lanes, past crypts and mausoleums, monuments, and gravestones. Some were well maintained, some had surrendered to the persistence of brambles, some had been freshly cleaned, most were stained with mildew and time.

He turned a corner, entered a smaller path. He found the numbers and counted. Walking slowly, he felt his heart begin to race as he reached the number in Leda's note. And then he was there. His mind lurched to keep up with his searching eyes. A grave, above it a sculpture of a nude, swooning woman, weeping. An inscription that read "Sylvie Verret." Jesus. He hadn't thought . . . he . . . Next to it, a newer stone. A simple marker. "Leda Verret."

His heart stopped.

"I'm sorry," she said behind him.

He spun around.

"Jesus! . . . God!" He staggered, caught himself on the iron railing around the graves.

"I'm sorry," she repeated.

He thought he was going to faint. Jesus, he was going to faint. But he didn't, he fought it, willing himself not to abandon this miraculous moment. His eyes clung to her face with the desperation of a dying man who believed that if he could only keep his eyes open upon this last lovely thing that he saw, then he could hold in abeyance this last lonely thing required of him.

"Jesus *God*," he said.

Chapter 41

Céleste was surrounded, but not touched, by a honey light that fell through an allée of chestnuts behind her that seemed to stretch into eternity. The sun filtered through them in broken streams while, scattered in the receding distance, glitters of amber foil fell rippling through the light. It was easier to believe she was an illusion.

He couldn't speak. His throat thickened; he swallowed, almost sobbed, swallowed again. She was more real than real, as if she existed in another, more heightened dimension all her own, a breathing hallucination, a reincarnation that had not yet lost its celestial traces. All that had been lovely about her was more lovely still. He could hardly bear it.

"Ross," she said, and the sound of her voice startled him, as if he hadn't heard her apologies a few moments before, "please."

"What in God's name is this?" he asked. Neither of them moved.

"I had to do it this way," she said. "Or, I thought I had to."

"Do what?"

"End it."

"End *what!*" He was, suddenly, furious. He was trembling with adrenaline and gratitude and anger. "*What,* goddamn it?"

She didn't move.

"When Sylvie was with you in Paris," she said, "I was in London. All of this . . . goes back to Paris."

"Jesus." He swallowed again just to steady his voice. "What *is* 'all of this'?"

"Can we . . . sit down" — she looked around — "over there?" She motioned to a bench across the pathway.

She moved sideways toward it, and he followed her, aware of the unsteadiness in his legs, aware of the jittery agitation in his stomach.

They sat at opposite ends of the bench. He noticed now that she was holding a large chestnut leaf, the only thing she had with her. She looked at it as she flattened it on her thigh, pressing it with strokes of her fingers.

"It . . . all of this started when you broke up with her."

"Sylvie?"

She nodded.

"Twenty . . . this goes back twenty-five years?"

"Yes, Ross, it does."

He was dumbfounded. She was nervous,

but determined. It was taking a lot out of her.

"When you broke up with her, you kept her on, working with you in the kilns —"

"I didn't 'keep her on,' " he snapped. "I was finishing a commission, she threatened to raise hell with the client if I didn't let her stay. I *needed* that commission. So she *stayed.*"

"When she finally left you, do you know why?"

"No, but it was a load off my mind."

"She was four months pregnant . . . beginning to show."

He looked at her coldly. "No. I didn't know that." Jesus, Sylvie. She was an enigma. She was an abyss.

"Five months after she left she had Leda."

"God . . . damn."

"That's right, Ross. Leda was your daughter."

"What! Wait!" He almost came off the bench. He could hardly get the words out. "How could you think that? Why would you think that?"

Céleste was looking at him with an obstinate expression, waiting.

"She told you that," he said flatly. He was stunned. "Sylvie told you that I was Leda's father."

"She always blamed you for Leda's deformity . . . for making her work around the gases from the kilns while she was pregnant."

" 'Making' her? I just told you, she threatened to scuttle the project if I *didn't* let her stay. And how could I have known she was pregnant?"

Céleste gave him a cold glance at the lameness of his remark.

"Jesus," he said, "this is all a horrible deception." It was beginning to come into focus, what Sylvie had done, the enormity of her lies.

"Listen. Céleste. Listen to me. Sylvie and I had not had sexual relations for six months — Christ, *longer* than that. Céleste, I caught her having an affair with another sculptor. Her affair, it wasn't even . . . discreet. A lot of people knew. I was too stupid to see it until I actually walked in on it. I went berserk. Beat the shit out of the guy. Almost . . . killed him. I didn't touch her after that."

"She said —"

"Stop! I'll tell you what happened. I don't give a damn what Sylvie said. After that she . . . she threatened to kill herself if I kicked her out. I let her stay for another two months. I wasn't living at the studio, so she moved in there. It was okay for a while, a

380

month, two. But when it was clear to her that I wouldn't have anything more to do with her, when she couldn't reignite the relationship, she started going crazy. She destroyed a couple of maquettes. I kicked her out. She threatened to make a scene with the client . . . ruin things. We compromised. I'd let her help me to the end of the project. She thought if she stayed around, she could change my mind about her. It was a stupid thing to hope for, only showed how unrealistic she was. She was always . . . just on the edges of reality."

"If this is true . . ."

"It's true," he said. "It's the truth. Leda is not my daughter. It's not possible. It's not true."

Céleste looked away. She stared down the allée of chestnuts and maples. She didn't look at him when she spoke.

"Sylvie . . . when Leda . . . when the deformity began to develop," she said, "Sylvie was beside herself. She began obsessing over the 'reason' for what was happening. You . . . she said you had forced her to work with the kilns with you. It was your fault."

"Céleste, even if that had been true, it would have affected the fetus, for God's sake. Leda would have been *born* with some kind of deformity. It wouldn't have been something that would have developed in adolescence."

"Always," she said, "all I'd ever heard from her were stories about how selfish you were, how cruel. You impregnated her, made promises to her, kicked her out. You abandoned her and Leda. You . . ."

She stopped and put a hand on her forehead as if she were feeling to see if she had a fever.

"Leda was thirteen. She wanted a reason for it, too. She wanted something to blame. She believed her mother. She was easily convinced. And I . . . I had heard these stories all these years. I believed her, too, I needed to believe, I needed to hate you to justify what Leda wanted us to do."

He was appalled. None of them, himself included, had taken a lot of convincing to do what they had done. He was no wiser than they were. But he was still shocked at what she had been willing to do.

"That's a lot of hate," he said, "to frame me for murder."

Céleste turned to him. "What?"

"What have you done with the videotapes?" It made him queasy to ask that, but he had to know.

"*Video*tapes?"

"Do you want me to 'buy' them from you, is that it?"

"What are you talking about, videotapes?"

"She told me you'd made videotapes of me getting rid of Lacan's body. You were going to use them to blackmail me. That's what this is all about."

"Oh . . . God . . ." She gaped at him. "Oh . . . Ross. There are no videotapes. There's nothing like that."

"She said the plan was yours."

"No! She came to *me*. I was desperate to get away from Michel . . . I *had* to get away from him. She knew. She knew how I felt, that I couldn't do it anymore, not for her, not for anything. God help me, I agreed to go along. I'm ashamed of it, Ross, but I did it. I wanted to get away from him so desperately. And I . . . I used what Sylvie had said all these years . . . I used all of that to justify what I was going to do."

He was skeptical.

"How was she going to blackmail me? What was Leda going to use?"

"She wouldn't tell me. She said she knew something, something from your past that you'd pay a 'fortune' to keep quiet. I assumed she knew something from Sylvie."

"No," he said. "There was nothing. Nothing like that. The only thing I've ever done in my life that I could be blackmailed for . . . is what I did for you."

Céleste turned away again and buried her face in her hands, but only for a moment.

"God," she said, looking up, "what has happened here? What have we done?"

"She told me . . . she said that you were the one who killed Lacan."

She spun around to him. "*You* know how it happened. It was the way we told you. How could I have done that?"

"She said he was asleep."

"No . . . no, no, no! I did *not* kill Michel Lacan."

They stared at each other, both of them realizing the magnitude of Leda's manipulation and deception. They were appalled at their own stupidity and gullibility.

He saw her disorientation. She was shaken, afraid. Abruptly she stood and started walking, not away, but in a confused, distracted wander. He hesitated, then went to her and took her arm and turned her around. The touch of her felt strange. It was something he thought he would never experience again, the texture of her skin, the living warmth of her.

She was distracted, as if he had awakened her from a daydream.

"Go on with it," he said. "I've got to know the rest of it."

Chapter 42

She stood in front of him, speechless. He couldn't imagine what else she might say. This was turning into a nightmare of another sort, but he believed that if they kept talking, there was a chance they would wake up in a less frightening world.

"This is unforgivable," she said.

"Just finish it."

She nodded but looked away from him.

"I couldn't go through with it," she continued. "I mean the blackmailing. I . . . I didn't have the stomach for it. I didn't have the heart for it."

She was tearing the leaf.

"You . . . weren't what I'd expected. At all. I hadn't expected . . . anything to change. What I found myself . . . what I was beginning to feel for you . . . I didn't expect any of that. It was outrageous. Inconceivable. Everything, all of it, was flying apart."

"You told her this."

"I didn't have to. She saw it happening. But, yes, eventually I said, no more. I was jumping out."

"Then Lacan showed up."

She nodded.

"Did you know he was coming?"

"No. I answered the door and there he was. I told you, I never knew. I had to let him know where I was at all times. He always knew where to find me."

"So . . . Leda's attack . . ."

"It had to have been spontaneous. I don't know what she was thinking. She didn't have anything to gain from it. My arrangements with Lacan are what she told you they were."

"She saw an opportunity to save her scheme," he said, "and to ratchet up the stakes. Did you know about the note she left in the bank box?"

He saw her brace herself, and her reaction answered his question.

"No . . ."

He told her what had happened, and she began shaking her head no.

"No, that's not true," she said. "No, he was dead. I know he was dead." She paused and composed herself. She started talking slowly.

"When Leda . . . burst into the room she hit . . . him with one violent swing of the pipe. The blood flew everywhere. . . . It didn't knock him out . . . his eyes flew open and then shut halfway. He just held himself up, his arms straight down on the bed . . . and he seemed as if he were trying to wake up . . . but he . . . but he grabbed me as if . . . as if he were trying to hang on to consciousness. I screamed . . . screamed and fought to get away from him, and Leda swung again and . . . it was only a glancing blow and . . . he nodded over me . . . blood everywhere, and I got clear of him, and she hit him a third time . . . and again . . . pounding at him."

She was staring away, her voice growing softer as she went on.

"Somehow I got across the bed and stopped her. We both stood there . . . dull with shock. Leda was making . . . I don't know . . . noises . . . verging on hysteria. I grabbed the pipe from her. I thought: If he's not dead, it's not murder; if he's not dead, it's not murder . . . over and over. I made her sit down and went to the bed and checked him."

She looked at him.

"He was alive. And then he died. I saw him die."

She buried her face in her hands again, but this time she didn't look up. They stood there, alone together in the autumn light. He was close enough to her to see the silver strands in her hair, to see the hollow in her neck where it met her collarbone and where he had kissed her so much, but never enough.

He reached out and drew her to him and held her. He pulled her hands from her face, but she turned her head away and then embraced him and buried her face in his shoulder. He thought the color of the light coming through the allée of autumn trees and the feel of her body as she cried were too much to bear. He would remember this when age had ravaged everything else from him and left him mute and empty. He would let nothing, not even escaping time, take this memory away from him.

He took her back to the bench and gave her a handkerchief and held her a long time. He didn't give a damn about anything else. After a while she regained her composure.

"I'm sorry," she said. "It's just . . . this is unbelievable."

"Why did you leave without even telling me?" he asked.

"Leda said you had figured out what we were doing, why we had come to San Rafael. You were shocked, angry. You didn't want to have anything else to do with me."

"She said pretty much the same to me," he said, "only she told me the scheme was yours, essentially to have me replace

Lacan as your benefactor."

The revelations kept coming. They were both in a state of dismay. As each layer of the story was peeled back, the proportions of Leda's scheme came into focus for him. It was not the complexity of the scheme that floored him, but the extent of her feelings that drove the scheme. It was hatred that had driven her, hatred for him. Such loathing was breathtaking, but to be the object of such loathing was sickening.

Céleste sat back in the corner of the bench, wadding his handkerchief, looking at it, looking at him.

"I told her," she said, "after I saw you that last night — I told her I was through. I was leaving. We argued. It went on for several days. Finally she said let's go back to Paris. We weren't thinking straight. I didn't care. I just wanted out of San Rafael. Paris was the only place I had to go.

"I didn't know, of course, about the message she'd left in the bank box. I wouldn't have left you like that, Ross. But . . . not knowing . . . thinking you wanted to have nothing to do with me . . . I decided you'd be better off if the two of us simply disappeared."

"You should've tried to talk to me anyway."

"I was so ashamed of what we'd done. It made sense to me that you wanted nothing more to do with us. I could imagine the betrayal you must have felt. And you didn't make any effort to try to see me. I could only believe that she was telling me the truth about it."

He felt a genuine bleakness in the face of all the misread communication. Leda had meant to deceive them, it was true, but she would not have been able to succeed if they had not been afraid of their own emotions, of their own feelings for each other. What were they holding back for? Why had they been afraid to simply tell each other how they felt? How could two reasonably intelligent adults who had seen so much life, who already had lived so many mistakes, persist in living them again?

"It's incredible," he said, "how we let this happen. We practically threw our lives away to her. I'll never know how that happened."

Céleste sighed a jerky sigh. She sat up straighter.

"Nothing changed for me after we got here," she went on. It was as though she wanted to get it all out, get it over with once and for all.

"I still couldn't live with it. Or her. One night, after another hateful argument, I told her I was leaving her. I just couldn't stand to be with her. I told her she would always have money, but I couldn't live with her. She flew into a rage, she was distraught . . . a madwoman."

She paused, swallowed. "Sometime during the early morning hours that night, she crawled into her bathtub and cut . . . the insides of her thighs . . . and her wrists."

"God." He was stricken by the image of Leda, reclining awkwardly, her hump forcing her to a position from which she had to watch her blood spilling out onto the white porcelain between her legs. Unless she had closed her eyes. But he knew that she hadn't. He knew that she had watched until her sight failed.

"The death certificate," he said.

She nodded. "I changed the name, photocopied it, sent it to you. In my mind, we no longer existed for you. It was over."

"But I would've thought Leda was still alive."

"I know. But I knew you'd never hear from her."

"Didn't you think I'd be waiting for the other shoe to drop? Sooner or later there's bound to be an investigation of some sort. I would've worried about Leda dealing with it. By this time I knew she was trying to destroy me, even if I didn't know why."

"I know, I know," she said. "I just wanted it over. It wasn't until after I'd sent the letter that I . . . that I started putting all of that together. The more I dwelled on it . . . I knew I'd done the wrong thing. But I couldn't bring myself to get in touch with you. At first . . . I thought I was being tough with myself. I thought that by making you think I was dead, I was being brutally self-disciplined."

"Then . . . why . . ."

"Why?" She shook her head. "It turned out that I didn't have the strength to live with that, either. The lies, the whole monstrous pile of lies we had tormented you with, haunted me. I couldn't get on with my life. I couldn't sleep. I couldn't think . . . and I couldn't *stop* thinking . . . of you. So I sent the letter asking for the meeting. I needed to tell you everything, no matter how shamefully it reflected on me. All that mattered to me after a while was that you know the truth and that you learn it from me."

She looked down again, and he did, too. She was twisting his handkerchief with such force that the backs of her hands were ribbed with the strained lines of taut tendons converging toward her wrist.

"I'm sorry . . . ," she said, "so sorry . . . it's

impossible to express how sorry I am . . . for what we have done to you."

As the afternoon light turned from bright gold to amber, they strolled through the cemetery's allées and avenues and talked. Sometimes the fallen leaves were so thick upon the ground that their feet never touched the cinder at all. They had no idea where they were going or where they had gone, and when they encountered others on the quiet lanes, they were unaware. A lifetime had passed since they had last spoken. They had been given back what they had thought they had lost forever, and such a gift had the power of resurrection. The world changed. Life changed. Now, a second time since they had met, they knew that nothing would ever be the same again.

Chapter 43

They left the Cimetière du Père Lachaise and took a taxi to the Marais. After Leda's suicide, Céleste had closed down Lacan's large house in the staid Chaillot district and had taken a flat in the Marais. It was an area that held happy memories for her from her early years in Paris after leaving school in London.

Céleste directed the taxi to a small neighborhood near her flat, and they walked to several shops, gathering cold meats, wine, cheese, and bread for dinner. In the early darkness they carried the food back to her building and took the elevator up to the third floor. Her flat was roomy and on the corner of the building so that the main room looked onto a leafy intersection, one side of the room overlooking one street, the other side of the room overlooking the cross street. There were shops along the streets and a few cafés.

"The views made it more expensive," she said, unpacking the food, "but it was worth it. In the evenings you can hear the tempo of the neighborhood changing. It might be too loud for some people, but it keeps me company."

They put the food out on the kitchen table and sat down. Ross poured wine for each of them and then sliced thin pieces from the small ham.

After taking his first sip of wine, he said, "Okay, now what about the police?"

She was sitting across the small table from him. She nodded.

"It was the day I sent the fax to you. Despite the fact I'd already decided to talk to you, I kept putting it off. The visit from the police changed that."

"Visit? They came here?"

"Yes. I'm sure they got my address from Lacan's accountant. When I moved here after Leda's death, I had to notify Lacan's accountant. My mail comes here now. His office had to know."

"Was there any reaction from the accountant?"

She shrugged and cut a slice of cheese. "I got a two-sentence letter: a sentence of condolence and a sentence acknowledging that they had received my change of address."

"Tell me about the police. That was . . . four days ago?"

She nodded. "He came here." She sighed heavily and took a bite of the cheese and chewed for a moment, thinking.

"He was an inspector with the Police

Judiciaire," she went on, "and his name was Raymond Vautrin. At first he didn't tell me Michel was missing. He said they wanted to talk to him and were trying to find him and when was the last time I saw him. As we had discussed, I told him . . . the time before last, which was . . . in May.

"He said wasn't it unusual that it had now been four months. I said yes. He said, well, had I done anything about his absence? Wasn't I worried? Had I reported it?

"I decided to get right to the heart of it, not even go to the trouble of having him worm it out of me. I told him what our relationship was like. I told him why I stayed with Michel. I told him that my life was only better the longer he stayed away. He could be gone for five years for all I cared. I wasn't going to try to find him because he was only misery to me, and I didn't go out of my way to find misery.

"He pointed out that Leda had been dead just over a month. There was no need to stay with Lacan anymore. Why hadn't I broken away? I said I had, I'd moved out of his place. He said, yes, but you're still cashing your checks from him. I said, yes, and I would continue to do so as long as they were sent to me, and even if they were sent to me for the rest of my life, it still wouldn't compensate me for what that man had done to me. But I wouldn't have anything more to do with Lacan. When the checks stopped coming, they stopped coming."

They were both quiet for a while. The occasional sound of traffic passing by under the trees drifted up and through the opened windows. After a few minutes Céleste got up and closed the windows, rubbing the chill off her upper arms as she came back to the table. She took a sip of wine and tore off a piece of bread and ate it.

"Then what happened?"

"Then he told me Lacan seemed to be missing. Missing from where? I asked. The man travels so much, who would know if he was missing? Vautrin said that he had missed three meetings with his accountant, and a corporation board meeting, which he'd never missed. I didn't know what to say."

She cut another slice of cheese and took a tiny bite of it, her eyes somewhere on the table, avoiding him, reluctant to continue. She poured a splash more of wine even though she had plenty in her glass.

"Then he asked me if I knew about the other women. No, I said. Yes, other women like me who received money from Lacan. In Lyon. In Antibes. Strasbourg. And . . . even another woman here, in Paris. I didn't know about Lyon."

"He got all of this from the accountant?"

"Apparently. They all had similar arrangements."

"You mean, financial payout."

She nodded.

"And did they have similar stories . . . their relationships with Lacan?"

She nodded again and then took a sip of wine. "But I was the only one who knew him by his real name. And I was the only one who had married him."

Silence.

"And there was something else," she said. "I think . . . at least it seemed to me from Vautrin's questions that they suspect Lacan of being mixed up in drug trafficking."

Ross stopped cutting a piece of ham. "What? Why, what did he say?"

"He spent a lot of time asking about Michel's names. Did I know of other names he might have used? Had I ever seen passports in any names other than the ones Vautrin had mentioned? I didn't even know Michel had passports in any other names. Had I ever seen packages addressed to some other name come to our address in Chaillot? Had I ever seen mail, packages, deliveries of any kind, arrive from Latin America or Asia or Sicily? Had Lacan ever asked me to carry packages to these places for him or to go to these places and receive packages?"

She stopped. "What does that sound like to you?"

He sat back in his chair and looked at her. "You know, don't you, that this is good news."

"Of course I know that. It hardly helps."

He understood how this must have made her feel, but at the same time, he was enormously relieved. The investigation into the disappearance of Michel Lacan was going to be complex and extensive, and more important, Céleste was going to be only one among many who might have had a motive to kill Lacan. In fact, she had no motive beyond the abuse.

"What about Lacan's will? Was that mentioned?"

"No."

"He already knew."

"I'm sure he did. The accountant would have been able to put him in touch with Michel's lawyers. It would have been easy to check."

Céleste tore off another piece of bread and ate it with disinterest. For the first time, Ross's hope that they might slip by being investigated to any great degree at all was grounded in something real. The question of drug trafficking was an unbelievable break.

"I'm wondering," he said, looking toward the windows across the street, other windows, other lives, other spaces dimly lighted, "I was wondering how difficult it will be for them to trace his movements during the time he went to San Rafael. Did he use his real name? Or one of the false ones? Or did he use one that the police know nothing about?" He looked at Céleste. "Did Vautrin ask about your stay in San Rafael?"

"No."

"But he must know about it. It's no secret that you went there. If he doesn't know now, he'll know later. He'll be running computer checks on all flights from France to Austin during the time you were there. He'll find Lacan's ticket. Unless Lacan flew in from somewhere other than France."

"Ross, please. Let's not do this. Let's not let this consume us. If this becomes everything to us, if it becomes all that we are, consuming all of our time, all of our thoughts, we won't have any lives left. And we've come through too much already to let that happen."

She reached across the table and put her hands on his.

"We've been given an extraordinary second — even a third — chance. Let's not . . . not waste it on this kind of obsession."

She was right, of course. That night, as they lay together in her bed, her words resonated even more clearly in his thoughts. Everything about their having met and fallen in love was wildly improbable. What they had been through, and what they had done, was unimaginable. It was inconceivable.

Yet it had happened. And they had survived. They shouldn't have, but they had slipped through the fine net of long odds as witlessly as they had been drawn into it in the first place. They had been rash. They had been blind. They had been selfish. They had been everything that people were who had needlessly wasted their lives. But they had not been destroyed. Not yet, anyway, and maybe they wouldn't be. They had a chance now.

Surely they would survive now with even a small chance, if they had survived when they had had none at all.

Chapter 44

"It could take . . . months, years, even," he said. He and Céleste were sitting in the sunshine in a small café across the street from her flat. They had slept late and had gone down for a breakfast of coffee and pastry.

They had talked far into the night about their future. What would they do now? Would it affect the investigation — that is, would it bring attention to Céleste that she would not otherwise receive — if she went back to San Rafael with him? If she were one of Lacan's other women, probably not. But Céleste was his wife, even though he didn't treat her with any more respect than he treated the other women. Still, it wouldn't look good in the media.

"It's no life at all, if we can't be together," she said. "Even if we meet surreptitiously, eventually they'll find out. It would look even more suspicious than if we were open about it. I'm not going to wait for this investigation to resolve itself. I'm going to divorce him now."

"What about Vautrin?"

"What about him?"

"Do you just go ahead with divorce proceedings without telling him?"

"I don't know why not. A divorce would appear as though I were assuming Lacan was going to return eventually. I could even say that: I don't care whether he returns or not. I want to be free of him. There wouldn't be any need for me to do it if I thought I was a widow. I'm not entitled to anything in Lacan's will, and I'm not going to seek anything. I just want to be free of him."

"How long will that take?"

"I have no idea."

"I've got to get back soon."

"How soon?"

"In a couple of days."

"Why?"

"We ought not to be together until the divorce."

She leaned toward him. "Ross, we have time. Whatever we do, let's not lose our grip on each other. I couldn't bear that. Not after everything we've been through."

He returned to San Rafael without her.

Amado, of course, was stupefied, and for once he was speechless. He simply stared and listened. Ross told him more or less the truth about what Céleste had done with Leda's death certificate, passing over the why of it with a story of misunderstanding and stress. He didn't mention Lacan at all, except to say that Céleste was divorcing him.

It was the middle of the afternoon, and they were sitting in the kitchen of Ross's house, drinking beer and eating fresh tamales that he had gotten in Rincon. On the other side of the screened door the patio was bright, but not as hot as before. While he was in Paris the first norther of the season had plunged down through the midwestern states and then had slowed in the Panhandle and settled gradually across Texas, breaking the back of the heat wave. The temperature highs were in the low eighties now, and the nights cooled down nicely. But there was still no rain.

Amado shook his head at these latest revelations and sipped his beer. He stammered a few questions to which Ross responded in varying degrees of evasion.

"And then, after the divorce, what?" Amado asked.

"Then we'll see."

"She'll move here?" Amado unwrapped a greasy corn shuck, removed the tamale, and dropped the shuck on a growing pile of them on a newspaper in the center of the table.

"Maybe."

"God," Amado said, taking half the small tamale in a single bite, "Ross, every time I talk to you you've got something else outrageous to tell me. When does this . . ." He searched for the right word.

"Insanity?"

"Yes, why not, when does this insanity end?" Amado wiped his hands on a paper napkin and picked up his Pacifico, chasing the peppery tamale aftertaste with a swig of the cold Mexican beer.

Outside, the mockingbird was alone in the bougainvillea, her choice of songs a soft, triple-note fluting that she repeated over and over, almost as if she were doing it absently, her mind elsewhere.

"It may never end," he said. "It may be the nature of her life."

Amado looked at him. "Aren't you a little apprehensive about . . . making all of that part of your life?"

"Yes."

"But . . ."

"I'm not as afraid of the 'insanity' as I'm afraid of life without her."

Amado nodded, regarding him thoughtfully. "And what about . . . this criminal matter, Ross? What happens to that?"

"It doesn't go away."

"And it won't."

"I don't think so."

Amado hesitated. "And I'm the only one who knows about it?"

"Just the three of us."

"Then it's a solemn thing."

"Yes, it is. A solemn thing."

He pitched once more into work on Leda's sculpture, which now was made even more complicated by the incredible revelations in Paris. But the complications served only to strengthen his fascination with the challenge that he now felt was something like a calling for him. He and Céleste corresponded almost daily by e-mail and talked on the telephone a couple of times a week. The divorce was going to take some time. Maybe four months.

He made good progress on the sculpture during November and most of December. For the week of Christmas Céleste flew into Austin. He picked her up, and they drove to San Rafael. It was a clear, warm Christmas, the kind that normally put him out of sorts. He liked Christmas to be cold and overcast and wet. Still, it was chill enough for a sweater during the day, and at night the temperature dipped low enough to require a slow mesquite fire in the fireplace.

During the day he tinkered with the small

sculptures of cicadas while Céleste read or talked to him while he worked. He had hidden the unfinished sculpture of Leda. He didn't want Céleste to know about it. Not just yet, even though it was essentially finished. They tacitly agreed not to talk about the risks of the investigation that was being conducted in isolated silence away from them. It was an odd feeling to have your future being decided for you by strangers in another country while you simply waited to be informed. But because of the oddness of their predicament, they convinced themselves that worrying was futile. There was nothing they could do.

In a way, it was a liberation. But as the holidays went by, he could not shake a sense that underneath their relaxed good pleasure was an acknowledgment of their provisional happiness. They had eluded so much misfortune, escaped so much tragedy that could have separated them forever, that to react to their present happiness with anything other than quiet gratitude would have seemed profane.

Céleste returned to Paris two days after Christmas, and the day after that the rain the Hill Country had been needing for so long arrived on the leading edge of an arctic cold front. It rained for two days and then

408

the temperature dropped below freezing, and he spent New Year's Eve iced in. Sleet whitened the ground on the first day of the new year and San Rafael was shut down, its hilly streets impassable. The fragrance of oak and mesquite fires sweetened the still air and mixed with the fog and mizzle that hung over town.

After the fourth day the weather station said they could expect at least another week of near freezing drizzle. No one was complaining.

He put chains on the Jeep and drove down Lomitas into town. He shopped for groceries, went by a coffee shop for more beans, and then stopped by Kirchner's for a cup of coffee and an almond croissant. From his window table he could see only the lower half of San Rafael. The upper parts were shrouded in a pale drizzly cloud.

After he got home and unpacked the groceries he went into his bedroom to check his e-mail and fax machine. There was an e-mail from Céleste wanting him to call her. Something had happened.

"Vautrin wants to talk to me again," she said. Her voice was not strained, but there was a forced calm about it. "He asked me if you were in the city. He wants to talk to you, too."

"When?"

"He said it wasn't urgent, but soon."

"Is that all? Nothing else?"

"He didn't say what he wanted to talk to us about, if that's what you mean. He did say that if you preferred, he could have someone with a law enforcement agency in San Rafael interview you. I didn't think you'd want that."

"No, you're right. But if someone here could do it, it sounds like routine stuff to me. I mean, if it was something serious, you'd think he'd want to do it himself."

"Yes."

"Okay, I'll go there. Try to arrange something for three days from now. I'll be in touch about when you can expect me."

Chapter 45

He booked a flight for early the next morning and then hired a charter flight out of San Rafael to Austin that afternoon. Considering the weather, it would be better to spend the night in a motel near the airport than to risk missing his flight the next day. He packed a small suitcase and threw the bag into the Jeep and headed for the airstrip south of town. This time he didn't worry about getting someone to stay at his place. The important events were going to be happening in Paris.

January was the coldest month in Paris and, after August, its wettest as well. Céleste had agreed to meet Raymond Vautrin at three o'clock at a brasserie very near her flat in the Marais. When they arrived at Brasserie Dupuis, Vautrin was already there, at a table near the front window.

As Céleste introduced them, he studied the inspector from the Police Judiciaire. He was in his late forties, dressed in a double-breasted dark suit, white shirt, dark burgundy tie. His hair was longish, but despite that he gave the impression of being a busi-

411

nessman of no particular distinction. He spoke excellent English and had a relaxed, easy manner. He smiled pleasantly, but Ross got the impression that he was a sober man.

"I'm sorry," Vautrin said, gesturing for them to sit opposite him at the table, "that you had to come to Paris for this, Mr. Marteau." They all sat down. "Marteau. Very nice French name."

There were dirty dishes in front of Vautrin. He had eaten lunch here.

"I'm always looking for an excuse to come to Paris," he said. "My great-grandfather was French, they say."

"You didn't know him?"

"No."

The waiter came and took away the dirty dishes and took three orders for coffee.

"Well," Vautrin said, crossing his arms and leaning his elbows on the table. "I'll bring you up-to-date on what has been happening in the investigation of Monsieur Lacan's disappearance," he said, looking at Ross. "But first, did he ever go to San Rafael?" he asked, turning his head to Céleste and addressing the question to her.

"No," she said. "At least, I never knew that he did."

"No." He nodded. "We couldn't find any

record of it either," Vautrin said. "That's interesting.

"Okay then," he continued, "as you may have already guessed, Monsieur Lacan seems to have been involved in the drug business. Trafficking. In a small way, but with very big people. He invested in shipments of cocaine from time to time, but mostly he just played at it. He was one of those men who liked living on the edge of a dangerous life while not actually being a fully involved part of it. When it came to violence, he much preferred to experience it in a different context."

The waiter arrived with their coffee, and Vautrin waited until it was served before he resumed.

"We don't know what happened to him," Vautrin said, then sipped his coffee tentatively and returned his cup to its saucer. "I, personally, believe he is dead. I'm sorry, madame."

It was not really an apology, but rather a remark of deference out of respect.

"We do not find any evidence," he said, continuing to speak to her, "of foul play in his disappearance. Although I am quite sure that there was."

"What do you mean?" Céleste asked.

"I think he might have been murdered."

Ross didn't look at her, but he knew Céleste had reacted. How? He couldn't imagine. Did she feign shock? Surprise? He watched Vautrin's face to see if he was convinced, but the inspector was far too experienced.

"Why?" Céleste asked. "If there's no evidence . . ."

"Evidence. Yes." Vautrin smiled. "Well, there's legal evidence that can be admitted into a trial, and then there's extralegal evidence. Circumstantial. Intuitive. Experientially informed evidence."

"So, then . . . what happens?" Céleste asked.

"Well, of course, we will continue investigating, but as more and more time goes by without new leads, my superiors will begin to lose interest. Soon they will be giving me other cases, and those investigations will be more demanding. After a while no one will look at this case very much. Rarely, even."

"That's it? It's over?"

"Not yet, no. As I said, I have my 'intuitions,' and I have never been comfortable with unresolved cases."

Vautrin took another sip of coffee. Outside, the rain began drumming down on the awnings, and Vautrin looked out at the sound. He watched the rain, and the corner

414

of his eye glinted in the gray light.

He turned back to them.

"I'm afraid," he said, "that it will be a long time before the estate can be settled."

"That won't affect me," Céleste said. "I'm divorcing him."

"Yes," Vautrin said, "I know that. Why?"

"I don't want to have anything more to do with him," she said. "Whether he's alive or not."

"I see. Still, you do have a little something coming to you. A divorce will void that."

"It's not worth it."

He studied her. "I understand that," he said nodding. "A new life is what you want." He glanced at Ross. "I can understand that."

To his surprise, Céleste showed a flash of anger.

"I'm not looking for approval, Monsieur Vautrin. I don't have to justify myself. I've earned the right to want something better than what I had."

"I was not being judgmental, madame." Vautrin was embarrassed that his glance had provoked her. "Not at all. Only . . . only I have a few more questions."

Céleste took a drink of her coffee, her hand unsteady with emotion. Now Vautrin looked at him.

"You've been very patient, Mr. Marteau," he said. "Thank you." He frowned and stared into his coffee cup for a moment, gathering his thoughts. When he looked up he looked at both of them, addressing them alternately with his eyes.

"When a man disappears like this, let's say he is murdered, it has been our experience — statistics bear it out — that most of the time the wife is a guilty party. And often — most of the time — the wife has a lover who was involved as well." He shrugged. "It's a fact.

"So you see my task. It's not personal. I am not being judgmental. I am doing my job."

"I understand that," Ross said. "You don't have to explain."

"With Monsieur Lacan, however, the situation is more complex than might be typical. There are complicating factors. Still, those factors do not rule out what I have just said. Of course, suspicion fell very heavily on you, madame. You must have known that."

"Yes, I assumed that," Céleste said.

Vautrin looked at Ross. "Did you ever meet Michel Lacan?"

"No, I didn't."

"Did you ever see him?"

"No."

"The last person we can find who saw Lacan alive was the woman he kept in Strasbourg," Vautrin said. "That was two weeks after you last saw him," he said to Céleste. "That was a long time ago. Three weeks before you went to San Rafael for the summer. Much of that time we think he must have been out of France. We're checking with our counterparts in Sicily, Colombia, Mexico, Eastern Europe, a few places in Asia. He could easily have disappeared in one of those places."'

He stopped to sip his coffee again.

"I'll be honest with you, madame. I think we will never solve this case. He traveled too much. Too many identities. He was too secretive. Too strange. It is so easy for people like that to come to a bad end in some obscure place — gone forever. I think Michel Lacan falls into that category."

"I don't understand why you're telling me all of this," Céleste said.

"You are his wife, madame, his sole heir, for another month, anyway."

"He didn't have any family?"

"No immediate family."

"Really?"

"None. Only second cousins."

"They will inherit his estate, then?"

"Theoretically. They will have to be

notified, and then they will have to make claims. The magistrate will have to go through the process of justifying those claims. It will take a lot of time. And there is so much money involved, I expect there will be a battle among the cousins about who gets what, how it is divided. A person could grow old waiting for this case to close."

"Isn't all of this irrelevant now?" Ross asked.

"We certainly thought so," Vautrin said, "until a week ago."

Ross braced himself and could almost feel Céleste doing the same, but neither of them responded. They simply waited.

"After your niece's suicide," Vautrin said, "you cleaned her things out of Lacan's home in the Chaillot district. You sold her clothes, threw away personal items you did not want to keep. The normal things one does after a death."

"Yes."

"The rest of the house you left for later."

"I just wanted out of there," Céleste said. "I got all of my things out, all of Leda's things out. It wasn't difficult. It was a big house, but I didn't live in all of it."

"How did Monsieur Lacan and your niece Leda get along?"

"They didn't," Céleste said. "They never talked. They didn't like each other. Each was barely tolerant of the other."

Vautrin nodded, his expression that of a consulting physician listening to a patient give him the facts of his symptoms. He was making calculations and judgments that he wasn't sharing . . . yet.

Vautrin bent and picked up a briefcase that had been resting against the leg of the table. He put it on the table, opened it, and took out a bundle of documents and handed them to Ross.

"We found these in another part of the house," Vautrin said, "in a room that she seemed to have used often. There was a desk there with scissors, tape, folders. The articles are about you. The notations are in Leda's handwriting."

Ross went through the clippings. There were articles from art journals, *Le Monde*, *Paris Match*, tabloids, various newspapers. He felt a chill wash slowly over his body, which responded like a tuning fork to a low-pitched hum from within.

"I'm sure you are already familiar with the articles themselves," Vautrin said. "But read the notations."

Scattered throughout in the margins, at various angles and in various colors of ink,

Leda had written:

ml says that r's favorite pastry is an almond croissant.

according to ml r hates this kind of publicity. . . .

he never listens to music while he is working — ml

doesn't like models talking to him while he's working

r's workday is regulated by the angelus bells in the chapel of san rafael — ml

meets amado about three times a week at graber's — ml

" 'Ml.' Michel Lacan?" Ross asked. "Is that what you think?"

Vautrin nodded.
"How would he know all of this personal information?" he asked as Céleste took the articles from him.
"I don't know," Vautrin said. "How would you explain the notes?"
"If you had known Leda, you wouldn't

420

have had to ask that question," he said.

"What do you mean?"

"The fact that she read these articles . . . made notes about me in the margins . . ."

"That's Leda," Céleste said, looking up from the articles. "Once we had decided on a sculptor, she went to great lengths to learn everything she could about him. In fact, the journal articles are mine. I shared them with her. Did you find the articles on the other sculptors?"

"No."

"We were considering three sculptors before deciding on Ross. We researched each of them this way. We got articles, bios from agents. Whatever we could. Articles, especially interviews, that gave details about the sculptors' personal life were her favorite. It gave her insight into their character that she couldn't get from the drier art journal articles that were more about the artists' work techniques."

"Then why does she use the initials *ml?*"

Céleste looked down at the notes and shrugged. "I don't know what she meant by that. Who knows what she was doing there."

Vautrin looked at Ross. He shook his head.

Vautrin considered their responses while looking back and forth between them. He seemed not to want to believe them, yet at the same time he seemed to have to admit to himself that what they were saying sounded reasonable enough.

"What's the matter?" Ross asked. "What did you think was going on?"

"I don't know," Vautrin said unconvincingly. "I thought you might have some ideas."

He shook his head again, and Céleste pushed the articles back across the table to Vautrin.

"Well," Vautrin said with a weary smile as he gathered up the papers, "this is one of those cases in which we shall never know all the answers." He shoved the papers back into his briefcase. "I think I'll be lucky even to think of all the right questions."

Chapter 46

Ross and Céleste left the brasserie and started back to her flat. Neither of them spoke for a little while as they walked along the wet sidewalk, huddled together under a single umbrella. The rain was light, only a drizzle.

"What the hell was that?" Céleste said finally. She was incensed. "He searched the house in Chaillot?"

"Sounds like it."

"That means he has some pretty strong concerns."

"I'm afraid so."

" 'Ml'? What was she doing? She *couldn't* have been talking to Lacan. How could she? About what, for God's sake? What would he know?"

Ross said nothing at first. His mind was swarming with possibilities. Vautrin hadn't seemed particularly threatening with his questions, but he was definitely on to something. But he gave up too easily. He didn't push them. He wanted only their reaction. And he got it. The question was, what did he think about it?

Indeed, the notes were interesting. The

whole issue of Leda and Céleste plotting against Ross was an embarrassment for both Ross and Céleste. Regardless of their relationship now, it was awkward that at one time she had been out to trap him, with sex, with extortion, with whatever she could. Ross suspected that part of her anger now was from her chagrin at having had that brought up in such a cold presentation.

Of course, Vautrin couldn't have known that. Clearly he suspected that Leda was intending to blackmail Ross, but it must have seemed to him an odd direction for the case to have taken. Still, it made sense from his point of view. Leda was dead, wasn't she? And Lacan was "missing," wasn't he . . . and presumed dead? Now, if they were involved together in a blackmail scheme against Ross, didn't their death and disappearance point straight at Ross? And what about Céleste? Had she colluded with Ross? Or had he kept it a secret from her? Though Vautrin didn't come right out and say all of this, he had let Ross know what he was thinking.

Ross took Céleste by the arm. "Come on," he said, "let's stop in here for a few minutes."

"We're just a block from the flat," she said.

"Please."

They stepped into a small neighborhood café unused to strangers and took a table next to the wall, both of them sitting at an angle that enabled them to see out the front windows a couple of tables away.

"What's the matter?" she asked, sensing a change in his manner.

"Lacan was worth a lot of money," he said. "Somebody's slipping Vautrin information. I don't think we ought to discuss this again in your flat."

She frowned at him but understood.

"God," she said, "do you think his suspicions have gone that far?"

"I don't know, but I'm worried about it."

"He wants you to be worried about it. That whole conversation, he was letting you know, wasn't he?"

Ross nodded. They ordered more coffee, but they didn't bother to drink it after the waiter brought it to them.

"You said someone's slipping Vautrin information. I don't see how that can be possible. There's got to be another explanation."

"Well, I don't see one right now."

"It's as if Leda is working from the grave to destroy you," Céleste said. "As if she set something into motion that's acquired a life of its own."

"There wasn't anything . . . unusual about her suicide, was there?"

"Oh, Ross. Really."

"Look, I'm questioning everything. It's something I should have done a long time ago. I'm in this mess now because I just floated along."

"No one would have been able to see this happening to them, Ross. People don't expect their lives to be targeted by that kind of deliberate malevolence. They don't live their lives on guard against that sort of thing."

"What do you think Leda was up to?" he asked.

"Up to? You know what she was up to."

" 'Ml.' What's that?"

"No idea. I was telling the truth. I don't know."

"Do you think she might have talked to him?"

"To be honest, no. I can't imagine it. They hated each other, and they didn't try to hide it."

He looked out to the people hurrying by in the gray afternoon. It was growing gloomy outside on the sidewalks. The rain came and went, sometimes a breeze blustered and kicked fallen leaves along ahead of it in the failing light. The cars and trucks and taxis turned on their headlights, and the street lamps came on in the twilight.

"Tell me how she first came to you with this proposition," Ross said. "How did Leda broach this subject with you?"

Céleste tapped her fingernails lightly against her coffee cup. She didn't want to do this. He understood that, but he didn't say anything to try to help her feel better. In fact, there wasn't anything to feel better about until they figured out what they were up against.

"She came to me and she said that —"

"When was this?"

"What?"

"When did she first mention this to you? You came to San Rafael in early May, a full month before I returned from Paris. How long had you been planning this before you showed up in San Rafael?"

"God." Céleste held her forehead in her hand and thought. "A month, maybe. We'd been discussing it . . . just about a month. She came to me just after . . . just after I'd had a serious . . . situation with Michel."

It always caused an empty feeling in his stomach for her to refer to Lacan by his first name. He could almost forget the things that happened between them if they always referred to Lacan by his last name, but her

427

use of the more familiar first name reminded Ross of their intimacies, of the "snail's trail" of Lacan's presence on Céleste's body to which Leda had so cruelly referred.

"She said, 'You can't go on with this anymore. I can't stand it. I've been thinking. I have some ideas you need to listen to.' "

"And she had this whole thing already worked out?"

"No, I don't think so."

"Well, about how much?"

She was surprised at his impatience. "I don't know. The overall concept. Not the details. The details came later, gradually."

"How gradually?"

"Where is this going?"

"I don't know."

She shook her head and looked down at her coffee. "Weeks, over a period of a few weeks."

"You said you'd been talking about it a month before you came to San Rafael."

"That's right. The reason it took a month before we did anything about it was that she had to talk me into it. And even then she probably couldn't have done it if . . . if Michel hadn't visited again and left me in a particularly bad mess. That last visit from him . . . scared me, scared me a lot." She paused. "I was frightened and angry. It was that, his last visit, that convinced me to go along with the scheme."

"How did she know what to do?"

"What do you mean?"

"How did she know what real estate agent to call to find a property to lease for three months?" He had a sudden flash of Nata telling him: *"She's coming in here four or five times a week for a month now. Same time. Your time."* "How did you know about Graber's?"

"Think about it, Ross. She had a ton of information. She read everything about you. She even called the little newspaper there in San Rafael — and in Austin — and had them send her copies of every article that they had ever printed about you. There was all kinds of information in those articles, you know those personality profiles. Interviews. Your favorite this, your favorite that. A day in the life of . . . In one of them there was even a photograph of you and Amado sitting at a table in Graber's garden with parrots all around. And another picture taken in front of Graber's at night standing under the little pale green neon sign."

"Jesus."

"She did everything she could think of to learn every detail she could about you. She wrote the Chamber of Commerce of San

Rafael, got everything they would send her about the town, maps, articles and brochures about the galleries and shops and restaurants. I knew all about it by the time I got there."

"You saw her do all of this?"

"A lot of it. She would go up to that room Vautrin was talking about — it was on the third floor — and she would pore over those articles, underlining, highlighting, assembling. That room was Leda's Ross Marteau headquarters."

He couldn't believe it. When he thought about it, yes, it made sense. His life was spread all the hell over the place. Fame. It was a by-product of his success and his own greedy drive to cater to wealthy, well-known clients. He had engineered an aura of success that became a self-fulfilling prophecy and allowed him to become wealthy in his own right. He was good media fodder. Someone could do a pretty good job of working their way into his life, given the right amount of motivation and guile.

Céleste grimaced and shook her head again. "But, God, I didn't even think of it when I was clearing out of there. If I'd thought of it, I would have thrown the stuff away, Ross. I'm sorry."

"No," he said, "none of that's your fault. I

don't think it comes down to that, as if none of this suspicion would have fallen on me if Vautrin hadn't found Leda's notes. I don't know why, but I have a feeling that he would be looking at me even if he'd never found those articles."

"That's the real question, isn't it?"

"Yeah. What made him search the house in the first place?"

That was the conundrum that had nagged at him even before they had finished their conversation with Vautrin. As far as Ross and Céleste were concerned, the questions raised by Lacan's disappearance should have been quieted by now. Even Leda's suicide should have been seen as nothing more than an additional tragedy in Céleste's life. One heard such stories, the death in a short period of time of several persons close to someone. Everyone knows someone to whom such things have happened. Usually you commiserated with someone like that, grateful that it hadn't happened to you. That's all it should have been in Céleste's life. Two tragedies so close together. And that was all . . . the end of it.

But that wasn't the end of it. Something had happened after Leda's death that had brought the two deaths together into a different frame of reference and tied Ross into the bundle. Ross had just enough connection to the two dead people to make it appear — if presented in the right context — that his relationship to them was in fact the red thread that tied the two deaths together.

The clever part of the illusion was that, in part, it was *not* an illusion. His life was connected to the two deaths, but he was not the *cause* of them, as the illusion implied.

And then — in a numbing, breathtaking realization — he knew! He *knew* what had happened.

"What's the matter?" Céleste asked suddenly.

He didn't know what he had done to make her react so quickly. Had he grunted as if he had been hit in the stomach? That's what he felt had happened. Had he lurched in his chair, physically shaken? He didn't know. But if he had not been sitting down, he would have had to.

"Sorry," he said, straining to gain control. If he had appeared discombobulated at that moment, he had to correct that impression. "I need to walk," he said. "We ought to go."

He paid, and they stepped to the door of the café, pausing under the long awning. The little round tables on the sidewalk in front of the café were abandoned, chestnut leaves plastered to them in random, windblown patterns; rain puddled, glistening, in the seats of the chairs. They could see the darkened windows across the street in Céleste's flat.

"I need to walk," he said again. "I've got to think."

"Fine," she said. "I don't mind."

"Alone," he said.

She snapped her head around at him.

"I just want to do it at my own pace. I just want to think."

She stared at him, and he saw in her eyes a painful mixture of confusion and fear and compassion. She reached up and put a hand flat against his face. Then she leaned forward and kissed him.

"I'll be waiting for you," she said.

Chapter 47

He watched her walk away. Just as she was about to step off the curb at the intersection to cross the street, a damp gust whipped up the corner of her raincoat, lifting it and her skirt with a flick, showing him the back of her leg. And then pedestrians crossed in either direction between them, and he lost sight of her as she crossed to the other side.

That one flutter of the dress epitomized the duration of their affair. In the span of his life he had known her for only a moment, but that moment had been saturated with passion and turmoil. The intensity of their moment was completely unexpected. He thought he had left that kind of thing behind forever. He had intended to. But this time it had sought him out, recalled from his past like the sudden appearance of a disturbing memory evoked by the cadence of a stranger's voice or the play of gray light on a rainy window.

The moment she entered the building, he hurried to the curb and hailed a taxi.

Staring out at the doleful evening as the taxi made its way to Montmartre, he thought of poor, wretched Leda. She might have been hating him still, poring over her clippings, staring into her mirrors at her naked buffalo's body and her incomparable beauty, had it not been for an event that he was about to confirm. He was reasonably sure what had happened, but he did not know how it had come about. He had a wild theory, but it seemed both too simple and too complex. Whatever the impetus, the encounter had given birth to fierce events and tragedy.

Who could imagine how Leda's life might have been lived except for that incident? Would time have gone by in the horrible monotony of her inwardly howling grief until the years claimed her beauty and, finally, her life? Or would she have eventually turned to the lonely solace of suicide anyway? Leda. For all her madness, she had been abandoned by loveliness in all its forms, and he could not bring himself to hate her for what that had done to her.

He left the taxi at the bottom of the small street and started up. He had taken a discarded newspaper from the backseat of the taxi and held it over his head with one hand as he turned up the collar of his raincoat against the mizzle. Everything was narrow and close here. He leaned into the sloping sidewalk, trudging past low stone walls with wrought-iron grilles and vines. He passed the doorway of a pharmacy, its bright interior throwing a pale bar across the wet sidewalk, and turned the corner, continuing upward.

The lane made a tight turn. The stone and brick residences stacked up in ascending tiers among trees. There were few lights, and those that burned dimly in an occasional doorway or from high windows threw sparkling glints off the wet surfaces in the shadows and darkness.

Finally he came to the address he was looking for and stopped across the lane from it, looking up at its darkened windows. Jesus, he had no idea how long he might have to wait. He stepped up off the sloping sidewalk into the doorway of a closed sewing shop and hunched his shoulders against the chill. He could see the glistening rainwater trickling down the falling sidewalk.

Half an hour passed. His wet feet grew cold. The chill around his neck was just beginning to be uncomfortable when he saw a solitary figure round the corner below him on the other side of the lane. The umbrella was tilted forward, obscuring the face; the pace was preoccupied, unhurried. The figure passed him by and turned into the doorway he had been watching. His breathing grew shallow. He waited, watching the windows on the second floor. When the lights came on, his heart flipped a double beat. He stepped out of the doorway and crossed the cobblestones to the other side.

In the cramped foyer of the building he scanned the mailboxes, peering intently in the bad lighting. He found the name: Leigh.

He avoided the lift and started up the marble stairs, the stairwell turning immediately around the caged lift shaft to the second floor.

At the door he removed his coat, lightly shook off the rain. He threw it over his arm and knocked on the door. Nothing. He knocked again. He heard footsteps approaching from the other side. Pause. Nothing. He knocked again.

He heard the dead bolt clack. There would be a chain. The door eased open.

He threw his shoulder into the door so hard that it ripped the chain from the door frame with an explosive crack and flung the woman staggering backward, arms flailing for balance, until she fell over an armchair and went sprawling to the floor on the other side.

But she was immediately scrambling to her feet, and in an instant they were standing in the middle of the room, facing each other.

"Jesus Christ!" She gaped at him in wide-eyed surprise, her auburn hair tumbled around her creamy face in a henna storm.

"Hello, Marian," he said.

The front room of the flat was comfortable and was clearly an artist's residence. The walls were crowded with paintings and drawings, and handmade pottery was scattered about on shelves and tables. The top of a long narrow cabinet was laden with stacks of sketchbooks, and a miscellany of unframed canvases leaned against each other in the corners. The room was lit by a single lamp. Marian's own raincoat was hanging on a hook beside the door, dripping on newspapers spread on the floor underneath it.

Ross reached behind him without taking his eyes off her and closed the door. She was rigid, having seen the anger in his face. He didn't care. She was making rapid calculations. Fear was slowly being displaced by a cautious curiosity. She began to recover her composure.

"It took you longer than I thought."

"Longer?"

"What's it been, a year?"

"Ten months."

"Oh. Seems longer."

"How did this happen?"

At first he thought she was going to play dumb, then he saw her change her mind and give it up.

"I'm going to have to have a drink for this," she said, and turned to a small table with liquor bottles and glasses. She picked up a short, heavy-based tumbler. "How about you?" she asked with her back to him.

He didn't answer. It was as if only a day had passed. She looked the same, her tight buttocks poured into her trademark black tights, the backs of her thighs taut beneath the second skin that encased her lovely legs all the way to the ankles. She was barefoot. Her tea rose blouse, just the right shade for her complexion, was pulled snug around her waist, its tail gathered and knotted above her exposed navel. She stood with one leg cocked . . . *déhanchement.*

She poured her drink.

"You're just going to do this straight up, huh?" she asked. "Like a man."

"How did you find her?"

"Find her?" she asked, turning around, a slow, amused grin taking shape. She still wore a hint of lipstick. "What makes you think *I* found *her?*"

"How did it happen, then?"

"Actually, she called me. Isn't that sweet?"

"The newspaper articles."

"Magazines. To be exact, it was the Paris *Match* that gave her the idea of finding me. You'll remember, that humiliating article, the one with the pictures of me throwing a fucking plate at you in the Brasserie Femme. And that other damn gossip rag that followed 'the breakup' in odious detail."

She tasted her Scotch.

"Leda guessed that I might harbor some animosity toward you. *Animosité,* she said. She thought, you know, that we might share that in common, she and I."

Another drink.

"She told me in our very first little conversation that she was your daughter." She offered an expression of mock shock. "And she *really* wanted to have some heavy conversation about Daddy."

"You didn't hold back anything, I hope."

"I talked my ass off. Listen, that gorgeous little hunchback — and what a weird combination she had there — had a voracious hunger for anything and everything about you. No detail was too small, no gossip too raw."

"You were careful to be truthful."

"Oh, I made damn sure she knew what Daddy was really like. Maybe I embellished a little . . . can't remember. What the hell, sometimes misconceptions slip in . . . that happens with celebrities."

She spoke with a combination of smiles and edgy looks. The ten months since he had seen her had served only to darken her bitterness.

"Just for the record," he said, "she wasn't my daughter. But she thought she was. I don't care whether or not you believe it. I just want you to hear it."

Marian shrugged indifferently, more interested in where he was going with this than what misconceptions Leda might or might not have had about life.

"She was a godsend to you, wasn't she?" he asked. "The perfect dupe."

Marian was still standing in front of the liquor caddy, one hip cocked, her left arm across her bare stomach, her tumbler hoisted beside her Technicolor face, elbow resting on the crossed arm.

"You know," she mused, "she was. It was astonishing, really. I had all this bottled-up malice, just boiling over with it, and nowhere to pour it out. Then one afternoon the telephone rings . . . hello? . . . it's her.

441

You've got to appreciate that kind of symmetry."

"You knew there was more on her mind than simple curiosity, didn't you?"

She took a drink, burying a smirk in her glass. She swallowed slowly, savoring it.

"Oh yeah, she had more on her mind, but really, she wasn't quite sure what. We met, I don't know, maybe eight, ten times over five or six weeks. When I saw how smart she was — and how dumb she was — I rolled up my sleeves and became her guidance counselor."

Chapter 48

"That's how she knew so many of the personal things," Ross said. "The articles explained most of that, but it didn't explain how she knew about the almond croissants, or how Céleste 'intuited' so much about Saleh. And it didn't explain Anita Beaton."

"The devil's in the minutiae."

"You got too carried away, Marian."

"Well, maybe Anita was a stretch, but Céleste had to meet her because Anita was going to be the best entrée into the San Rafael circles where she was likely to run into you. I had heard Anita talk about a friend of hers here in Paris. I called a friend of mine who called a friend of hers who called Anita's friend and gave her the old friend-of-a-friend story. It wasn't very slick, but it kept me out of the picture . . . and it worked, didn't it?"

A chilling thought ran through Ross's mind, something that hadn't occurred to him until this very instant.

"And how did you meet Céleste?"

The question caught her by surprise, and she stared at him. In that moment he realized that she didn't know that he didn't know that she had never met Céleste. They both understood at the same instant what had happened.

"Shit," Marian said with a slow, crooked grin of self-reproach for having missed a golden opportunity. "I wish I'd known that. I could have messed with your head, oh, I really could have."

He was enormously relieved, more grateful for this than anything he'd been grateful for in his life.

"You didn't talk to Leda after she returned to Paris, did you?"

Marian thought about it but couldn't see a downside to admitting that she hadn't. Still, she didn't say no, but he could see it.

"Do you know what finally happened?"

"I do now."

He wasn't sure what she meant by that, but he didn't want to be the one to say what *had* happened. Certainly not to Marian.

"It didn't come off exactly the way you'd planned," he said.

"That doesn't surprise me. Leda was certainly capable of screwing up things. If she screwed up — whatever it was — that wasn't part of the plan."

"But you do know something went

wrong, don't you? That's why you contacted the Police Judiciaire."

This was getting interesting. Ross tossed his raincoat onto the chair that Marian had fallen over and walked to the liquor table and poured a drink for himself after all. He turned to her.

"Anonymous call," he said.

"I wasn't getting any news," she said with a shrug. "When that stupid hump sliced herself up in her bathtub, that was the end of it. I hadn't had any confirmation. I wanted to know how far she had gotten with our plans before she killed herself."

Ross sipped the Scotch and looked at her. "You don't know what happened, do you?"

He could see that this made her furious.

"I know what was supposed to have happened," she said, "and seeing you standing here means it hasn't come full circle yet."

"You put it all into her head, didn't you? All of it."

"Oh no. She had some vague plans of revenge when she came to me. I might've helped her refine her ideas a little."

She moved around to a settee in front of the windows that overlooked the street and sat down. She sat on the edge of it, her knees spread, her hands hanging down between her legs, holding the drink. He thought he

445

sensed a growing uneasiness in her despite her bravado.

"I'm not sure where the line is between what you planned and what went wrong," he said. "I think we need to clear that up."

He could tell her curiosity was eating at her.

"Look," she said. "I know Lacan's disappeared —"

"How do you know that?"

She grinned but didn't answer. "I'm guessing he's not on vacation, and I'm guessing he's not ever going to come back from wherever he is."

It was raining hard outside now. He could hear it slapping on the leaves of the trees and splashing in the street.

"How could you be sure he would show up in San Rafael?"

She nodded. "Yeah. Well, he would be about due a little rough nooky after a month or so, wouldn't he? I think that was about his schedule, wasn't it? The odds were good."

She was smirking again. She knew it tortured him to hear her talk like that about Céleste. He looked at her. One of them was going to have to step out further than either of them wanted to in order to advance the conversation. But he knew that neither of them was going to admit that Lacan was supposed to have been killed. He knew now that Marian didn't know for sure if that had happened. She knew only that he had disappeared.

"Something went wrong for Leda," he said, holding his drink as he walked to a picture on the wall and looked at it. Then he turned and came back toward her. "But she was young, and I guess you'd forgotten to mention to her that there's no such thing as a perfect scheme."

Marian pursed her beautiful lips and watched him. She was lovely to look at, a paradox of package and content.

"You mentioned," he said, "that Leda was both smart and dumb. Well, she was smart last of all."

"Okay."

"She locked all her doors behind her, Marian. Even the one you walked through. She was like that, obsessive. You must've seen that for yourself."

Marian's eyes were fixed on him now, following him as he paced back and forth in front of her.

"Maybe you didn't know exactly what she was going to do," he continued, "but you put a lot of ideas into her head, and you knew that whatever she ended up doing, it wasn't going to be good for me."

Marian smiled. "I did get that feeling. It made me wet, just knowing how lucky I was to be able to contribute to that . . . whatever it was."

He took a few steps to a cabinet, its shelves filled with Marian's glazed pottery. He took a piece down and looked at it. Suddenly he saw the explosion of turquoise fireworks, the shower of shards falling around him like green hail.

"Unfortunately," he said, turning to her again, "you knew me better than you knew her."

Marian was blank.

"The truth is," he said, "Leda locked her doors from *both* sides — and she kept all the keys herself. She wasn't quite as dumb as you thought. Her scheme required the help of several people, and she was smart enough to take precautions to make sure that none of them — none of them — could talk about this without incriminating themselves. Even if they didn't know what finally did happen." He paused. "Everyone became an accomplice."

"Accomplice?"

"She taped your conversations, Marian. Not all of them, just the crucial ones."

She tried to smile, but it soured. "I don't believe you."

He drank in one swallow the remaining bit of Scotch in his glass and walked to the liquor table, where he put it down.

"You did all this work cultivating Leda, helping her set up this elaborate maze of lies, and then she goes off to the States . . . and that's it. You don't hear another word. You don't see anything in the news. You don't get a call. You don't get a letter. Just silence. You get antsy, can't stand it. The best you can do is place an anonymous call to the Police Judiciaire."

He stepped to the armchair and picked up his raincoat.

"That was your first big mistake."

He held the coat in his arms and looked down at her.

"But you never really knew for sure exactly what had finally happened . . . or had not happened. That was another big mistake."

Pause.

"I've got the tapes, Marian."

"Bullshit!" She jumped to her feet, her face contorted. "Bull*shit!*"

"Don't believe me," he said. "That'll be your last mistake."

He saw her trembling. He saw her jaw set. He saw her eyes go blind.

She lunged at him, and before he could

raise his arm she hit him on the side of the head with her tumbler of Scotch. He absorbed the shock, felt the top of the tumbler smash and cut, and blinked his eyes against the Scotch. She swung at him again, still gripping the weighted bottom of the broken tumbler, and he deflected the blow, which glanced past him in front of his face. Instead of raising her arm again, she flailed at him, recoiling with a back stroke. He wasn't ready. She swiped the sheared glass across his throat. He felt the clean separation of tissue, felt the release of pressure in his carotid artery as if a pressured water hose had blown a hole. He heard the rush of spewing inside his head.

She fell back, eyes bulging, her tongue frozen in the center of her wide-gaping mouth.

He could feel the blood spurting. With the raincoat still draped over his forearm, he reached up and felt the warm jet hit his hand. He grabbed his neck and felt it gushing through his fingers.

He stood there, stunned by the irreparable moment but resolved not to slip into shock. He held his breath, not wanting to know that he couldn't breathe. Gripping his throat, he felt something weighty pulling at him and he sank to one knee. Marian staggered back, dropping the glass. He heard it hit the wooden floor and looked up at her. Her expression was seized by disbelief, as if she were watching him being transformed into something unrecognizable, her beauty adorned in astonishment.

He was surprised at the sound of it, the enormous rushing in his ears. And he was stunned by the volume of blood and by its exuberance in escaping him. Feeling a little weak, he slowly slipped down on the other knee, then leaned to one side and rested on an elbow, still holding his throat and his raincoat. Already the first of his escaping blood was cooling, and he could feel it cold on one hand while the fresh blood still gushed hot through the fingers of the other. He was very tired. He needed to rest for just a second. He slumped over on his side.

Oddly, he didn't feel as though he needed to breathe. Holding his breath was no trouble at all.

But he was so tired. He rolled over, no longer having the strength to remain on his side. She stepped toward him and looked down. He stared up the length of her. Marian foreshortened, the long beautiful length of her. There was no regret in her face. No fear. But there was uncertainty. His gaze focused on her navel, a smoky spot in her white midriff. As the darkness grew from there and spread outward to encompass everything, he saw her ripping open her blouse, tearing at her tights.

She waited for him by the window, looking down at the rainy street. Any moment she would be surprised to see him, walking under the bare and dripping branches of the linden trees, his footsteps cushioned by the carpet of fallen, wet leaves.

It was still early. They would go out to eat at a brasserie, and they would talk. There was so much to talk about.

The employees of Thorndike Press hope you have enjoyed this Large Print book. All our Large Print titles are designed for easy reading, and all our books are made to last. Other Thorndike Press Large Print books are available at your library, through selected bookstores, or directly from us.

For information about titles, please call:

(800) 223-1244
(800) 223-6121

To share your comments, please write:

Publisher
Thorndike Press
295 Kennedy Memorial Drive
Waterville, ME 04901